This copy of

# *A Muse 'N Washington*

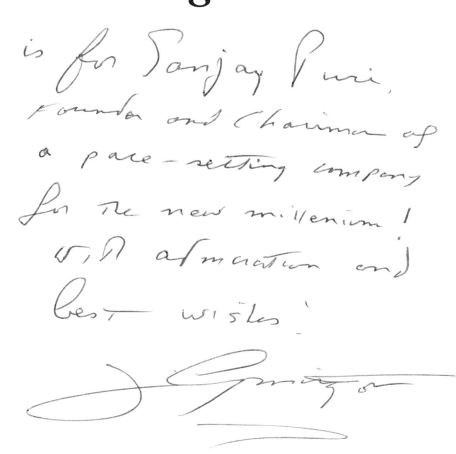

is for Sanjay Puri,
Founder and Chairman of
a pace-setting company
for the new millenium!
with admiration and
best wishes!

# ALSO BY THE AUTHOR

## The Stately Game:
Getting Along with Russians, Arabs, Israelis,
Canadians, Asians, Latins, Africans, and Americans.
Behind the Scenes with the Former
U.S. Chief of Protocol.

# A Muse 'N Washington

## Beltway Ballads and Beyond

Fifty Years of Politics
and Other Pleasures
In Poetry,
Prose and Song

With a Foreword by Hugh Sidey

☆☆☆

## James W. Symington

☆☆☆

Pentland Press, Inc.
England • USA • Scotland

This book is available for sales promotions, business, fund-raising, or educational use. For information contact Pentland Press, Tel. (919) 782-0281. This book may also be purchased directly on the Internet at "amazon.com." No part of this book may be used or reproduced in any manner whatsoever without written permission except in the case of brief quotations. For information write Literary Enterprises International, 1255 New Hampshire Avenue, N.W., Suite 511, Washington, DC, 20036.

Cover photo: Outnumbered but still smiling—President George Bush, Senator John Warner (R-VA), Congressman Robert Michel (R-IL), and the author (D-MO)—Alfalfa Club Dinner, Washington, DC, January 25, 1992.

*Photographs are credited in the order in which they appear:* White House photo, Peggy McMahon, Democratic National Congressional Committee, no credit, no credit, Al Rupp, Herb Weitman, no credit, *Meet The Press*, no credit, no credit, no credit, Democratic National Congressional Committee, no credit, Al Rupp, United Press International, Inc., no credit, no credit, City News Bureau, Inc., no credit, no credit, no credit, no credit and *The Evening Star*, no credit, no credit, no credit, no credit, no credit, no credit, no credit, no credit, no credit, Time Incorporated, *The News*, no credit, United Press International, Inc., *The Saturday Evening Post*, no credit, no credit, no credit, Peggy McMahon, no credit, White House photo, White House photo, *Eastern Sun* (Malaysian Edition), Associated Press, White House photo, no credit, Joseph Mileger, Charles E. Guggenheim.

PUBLISHED BY PENTLAND PRESS, INC.
5124 Bur Oak Circle, Raleigh, North Carolina 27612
United States of America
919-782-0281

ISBN 1-57197-142-4
Library of Congress Catalog Card Number 98-067435

Printed in the United States of America

*For My Grandchildren*


To Evie, Hayley, Dylan, and Sawyer*
From your fond ancestral lawyer
Whose observations of his times
Are here preserved in metered rhymes.
This collection also shows
How some demands drove him to prose.
In his own century immersed
He's looking to the 21st.
When he'll be sitting on a porch,
Having lightly passed the torch
To your dear parents who in turn
Will teach you all to love and learn
So your good deeds will be well reckoned
On into the 22nd.**


Washington, DC—1999


*Before this work was tucked away, we were blessed with Harriet Hay.
**Also to my wife of forty-something years, who brought some verse to life with music of the spheres.
Indeed I'm much indebted, for when I'd write a wrong, Sylvia would get it and turn it into song.

**Here's the scoop!**

Howard Johnson's, during U.S. Senate campaign.
St. Louis, Missouri, July 1976.

# Foreword

A search for the origins of Jim Symington's penchant for public service and bemused commentary thereon leads to a veritable grove of family trees with roots that reach deep in history. In fact, I'm inclined to wonder if there might have been one of his ancestors in Philadelphia on an evening in 1776 sharing a glass of claret with Mr. Jefferson and murmuring, "I like your words, Tom. 'We hold these truths to be self-evident, that all men are created equal . . .' By all means use them in the Declaration."

Nor would I be surprised to learn that a fresh young scholar had discovered a Symington cousin was holding the thread for Betsy Ross, whispering, "Sew, Betsy, as if the Union depended upon this flag."

In four decades of wonderfully gratifying friendship with Jimmy, I have been startled time and again by the parade of his progenitors across the American scene. His maternal ancestors, the Wadsworths of upstate New York, served in the Revolution and the Continental Congress. A Symington forebear from Baltimore quarried the cornerstone of the Washington Monument. His great granddad, John Hay, President Lincoln's observant and devoted private secretary, later served as Secretary of State for Presidents William McKinley and Theodore Roosevelt. The two main family branches, one Confederate and one Union, faced each other at Gettysburg.

Armed with the batons of five Congressmen and Senators, including his father, Stuart, and his grandfather, Jim Wadsworth, he set off on his own lively trek through life, law, and government. As both a keen participant and cheerful observer, he faced the turbulent challenges of the New Frontier and Great Society from high offices in the Departments of Justice, State, and the White House, before brightening the halls of Congress for four successive terms as a Missouri Representative.

The weight of his heritage and his personal agenda could suggest a man of grave countenance, stern voice, and bespoke suits. But the enduring genius of Jimmy Symington is that he took this journey (and is still traveling) with warmth, laughter, a guitar, and a myriad of tunes on his lips (some written with his talented wife of forty-five years, Sylvia). The world and its afflictions were serious, indeed, but his healing responses included great amounts of wit, joy, and song. He brought us the gentle insight of the poet when the thunder grew loudest. He gave us laughter when the reservoir of humor seemed to be drying up. He has sung and soothed and more than earned the right to march alongside the gallant men and women who charted his path.

—HUGH S. SIDEY

# Contents

Page

*Foreword* . . . . . . . . . . . . . . . . . . . . . . . . . . . . . . . . . . . . . . . . . . . . . . . . . . vii
*Acknowledgments* . . . . . . . . . . . . . . . . . . . . . . . . . . . . . . . . . . . . . . . . . . . xv
*Introduction* . . . . . . . . . . . . . . . . . . . . . . . . . . . . . . . . . . . . . . . . . . . . . . xvii

## On Washington Life
Washington — It's Time You Had A Song . . . . . . . . . . . . . . . . . . . . . 1
Farragut Square — At 17th And Chaos . . . . . . . . . . . . . . . . . . . . . . . 3
There's Pandemonium In My Condominium . . . . . . . . . . . . . . . . . . . 5
This Club Is Your Club . . . . . . . . . . . . . . . . . . . . . . . . . . . . . . . . . . . . . 7
A Birthday Salute To The Smithsonian's Dillon Ripley . . . . . . . . . . . . 8
Bless The Mall . . . . . . . . . . . . . . . . . . . . . . . . . . . . . . . . . . . . . . . . . . . 12
Remember The Fish Is Our Friend . . . . . . . . . . . . . . . . . . . . . . . . . . . 13

## On Politics
Uncle Sam's Dream — The '96 Election . . . . . . . . . . . . . . . . . . . . . . . 19
Presidential Advice — A Contract For White House Memoirs . . . . . . . 20
Ode To The Royalty Oath . . . . . . . . . . . . . . . . . . . . . . . . . . . . . . . . . . 21
Term Limits (1) And (2) . . . . . . . . . . . . . . . . . . . . . . . . . . . . . . . . . . . 23
Have You Ever Thought About Politics? . . . . . . . . . . . . . . . . . . . . . . 25
Hello Young Voters . . . . . . . . . . . . . . . . . . . . . . . . . . . . . . . . . . . . . . . 27
A Struggle For Presidential Delegates . . . . . . . . . . . . . . . . . . . . . . . . 31

## On The Press
The Ballad Of Hightower, Roberts And Ward . . . . . . . . . . . . . . . . . . 35
Proposed Contempt Citation Against CBS . . . . . . . . . . . . . . . . . . . . . 36
Elegy For A Muckraker . . . . . . . . . . . . . . . . . . . . . . . . . . . . . . . . . . . . 38
Snoop On Us? . . . . . . . . . . . . . . . . . . . . . . . . . . . . . . . . . . . . . . . . . . . 39
The *New York Times* . . . . . . . . . . . . . . . . . . . . . . . . . . . . . . . . . . . . . 40

## On Romance And Its Hazards
Distraction . . . . . . . . . . . . . . . . . . . . . . . . . . . . . . . . . . . . . . . . . . . . . 45
"Let's Do Lunch" . . . . . . . . . . . . . . . . . . . . . . . . . . . . . . . . . . . . . . . . 46
Gypsy Toot (A Fantasy) . . . . . . . . . . . . . . . . . . . . . . . . . . . . . . . . . . . 47
April Skies . . . . . . . . . . . . . . . . . . . . . . . . . . . . . . . . . . . . . . . . . . . . . . 49
Having Just Phoned You . . . . . . . . . . . . . . . . . . . . . . . . . . . . . . . . . . . 50
Pretend (A Song) . . . . . . . . . . . . . . . . . . . . . . . . . . . . . . . . . . . . . . . . . 53
Bonnet And Sandals . . . . . . . . . . . . . . . . . . . . . . . . . . . . . . . . . . . . . . 54
How's Bayou . . . . . . . . . . . . . . . . . . . . . . . . . . . . . . . . . . . . . . . . . . . . 57
Weekend Pass . . . . . . . . . . . . . . . . . . . . . . . . . . . . . . . . . . . . . . . . . . . 58
Song Of The Lonely Swiss Guide (A Yodel Song) . . . . . . . . . . . . . . . 59
I Seek A Greek . . . . . . . . . . . . . . . . . . . . . . . . . . . . . . . . . . . . . . . . . . 60
Two Bodies . . . . . . . . . . . . . . . . . . . . . . . . . . . . . . . . . . . . . . . . . . . . . .62

## On Lawyers And The Law

A Dialogue With Socrates . . . . . . . . . . . . . . . . . . . . . . . . . . . . . . . . . . 65
Respect For The Lawyer . . . . . . . . . . . . . . . . . . . . . . . . . . . . . . . . . . . 68
Suggestion To The IRS . . . . . . . . . . . . . . . . . . . . . . . . . . . . . . . . . . . . 71
Modern Law And Lawyering — A Lawyer's Lament
    Part I   — As I Walked Out Of Columbia One June Day . . . . . . . . 72
    Part II  — Hush Little Barrister . . . . . . . . . . . . . . . . . . . . . . . . . 73
    Part III — Old Uncle Tom Cobbs And All . . . . . . . . . . . . . . . . . . 74
    Part IV — The Nightmare . . . . . . . . . . . . . . . . . . . . . . . . . . . . . 75
Medieval Law
    If . . . . . . . . . . . . . . . . . . . . . . . . . . . . . . . . . . . . . . . . . . . . . . . 76
    The Idylls Of A Socage Tenant, Or Roar Of The Serf . . . . . . . . . . . 77
The Confederate Constitution — Hints Of The Future . . . . . . . . . . . . 78
Trials Of Our Time . . . . . . . . . . . . . . . . . . . . . . . . . . . . . . . . . . . . . . 81

## On Congress

A Funding Son Looks At The Founding Fathers . . . . . . . . . . . . . . . . . 85
The Federal Records Center Fire — A Special Bill . . . . . . . . . . . . . . . 89
A Farewell Salute To Senator Paul Douglas . . . . . . . . . . . . . . . . . . . . 91
The Flip Side Of The Moon . . . . . . . . . . . . . . . . . . . . . . . . . . . . . . . . 92
Congressional Remarks:
    A Proposal To Eliminate Tax Inequities Concerning
        Wine Production For Personal Consumption . . . . . . . . . . . . . . 94
    The Outlook Was Not Brilliant . . . . . . . . . . . . . . . . . . . . . . . . . . . 95
A Farewell To Constituents . . . . . . . . . . . . . . . . . . . . . . . . . . . . . . . . 97

## On America

Thirteen Stripes And Fifty Stars . . . . . . . . . . . . . . . . . . . . . . . . . . . . 101
Centennial Of The Statue Of Liberty — The Spirit Of '86 . . . . . . . . . 102
The Genesee Valley . . . . . . . . . . . . . . . . . . . . . . . . . . . . . . . . . . . . . 104
This Star-Filled Night (A Cowboy Christmas Song) . . . . . . . . . . . . . 105
The *Constellation* . . . . . . . . . . . . . . . . . . . . . . . . . . . . . . . . . . . . . . 106
My State — Missouri
    I'm From Missouri . . . . . . . . . . . . . . . . . . . . . . . . . . . . . . . . . . . 108
    Nyet . . . . . . . . . . . . . . . . . . . . . . . . . . . . . . . . . . . . . . . . . . . . . 109
    The Buford Mountain Song . . . . . . . . . . . . . . . . . . . . . . . . . . . . . 111
    The Mississippi — Father Of The Waters . . . . . . . . . . . . . . . . . . 113
    The City By The River . . . . . . . . . . . . . . . . . . . . . . . . . . . . . . . . 115
    Another Kansas City Day . . . . . . . . . . . . . . . . . . . . . . . . . . . . . . 116

## On Diplomacy

It Takes Time To Know A Country . . . . . . . . . . . . . . . . . . . . . . . . . . 119
The Fair Invader . . . . . . . . . . . . . . . . . . . . . . . . . . . . . . . . . . . . . . . 121
Averell Harriman — La Plume de Détente. . . . . . . . . . . . . . . . . . . . 122

Alliance For Progress ........................................... 125
Out Of The Night That Covers You ........................... 128
Miss Ortiz Regrets ............................................ 130
On The Road To Samarkand ................................... 131
Hail To The Grand Duke Alexis .............................. 133
Through Russia With Guitar ................................... 135

## On War And Peace

Vietnam, The Songless War (Let Saigons Be Saigons) ............ 139
First Poems
    Letter To Hitler .......................................... 141
    To Carry A Song .......................................... 142
A Warning To Stalin — An Appeal To God ..................... 143
We're Going To Win The World ................................ 145
The Bomb — Stone Age Revisited ............................. 147
Conventional War ............................................ 148
Prophet Of Promise .......................................... 149
War And Preparedness ....................................... 150

## On Technology

Reproduction ................................................ 159
Here Come The Clones ....................................... 160
Computers Are Here To Stay ................................. 161
The Ballad Of John Smithers ................................. 163
Commercial Airflight In 1985 (A Thirty-Year Projection) .......... 166

## On Education

Dictionerror ................................................. 169
School Days — "Hail To The Class Of '40" ..................... 170
Senior Class Prophecy ....................................... 172
Headmaster — Past, Present, Forever ......................... 173
"Ol' Miss" — A Memoire ...................................... 174
Latin ........................................................ 178

## On The Family

A Hayride With Lincoln ...................................... 181
A Child Can Grow ........................................... 189
The Bills .................................................... 192
A Fifth Wedding Anniversary Letter To Miami's Kenilworth Hotel ... 193
Twenty-Fifth Wedding Anniversary — Lord Byron's Challenge .... 195
Remarks At Services For Senator Stuart Symington ............... 196
Selections From The Poems Of Eve Symington .................. 200

# On Music

Beethoven . . . . . . . . . . . . . . . . . . . . . . . . . . . . . . . . . . . . . . . . . . . . 207
Debate On The Arts . . . . . . . . . . . . . . . . . . . . . . . . . . . . . . . . . . . . . 209
Even Monkeys Muse On Music . . . . . . . . . . . . . . . . . . . . . . . . . . . . 210
Nostalgia From Radioland — Rocktime Cowboy Joe . . . . . . . . . . . . 212

# On Sports And Fitness

Skipping — On The Road To Fitness . . . . . . . . . . . . . . . . . . . . . . . . . 215
Boxing — The Johannsen-Patterson Bout . . . . . . . . . . . . . . . . . . . . 217
Soccer Lessons Of '74 . . . . . . . . . . . . . . . . . . . . . . . . . . . . . . . . . . . . 219

# On The Passing Of Time

Runners To Come . . . . . . . . . . . . . . . . . . . . . . . . . . . . . . . . . . . . . . . 225
Time . . . . . . . . . . . . . . . . . . . . . . . . . . . . . . . . . . . . . . . . . . . . . . . . . . 229
Fiftieth Birthday Salute — The First Fifty Years . . . . . . . . . . . . . . . . 230
The Apple Tree . . . . . . . . . . . . . . . . . . . . . . . . . . . . . . . . . . . . . . . . . 231

# Pride and Presidents

## ☆Truman☆

Whistle Stop . . . . . . . . . . . . . . . . . . . . . . . . . . . . . . . . . . . . . . . . . . . 235
Harry's Way . . . . . . . . . . . . . . . . . . . . . . . . . . . . . . . . . . . . . . . . . . . 235
Joe McCarthy
    The Knight Behind Christmas . . . . . . . . . . . . . . . . . . . . . . . . . . . 240
    Schine . . . . . . . . . . . . . . . . . . . . . . . . . . . . . . . . . . . . . . . . . . . . . . 244

## ☆Eisenhower☆

Pridelands — A Sad Tale Concerning A Simple Farmer
    And Some Great Decisions . . . . . . . . . . . . . . . . . . . . . . . . . . . . . 245
Eisenhower . . . . . . . . . . . . . . . . . . . . . . . . . . . . . . . . . . . . . . . . . . . . 251
Ivory Tower . . . . . . . . . . . . . . . . . . . . . . . . . . . . . . . . . . . . . . . . . . . 252

## ☆Kennedy☆

The Plaint Of JFK . . . . . . . . . . . . . . . . . . . . . . . . . . . . . . . . . . . . . . . 253
McGovern . . . . . . . . . . . . . . . . . . . . . . . . . . . . . . . . . . . . . . . . . . . . . 255
Tiptoe Through The Issues . . . . . . . . . . . . . . . . . . . . . . . . . . . . . . . . 256
John Fitzgerald The Second . . . . . . . . . . . . . . . . . . . . . . . . . . . . . . . 257
Affectionate Reply To Jim And Sylvia Symington . . . . . . . . . . . . . . 258
Bethany Beach . . . . . . . . . . . . . . . . . . . . . . . . . . . . . . . . . . . . . . . . . . 260
April Shahs . . . . . . . . . . . . . . . . . . . . . . . . . . . . . . . . . . . . . . . . . . . . 261
Oh, Arthur Schlesinger . . . . . . . . . . . . . . . . . . . . . . . . . . . . . . . . . . 262
The Young Champion . . . . . . . . . . . . . . . . . . . . . . . . . . . . . . . . . . . 263

# ☆Johnson☆

The Johnson Years . . . . . . . . . . . . . . . . . . . . . . . . . . . . . . . . . . . . . . . . 265
Exile . . . . . . . . . . . . . . . . . . . . . . . . . . . . . . . . . . . . . . . . . . . . . . . . . . 267
On The Road With LBJ . . . . . . . . . . . . . . . . . . . . . . . . . . . . . . . . . . . . 269
We're Landing, Mr. President . . . . . . . . . . . . . . . . . . . . . . . . . . . . . . . 272
Suggested Arrival Statement For Sen-Sen . . . . . . . . . . . . . . . . . . . . . 274
Moyers' Lament . . . . . . . . . . . . . . . . . . . . . . . . . . . . . . . . . . . . . . . . . . 276
Quiet Flows The Billy Don (A Farewell To Bill Moyers) . . . . . . . . . . 278
The Saga Of Charles Robb . . . . . . . . . . . . . . . . . . . . . . . . . . . . . . . . . 280

# ☆Nixon☆

On Nixon (Letter To Parents) . . . . . . . . . . . . . . . . . . . . . . . . . . . . . . . 282
Oh, Christmas Peace! . . . . . . . . . . . . . . . . . . . . . . . . . . . . . . . . . . . . . 283
The Watergate Period . . . . . . . . . . . . . . . . . . . . . . . . . . . . . . . . . . . . . 284
Wallowin' In Watergate Tonight . . . . . . . . . . . . . . . . . . . . . . . . . . . . . 286
Johnny Dean (Lines Penned Awaiting Indictment) . . . . . . . . . . . . . . 287
The Doctrine Of Executive Pilferage . . . . . . . . . . . . . . . . . . . . . . . . . 289
1973-74: The Impeachment Years . . . . . . . . . . . . . . . . . . . . . . . . . . . 290

# ☆Reagan — Bush☆

Battle Hymn To The Republic Of American Women . . . . . . . . . . . . . 292
Questions For Grandpa (2000 A.D.) . . . . . . . . . . . . . . . . . . . . . . . . . . 296
Making A Mesopotamia . . . . . . . . . . . . . . . . . . . . . . . . . . . . . . . . . . . 298
Christmas In Iraq . . . . . . . . . . . . . . . . . . . . . . . . . . . . . . . . . . . . . . . . 299
Riyadh Rose . . . . . . . . . . . . . . . . . . . . . . . . . . . . . . . . . . . . . . . . . . . . 300
Broccoli . . . . . . . . . . . . . . . . . . . . . . . . . . . . . . . . . . . . . . . . . . . . . . . . 301
The Chute Fits . . . . . . . . . . . . . . . . . . . . . . . . . . . . . . . . . . . . . . . . . . 302

# ☆Clinton☆

A Sonnet To The 1992 Election . . . . . . . . . . . . . . . . . . . . . . . . . . . . . 303
The First Hundred Days . . . . . . . . . . . . . . . . . . . . . . . . . . . . . . . . . . . 304
Presidential Bypass . . . . . . . . . . . . . . . . . . . . . . . . . . . . . . . . . . . . . . . 305
Republican Reverie . . . . . . . . . . . . . . . . . . . . . . . . . . . . . . . . . . . . . . . 306
On The Truman Balcony . . . . . . . . . . . . . . . . . . . . . . . . . . . . . . . . . . . 307

*About The Author* . . . . . . . . . . . . . . . . . . . . . . . . . . . . . . . . . . . . . . . 311
*List Of Photographs* . . . . . . . . . . . . . . . . . . . . . . . . . . . . . . . . . . . . . 315
*Index* . . . . . . . . . . . . . . . . . . . . . . . . . . . . . . . . . . . . . . . . . . . . . . . . . 319

# Acknowledgments

I would first like to express my appreciation to Messrs. Smith & Corona for the sturdy device they fashioned, and which since 1948 shares some of the blame at least for all the first drafts. Civilizing same became the task of my long-time secretary, Lucinda Shaw, whose patience and good cheer have sustained my working hours for two decades. The initial culling, sorting, and categorizing fell to my niece, Anne Symington, who also suggested the title. To bring the project to fruition, however, required a rare combination of literary acumen, computer skills, perseverance, and barrels of midnight oil, all of which were happily provided by one pair of twin sisters, the Misses Deborah E. Berliner and Diane T. Berliner.

Mindful that spousal tolerance is the cement that holds America together, I would like to thank my wife, Sylvia, for her inexhaustible (so far) supply of that precious commodity.

# Introduction

Versifying, or, if you will, making matters verse, is an affliction for which there is no known remedy. It usually strikes only the culprit whose preoccupation with it limits the time available for productive activity. Only when it is published does it pose a threat to the wider community.

Accordingly, Alceste (Molière's *Misanthrope*), when prevailed upon to review the poetry of his young rival, observed that were he, himself, to be so unfortunate as to write such verse, he "should take care not to show other people the results." This is sage advice to anyone whose future hangs in the balance. As that is not my problem, I no longer feel obliged to suffer alone. Hence these observations . . .

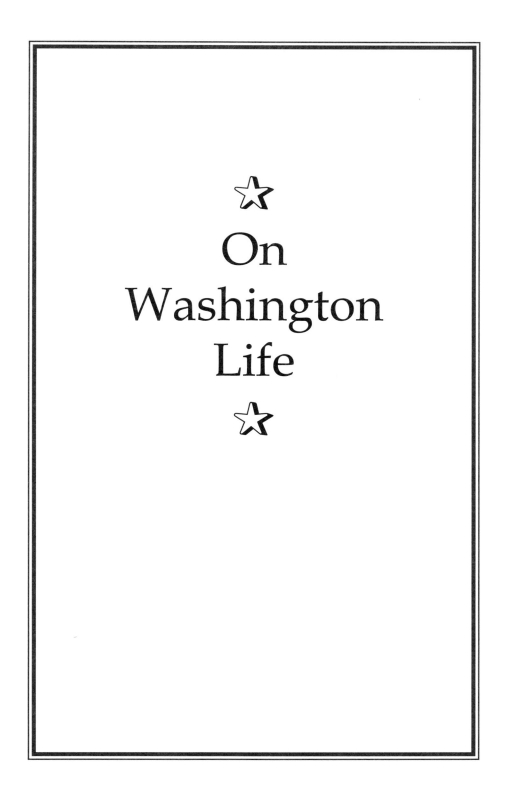

# On
# Washington
# Life

# WASHINGTON — IT'S TIME YOU HAD A SONG

I've got Washington on my mind.
It's the city where you can find
Eternal verities
Between the cherry trees;
A city the whole world clings to,
But nobody ever sings to.

Washington,
It's time you had a song.
From Cardozo to Spring Valley
The muse of Tin-Pan-Alley
Has neglected you too long.

Washington,
Like an aging débutante,
You smile there on the shelf,
While every passing minstrel
Warbles mainly to himself.

Tourists gossip of you,
What do they know?
They may say they love you
Before they go.

When they've gone
Back where they belong,
Memories remind you
Of dreams that came to find you,
And this will be your song.

People staring at you,
What do they see?
Here and there a statue,
Not you, not me.

When they've gone
Back where they belong,
Memories surround you
Of dreams that finally found you,
And this will be your song.

Washington, DC —1962
Music: Sylvia Symington

# FARRAGUT SQUARE — AT 17th AND CHAOS

Somewhere in vaulting towers of concrete and steel, sealed from the normal sounds of the street, skilled private attorneys are said to be engaged in the systematic subversion of the public interest. Are Washington lawyers engaged in a successful conspiracy of this kind?

The answer is that sustained intrigue requires concentration, concentration requires a controlled environment, and the environment in which Washington lawyers do their day's work may be said to be totally out of control. Let us take for example Farragut Square (at 17th and K Streets), the industrial park of the legal profession. Morning at Farragut Square begins innocently enough. But this could be said of morning in many parts of the world. By nine or nine-thirty, when lawyers officed around the Square have had their coffee and settled down to their respective connivances against the commonwealth, the first of five daily hook-and-ladder runs is made down K Street and up Connecticut or down 17th. The miracle of technology has supplemented the familiar siren sound with a whirling doppler whistle and a hydraulic horn-blast that has reportedly popped a client's cuff-links out of his shirt, knocked pictures down, and done spinal damage to at least one filing clerk and a senior partner. These devices are also fitted to squad cars and ambulances, so that only the trained ear can detect whether it is a law or a back that has been broken. And who but the most hardened or hard of hearing can suppress momentary compassion for the injured or fleeting speculations on the vicissitudes of life?

Next, the first of several daily demonstrations forms up along the Square. These generally call for the overthrow of one of the world's 140 governments, so it is necessary to schedule at least two or three a week in order to get them all in during a given calendar year. These mobilizations are led by individuals chosen for their lung power and lack of shyness. Nor are they too proud to use hand-held, battery-powered megaphones. It sometimes requires a response of over one thousand loyal followers to match the sonic level of their captains. These groups frequently wear masks lest their parents or governments find out what they are doing during school hours. On off days, Americans are permitted to demonstrate. They, too, display a dizzying array of viewpoints on key issues of our time, and some not so key. The common bond that unites these gatherings is wrath, albeit they are not choler coordinated.

Yet, it would be both unjust and untruthful to infer that only the angry are heard on Farragut Square. Happy people also gather there, though the reason for their contentment can be annoyingly obscure. And powers of concentration that can survive sirens, shouts, and explosions, have been known to collapse at the tinkling of a tambourine. The playful bells and chants of the Hari-Krishna sect provide sonic intrusions of this milder sort, as do the noon Salvation Army lecture and hymns.

Young women spreading their picnic blankets on the grass provide a visual diversion that can terminate the most scholarly reflections. There is also a certain wild joy to the onrush of official limousines and motorcycle outriders, flags akimbo, carrying fretful state visitors to their rendezvous with ambiguous joint communiqués. The long lines of horn-blowing cars kept waiting by these diplomatic excursions can be forgiven by anyone interested in world peace. This cannot be said of the periodic acid-rock concerts, however . . . all in the ever patient shadow of Farragut.

Facing south with a pigeon on his head, the Admiral retains his composure, mutely damning not only the torpedoes, but the electric guitars, the steel drums, the wandering flutes, the swooping sopranos, the traffic altercations, and the occasional lone evangelist urging repentance through a bull horn. But that's easy enough for him. For the mean, average American, and that includes most of us, it is an immersion in cacophony unequalled in the Western world or that of the East—Tokyo, Istanbul, and Chicago notwithstanding.

An air raid might rival the existing competition depending on the calibre and accuracy of the bombs dropped. On those special days when the entire Farragut Square orchestra tunes up, and every one of its instruments is playing, including the screams of the innocent, even war might go unnoticed.

What can be concluded from all this is that sustained thought, much less effective concentration by the dreaded legal minds of Washington, is effectively blocked during normal working hours. No significant long-term damage can be inflicted by persons gripping their chairs and staring fixedly ahead. The public interest is therefore safe, and kept so by the public, in its infinite wisdom. So there is no need to ask for whom these decibels toll. They toll for us all.

Published in the *Washington Post*—November 6, 1978

*The living conditions in our nation's capital can be no less unnerving than the working environment:*

# THERE'S PANDEMONIUM IN MY CONDOMINIUM

I come to town so innocent
Got a job and paid my rent.
'Till a real estate fella come along.
Said, "Man you're doin' the thing all wrong—
Why, what you need is your own space,
And with a little down payment you can *buy* a place
Along with folks you'd like to know.
Together you'd be runnin' the whole darn show.
So jest you leave a check with me,
And that'll be your equity."
I did like he said; Now I suspect
He must rank me among the ingrates.
But to tell you the truth I didn't expect
An asylum run by the inmates.

There's pandemonium in my condominium
And I can't find no peace.
There's pandemonium in my condominium
Won't somebody call the police?

The couple upstairs are having a fight.
And their washin' machine ain't workin' right.
So while they're yellin' up and down the halls,
There's rusty water runnin' down my walls.
Folks next door 'r even more to blame,
The old man's runnin' a numbers game.
If the cops check it out well like as not
They'll find the whole family smokin' pot.

There's pandemonium in my condominium
And I can't find no peace.
There's pandemonium in my condominium
Won't somebody call the police?

The plumber's gone, the electrician too
The minute you find 'em somethin' to do.
The super's quit and my stove won't work,
And the elevator's gone berserk;
There's a cryin' baby and a whinin' pup
I'm gonna cash it in and give it up.
Head back to my home in Tennessee
Where no real estate man'll be connin' me.
Where there ain't no high rise but the hills,
No fake lakes, and no water bills.
But before I leave my dream home here,
Let me say it again, boys, loud and clear—

There's pandemonium in my condominium
And I can't find no peace.
There's pandemonium in my condominium
Won't somebody call the police?

Washington, DC—1994
Music: Jim Symington

Early in the Kennedy Administration a new luncheon club appeared in Washington. It was the brain-child of its "once and future" president, syndicated columnist Charles Bartlett.* He and fellow founding members named it the Federal City Club, and determined that its membership would not be impoverished by restrictions inherited from another age. The only criterion for membership was and remains "demonstrable interest in public affairs." At each annual dinner a vote is taken on whether or not the Club song should be sung. The vote is usually very close. Sung to the tune of Woodie Guthrie's immortal "This Land Is Your Land," the lyrics follow:

## THIS CLUB IS YOUR CLUB

This Club is your club,
This Club is my club.
A kind of poor club,
A no club-tie club,
Which draws its members,
So wise and witty,
From all over
The capital city.
They've learned what love meant
If they've served gov'ment.
And peace of mind
If they've resigned.
From the Rock Creek Forest
To Potomac Waters,
This Club was made for you and me.

Washington, DC — 1963

*It was Charlie's encounter with discrimination at another established club that prompted his initiative. A decade after founding the Federal City Club he was honored at its annual dinner, thus joining a pantheon of prior honorees, including Walter Lippmann, George Ball, Averell Harriman, Alice Longworth, Nelson Rockefeller, Elliot Richardson, William Ruckelshaus, and Henry Kissinger.

*Among the milestones passed in 1993 was the 80th birthday of S. Dillon Ripley, ornithologist and Secretary Emeritus of the Smithsonian Institution. His long, illustrious service and invaluable contributions warranted a birthday salute.*

*Hosted by his successor, Secretary Robert Adams, it was held at the Smithsonian on September 19, 1993. The principal focus of the commemorative recitation prepared for the occasion was Mr. Ripley's lifelong preoccupation with birds. This was followed by a song that recognized his enduring contributions to the Great Mall.*

# A BIRTHDAY SALUTE TO THE SMITHSONIAN'S DILLON RIPLEY

Handsome and well-built, he
Is evidently guilty,
And without apology,
Of blatant ornithology.

The name is Dillon Ripley,
And he's strictly for the birds,
From Galápagos to Gallipoli,
He's always found the words

To describe their habitations,
Their mating calls and songs,
Their annual migrations,
And where each nest belongs.

As a child, what a fit he
Had in New York City
When strolling in the aegis
Of the Plaza or St. Regis,

Or possibly the Ritz,
He discovered two tom-tits
Never spotted north
Of Park and 34th.

This set him on a course,
With no trace of remorse,
Of spying on their perches
In several local churches.

Next thing that we knew,
Everything that flew
Would be before it died
Dillon Ripley-fied.

Through India's swamps and copses,
Completely undeterred,
He authored a synopsis
Of every single bird.

When informed the starling
Was nobody's darling,
He brushed the thought aside,
And cheerfully replied,
"There never was a bird
That shouldn't have occurred.

Millions of God's creatures
Have depressing features;
Be happy they don't fuss
When they look at us!"

He revels in the cackle
Of the ordinary grackle,
Gets a maniacal rush
From the heron and the thrush.

And if the moody cormorant
Reminds him of a former aunt,
He sturdily maintains her right
To engage in daily flight.

To the dilettante and dabbler
Distinctions can be blurred,
Between the spiny babbler
And the chatty mynah bird.

It was up to him to court 'em,
Catalogue and sort 'em
So you ladies and you gents
Could tell the difference.

In search of rara avis
Smithsonia preferred
Not to hire a novice,
But a Secretary Bird.

Having found their Daedalus,
Further search was needless.
S. Dillon, all aboard,
Spread his wings and soared.

Disdaining what the rabble wished
He instantly established,
With his academic buddies
And appropriated dollars,
A Center for the studies
Of Woodrow Wilson scholars.

The Doric and Ionian
Halls of the Smithsonian
Echoed to the clamor
Of the chisel and the hammer
As Dillon's next immersion
Resulted in the Hirshhorn.

Chanting a Te Deum
For the Air and Space Museum,
He contributed his salary
To the National Portrait Gallery.
For directing these adagios
And protecting tous les oiseaux,
France gave him le bonheur
De La Légion d'Honneur.

Earlier in Britain, he
Endured the usual litany,
And with a cup of tea
Was knighted O.B.E.
These honors in his hand
He made it back to land
Where Reagan stood to greet him,
With the Medal of our Freedom.

So let us raise our glasses
To our man on Parnassus,
Not only our emeritus,
But our very lux and veritas.

Hail to the Secretary
S. Dillon and his Mary,
We of their aviary
Sing howdy, cum laude, all hail!

Washington, DC—September 19, 1993
Background Music:  Sylvia Symington

# BLESS THE MALL*

Bless the Mall, Bless the Mall,
And the man standing on it so tall,
High in his tower, the quietly powerful
Ripley conceiving it all.

Bless the Mall, Bless the Mall,
Where winter and summer and fall,
At lunch in his kiosk and munching a brioche
Was Ripley achieving it all.

What we got, on the dot
Was the art of the world on the spot.
Asian, American, African too,
From Ripley, believe it or not!

Bless the man, yes, the man
Who answered Smithsonia's call,
And under the stress of a querulous press,
Survived each Congressional brawl.

Got the dough, as we know,
And the welcome permission to go
With the plan of his vision, This man of decision,
I confess, serendiply, named S. Dillon Ripley,
Met every test and never could rest
Till he'd thoroughly blessed — the Mall!

Washington, DC — September 19, 1993

*Melody: *Bless Them All*, an old Army standard.

*With the completion of the new National Aquarium in Baltimore there was a move to close the modest little one in the Department of Commerce in Washington. Mrs. Malcolm ("Midge") Baldridge, wife of the Secretary of Commerce, decided on a benefit to raise funds to preserve the threatened facility. It was held in the Department's auditorium, and was called "Splash."*

*Mrs. Baldridge thought it needed a song, and asked me to write one about fish. "What should I say about fish?" I asked. "Just say something nice about them," she said. And that is what led to . . .*

## REMEMBER THE FISH IS OUR FRIEND
### Preface

With typical mammalian lack of tact
We generally tend to blink the fact
The gill-breathing vertebrate,
You've heard of it —
Fish
Is not just a dish
That feeds us.
It precedes us
By more millennia
Than any o'ya.
A little respect it's time we showed.
Hence this memorial, piscatorial
Ode.

They want a hep tune
For Neptune,
Something propitious
For the fishes,
While old Poseidon's bidin' his time.
This life aquatic
Was never static,
From the carp on to the tarpon to the haddock,
Since we crawled from the primeval slime.

We've had devotion to the ocean,
We're fond of the pond,
Get the shivers from the rivers,
And the shakes from the lakes . . . .

'Cause we've been there,
We've been in there,
Maybe committed original sin there;
Left a morsel of our dorsal little fin there.
And certainly some kin there.

So let's visit,
See who is it;
Not just kill it for a fillet in the skillet.
Remember the fish is our friend.

We can bring 'em to gaff,
But they'll have the last laugh,
'Cause they're in the swim to the end,
Yes, the whole of mankind
Should love the gills we left behind,
So remember the fishes,
Remember the fishes,
Remember the fish is our friend.

Washington, DC—August 31, 1982
Music: Sylvia Symington

Art Buchwald, dean of Washington's humorists, as auctioneer for a public television fundraiser calling for bids on an evening of folksongs with the author. Washington, DC, 1970.

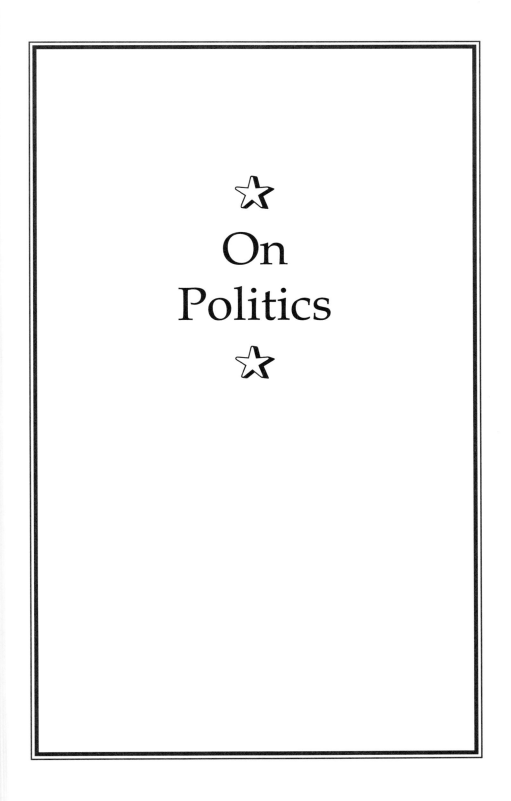

# On
# Politics

# UNCLE SAM'S DREAM — THE '96 ELECTION

Opening one eye is Uncle Sam

Startled from his slumber by a dream

Of dazzling contradictions, show and sham,

Pots and kettles letting off their steam,

Resignations, mea culpas, sighs

Uttered in the glare without a gleam,

And fashioned by the smart if not the wise.

Titanic challenge patiently stands by

As butterflies are captured and displayed.

Talismans are ready and held high

So the children needn't be afraid.

Rest easy, Uncle, have another snore.

Reality awaits beside your door.

Washington, DC — November 6, 1996

# PRESIDENTIAL ADVICE —
# A CONTRACT FOR WHITE HOUSE MEMOIRS

Having observed for the past seven presidencies the growing inclination of White House insiders to reap subsequent financial profits from their brief association with our chiefs of state, and having wondered how to deal with this commercialization of trust without offending the First Amendment, I have finally arrived at a reasonable solution that should appeal to all fair-minded folks.

The contract of White House employment could contain a provision that if, within ten years of such employment, the employee should take it upon himself or herself to write a book or article about the employer, the royalties thereof shall be shared with the employer or his heirs or assigns according to the following schedule: seventy percent to the employer if the revelations are in the main negative; fifty percent if it is an even-handed work; thirty percent if it is an obsequious whitewash.

These figures are adjustable, and any question concerning which category the work falls in could be resolved by a three-person arbitration team; one person selected by the ex-employee, one by the employer, and the third by the two so chosen. Appeals would lie to a public poll conducted by an acknowledged professional firm in that field, all expenses to come off the top.

The only appointee to whom this equitable solution might not commend itself would be one who will neither undertake to provide trustworthy service nor share with his erstwhile employer the rewards of broken trust. Are such persons necessary to government? They may well argue that the public benefits from their valuable insights! This may be true, and in that case, the true patriots could share them for free. The Internal Revenue Service could then determine the amount of deduction that can be taken for such a generous gift to the people of the United States.

A Letter to the *Washington Post* — Published May 5, 1979

*In addition to the required oath of office, the idea of a personal-loyalty oath to the appointing authority occasionally surfaces. In lieu of such a distasteful requirement, I have proposed a Royalty Oath to complement the previous contract. This suggestion has been ignored by at least four Presidents. President Bush received it in the form of a few lines addressed to his Chief of Staff, John Sununu:*

## ODE TO THE ROYALTY OATH

Dear John Sununu
We importune you
Knowing that soon you
'll be staffing.

We hope and believe you
'll want staffers who grieve you
To quietly leave you
Laughing.

To ensure the event
See that wisdom is spent
On ways to prevent
Them from writing . . .

The angry critique,
How the Prexy was weak,
And controlled by a clique
Worth indicting.

To muffle such foes
Or soften their prose
I would propose
Each contractor

Write if they dare,
But promise to share
The proceeds with their
Benefactor.

Their bottom lines
To his heirs and assigns,
Or grander designs,
Or both.
The power to spoil
The fruit of their toil
Lies, thus, in a royalty oath.

Washington, DC — November 21, 1988

# TERM LIMITS (1)

If we reach the point of constitutionally-approved term limits, they should, indeed, like federal liquor laws, be subject to local option. Any state or congressional district which has insufficient confidence in its own electorate to entrust to its judgment the question of fitness of its elected officials after a certain number of years, would be empowered to impose whatever limit it wished. Some might think that in two years infection sets in, and the patient should be quarantined. On the other hand, no state or district would presume to make such a judgment for the others. The two Houses could ameliorate the perceived advantage of tenure by elevating to their leaderships and committee chairmanships a selection, drawn from a hat to take the politics out of it, of the most recently elected class of members; a variation, if you will, of a familiar accounting formula, to wit: Last In First Up (LIFU), and a welcome departure, to be sure, from the flawed principle, FIFU.

States' righters will finally have something to applaud, and the country can get on to other business.

# TERM LIMITS (2)

Since my last communication on this aspect of congressional accountability, I have been advised that my formula makes only a half-hearted strike at the principal weakness of the current system of choosing federal representatives. As explained to me by its detractors, it is a system which encourages promises and more promises by persons seeking election, reliance on those promises by a defenseless electorate, and subsequent disappointment. It also requires the root of all evil, money. This dreary process can be obviated by employing the same technique we use to encourage young Americans to serve their country in time of need, a draft.

Citizens twenty-five years or over (thirty for the Senate) would be subject every two (six) years to a letter beginning, "Greetings — You have been designated the Congressperson (Senator) for the such and such congressional district (state). If you wish to plead special circumstances to avoid this obligation, please use the attached form. A final determination will be made in thirty days. Congratulations and good luck."

This approach removes the choice from the circus atmosphere in which it is now immersed. It eliminates entirely the need for campaign spending and the requisite fundraising activities which bring discredit on the system. Further, it will gratify those who believe anybody can do the job. Congress will most certainly be peopled by a very broad spectrum of citizens—including no more lawyers than their ratio to the whole—whose obligation to their constituents is unaffected by prior contact. The question of term limits becomes moot, as the likelihood of any sitting member receiving a second letter of this nature is almost mathematically impossible. Moreover, the rules could forbid it.

Washington, DC—February 19, 1997

# HAVE YOU EVER THOUGHT ABOUT POLITICS?*

Have you ever thought about politics?
Have you never wanted to serve?
It's a wonderful life for you and the wife
If you've got the nerve.

Can you tell by reading the paper
That the system's going astray?
Are you one of the kind with a lot on his mind
That he just won't say?

> Tell us it isn't so
> And that you're willing to fight
> To help society grow
> Strong and in the right.

We hope you'll think about politics
For whether you lose or you win
It's a challenge for you, to dare and to do
Or to be done in.

Sure it's a kind of a gamble
But if service means more than fame
The old croupier can win every play
But not your good name.

Is the label of politician
One we tend to malign?
Then carry it so the folks will know
That it can shine.
Come on into politics —
The water's fine!

Washington, DC — 1963
Music: Sylvia Symington

*A song.

Strumming for father, Stuart Symington's Senate race.
Tarkio, Missouri, 1952.

*Campaigning for Congress is not a poetic experience. I was told no muse is good muse. In the final week of my first campaign I allowed myself one departure from this discipline with a gentle appeal to the tune of "Hello Young Lovers":*

## HELLO YOUNG VOTERS*

Hello young voters wherever you are,

I hope your choices are few.

It's getting late, so please concentrate

On Hubert and Ed,[1] and me, too.

St. Louis — October 1968

*For a comparison of the Continental Congress and the one the author joined, the 91st, see pages 85-87; and for "less serious" speeches on the floor of the House, see pages 94-95.
[1]Vice President Hubert Humphrey and Senator Edmund Muskie (D-ME), the Democratic national ticket.

## ORATORY

When campaign rhetoric grows loud
Beware the consequences.
It's easier to bring a crowd
To its feet than to its senses.

Author's declaration of candidacy for Congress.
Chase-Park Plaza Hotel, St. Louis, Missouri; April 1, 1968.

Above: Opening of first Congressional campaign headquarters. Clayton, Missouri; May 19, 1968. Left to right: Author with wife, Sylvia; mother, Mrs. Stuart Symington; and campaign manager, Morton Bearman. Below: Sylvia at the headquarters.

The author, his wife, and volunteer workers with the campaign
bus in first Congressional race. Clayton, Missouri, 1968.

*In 1960, Senators John Kennedy, Lyndon Johnson, Hubert Humphrey, and Stuart Symington (my father) were contenders for the Democratic Presidential nomination. At the New Mexico Democratic Convention that summer in Sante Fe, Senator Kennedy appeared in person, Speaker Sam Rayburn appeared on behalf of then-Senate Majority Leader Johnson, and I was there for my father. The event was covered by William H. Lawrence for the New York Times, in part as follows:*

## A STRUGGLE FOR PRESIDENTIAL DELEGATES
### "Kennedy Raiding Johnson Ground"

Senator John F. Kennedy of Massachusetts mounted a Democratic delegate raid today deep in the southwestern backyard of Senator Lyndon B. Johnson of Texas. The struggle was before the New Mexico Democratic Convention, which is scheduled to choose delegates with seventeen votes to the Los Angeles nominating convention next month. . . .

The importance of the New Mexico battle was demonstrated by Senator Kennedy's personal participation and [the] last-minute decision [made] yesterday to fly House Speaker Sam Rayburn here to lead the Johnson campaign. James Symington was here to represent his father, Senator Stuart Symington of Missouri, who was seeking second-choice support if Senators Kennedy and Johnson falter and fail at Los Angeles. . . .

Speaker Rayburn, Senator Kennedy, and Senator Symington's son addressed the convention this morning, but each avoided a harshly partisan appeal. . . .

*New York Times* — June 5, 1960

*Indeed, having not one New Mexico delegate or even the hope of one it seemed best to enjoy the moment, as follows:*

## REMARKS BY JAMES W. SYMINGTON
## BEFORE THE NEW MEXICO
## STATE DEMOCRATIC CONVENTION

Mr. Chairman, Senator Kennedy, Senator Anderson, Speaker Rayburn, and would-be delegates to the Democratic National Convention. As the able and distinguished William Shakespeare wrote in his most memorable work, *Hiawatha*, "The sins of the fathers are visited on the sons," and I must say mine have overstayed their leave lately. Looking about, I realize it's an impertinence for me to clear my throat, much less speak. Indeed, I'm tempted to ask a moment's silence for absent friends—and in my case—relatives. It seems incredible, but the fact is, I'm here to help my father find work. I confess the Presidency is not necessarily the kind of work my brother and I would have chosen for Dad, but you know how fathers are. They have to feel their own way along life's road, and we can only hope to guide and help when we can.

All seriousness aside, look at the alternatives before you. Since the advent of Alaska, Texas has eyed her neighbors with a more than casual interest—in fact, hunger. A vote for the incomparable Majority Leader of the Senate may well be a vote for annexation. On the other hand, will it be said by historians that the mighty mavericks of New Mexico were meekly coralled by the cowboy from Cape Cod?

Politics aside—an unlikely scenario—if you would like to nominate someone trained and prepared for the job, I have just the fellow for you. Unanimously confirmed six times for posts in President Truman's Administration, he has clearly received an unprecedented seal of approval from the "world's most deliberative body," one with which Presidents must, on occasion, deliberate. As the nation's first Secretary of Air, he had his eye and his hand on our country's vital security needs. Subsequently, as Chairman of the National Security Resources Board, he had a similar overview of the nation's economy, as it related to security.

National security and the economy, not bad places to start when Presidential qualifications are at issue. Meanwhile, we are beset with slogans and quotes of many colors. For example: "A time for greatness"—when even a little mediocrity would be an improvement.

Finally, the generational gap that divides me from my father has presented some unique challenges. At a recent Democratic rally, a very sweet lady took me aside and said: "We do wish the Senator could have made it, but it's so nice to have his brother with us, and thank you for coming, Mr. Kennedy." It happened again last night. "Ain't you Jack Kennedy's brother?" I was ready this time. I looked the elderly gentleman in the eye and replied: "Yes, sir, but I've switched my support to Stuart Symington of Missouri."* And that, folks, is what I hope you will do.

And I thank you.

Santa Fe—May 28, 1960

---

*For remarks given in eulogy of Senator Stuart Symington, see pages 196-97.

☆

# On
# The Press

☆

*The press as an institution has produced an array of titans. A joint retirement for a distinguished trio of reporters inspired:*

## THE BALLAD OF HIGHTOWER, ROBERTS AND WARD*

I'll tell you a tale in this hour of our Lord
About three old pens that have mastered the sword,
Valiantly scribbling while others have snored,
And belonging to Hightower, Roberts and Ward.

A Pulitzer prize winner Paul Ward was he
Who helped free the French without leaving DC.
He left nothing unsaid and little undone
In his 41 years on the *Baltimore Sun.*

The next accolade is for Hightower who
Pulled in a Pulitzer in '52.
He's traveled quite widely for you and for me
But more particularly for the AP.

Finally Roberts whom archivists will
Reflect he was born on Squirrel Hill,
Yet many a Secretary of State
Trembled to hear that scratch on his gate.

So let's raise our glasses and with one accord
Toast a trio whom Presidents never ignored
Who made press spokesmen nervous and nobody bored—
Here's to Hightower, Roberts, and Ward.

Washington, DC—1970

*Columnists John Hightower, the Associated Press; Chalmers Roberts, the *Washington Post;*
and Paul Ward, the *Baltimore Sun.*

*The line between media viewpoint and bias is both subjective and irrelevant. The Constitution protects both. Hence these remarks before Congress in dissent from the Commerce Committee's vote of censure of CBS for refusing to produce in their entirety all interviews conducted for a program on the Pentagon.*

## PROPOSED CONTEMPT CITATION AGAINST CBS

Mr. Speaker, it is asserted that the editing by CBS of its program, "The Selling of the Pentagon," was so flagrantly deceitful and injurious to a proper public understanding of the subject matter as to invite congressional inquiry. Congress certainly has a legitimate interest in preserving the integrity of usage of public airwaves and channels by their licensees. And, as in other areas of legislative concern, it has a broad power to compel the production of information it deems essential to its lawmaking function.

If we do choose to exercise that power, as is suggested today, we must recognize that the underlying assumptions we make as to its reach will be subject to judicial review and possible reversal. So, the first question to consider ought not to be whether the asserted power actually exists in this case, but whether, on the perilous assumption that it does, it ought to be exercised in this fashion. Discretion may be the better part of congressional valor where the constitutional line to be approached is seen to divide us from First Amendment territory.

Even assuming that the subject program was deliberately edited with such deceptive results as to invite our inquiry, the question then arises as to whether an absolute necessity exists to compel production of the outtakes in order to complete that inquiry. It would seem, in view of the availability for comparison of the full transcripts of the principally contested materials, that no such necessity is shown. Congress certainly ought not to compel production of information it already has. Nevertheless, we are told we must serve notice now, by asserting this power, that it exists, else we will lose it. But Congress cannot ever lose a power it has, much less power it never had.

Indeed, in a larger sense, any congressional initiative which springs from the premise that government has the power to guarantee the "responsible" use of journalistic judgment springs from a false premise. Government is powerless either to render journalism "responsible" or to restore public confidence in it. Only the journalists have that power. Government can certainly erode public confidence in the press and other media, and one way to do so, paradoxically, is to announce that it has taken measures to keep them honest. Few would be reassured by such an assertion. In our society the government and the press cannot at any given moment know precisely where their respective boundaries are. They must coexist in a state of dynamic tension. Maintenance of this delicate balance cannot be achieved by fiat or force any more than a fine watch can be tuned with a hammer. Does this place the public at a disadvantage? It will be temporary. The threat of public disbelief should hang far heavier over the media and its sponsors than any congressional subpoena. No doubt public respect today for the media is at a low ebb. It would be inaccurate certainly to say the media need no apology, or that their apologists are in abundance in the Congress.

If and when their practices should invite governmental challenge, such challenge might be issued with better grace on behalf of some other aggrieved party than the government itself. The First Amendment problem is most acutely raised when the material to be censored or condemned is deemed injurious to the censor.

In 1861 President Lincoln wrote Thurlow Weed:

*Do you gentlemen who control so largely public opinion, do you ever think how you might lighten the burdens of men in power — those poor unfortunates weighed down by care, anxieties, and responsibilities?*

It is a wistful question, with sympathetic echoes in our time. But Lincoln did not confuse or equate his own discomfiture with public injury. Nor should we. An educated and vigilant citizenry is the best and perhaps the only defense against the broadcast of falsehood, whether it emanates from a private source or a public one.

*Congressional Record* — July 12, 1971

*Admittedly, not all "investigative" reporting serves a useful purpose. Hence this "elegy" written during the Democratic National Convention in 1972, but applicable to a genre of reportage that has grown and flourished.*

## ELEGY FOR A MUCKRAKER

Pity the poor muckraker.
From sun to setting sun,
As long as good men stand admired,
His work is never done.

What a lonely calling!
Others stand aghast,
While he injects the throbbing present
With the venom of the past.

Who are his companions,
The partners of his grief?
The envious, the malcontent,
The gossip and the thief.

Less favored than the ghoul
Who only robs the grave,
He tears the tissue from good names
History sought to save.

His pen a dripping scalpel,
His ink—formaldehyde,
As he performs his autopsies
On privacy and pride.

Charity is silent,
Conscience deeply sleeps.
And as he searches out his victims,
Journalism weeps.

Miami, Florida—1972

*Undeterred is the tendency for "investigative reporting" to go not only "behind the scene," but outside the theatre, into the home, boudoir, closet, bed, and bath. The First Amendment being not only the first but the last refuge — and a very substantial one at that — of purveyors of such reportage, the solution would seem to lie, not in fiat, but in simple arms-length negotiation between people of good will engaged in equally noble enterprises. Hence this letter to the Baltimore Sun outlining a proposal for POPSICLE, a private, non-profit organization that would conduct such negotiations as, if, and when circumstances should require.*

## SNOOP ON US?

The following proposal is predicated on the assumption that the role of the media in a democratic society is as vital to the health of that society as that played by politicians and public officials. If the media would insist that its role is of a lesser order of importance and therefore subject to a less stringent code of conduct, it could question the idea with a straight face. The proposal is as follows:

An organization would be formed entitled POPSICLE (Protectors of Public Servants Against Innuendo, Calumny, Lies and Eavesdropping). It would raise ten million dollars a year in one-dollar contributions from ten million Americans who read papers and watch and listen to the news, and who are more interested in good government than unremarkable private lives. Restricting contributions to one dollar will prevent any single contributor from exercising or appearing to exercise undue influence on the work of POPSICLE.

What is this work? POPSICLE will hire private investigators, using state-of-the-art technologies, to track the comings and goings of selected media personages, including the officers, directors, and staff of broadcasting networks as well as reporters, columnists, editorial writers, publishers, and indeed all persons bearing responsibility for sharing "vital" information with the public.

Data gathered, including photos, taped conversations, et cetera, would be closely held unless and until the target individuals directly or indirectly countenance the invasion of privacy of a public official. Then there would ensue a negotiation which may or may not result in diminished interest in pursuing the referenced reportage.

Its principal value will be to the credibility of the press because the public will know that the authors, publishers, and broadcasters of this kind of "news" that actually makes it through to publication are themselves POPSICLY-certified free from any parallel taint; that the purveyors of such disclosure have nothing equivalent to hide themselves; that when a kettle is called black, it's no pot talking but a spotless silver tureen.

Published in the *Baltimore Sun* — April 19, 1982

*President Kennedy expressed his distaste for the editorial biases of the New York Herald Tribune by cancelling his subscription. This raised the profile and prospects of its already very visible competitor, whose employees promptly went on strike. But the nation was more dependent than ever on:*

## THE *NEW YORK TIMES*

Nowadays it's more or less agreed
No matter what your color, race or creed,
If you want to get ahead
It's like the fellow said
It's not what you know, it's what you read.

So . . .

I'm reading the *New York Times*
It's seething with reasons and rhymes.
The ways of the world are all unfurled
When I open my *New York Times.*

I've found many a strange new noun,
And some of them upside down.
But between the misprints there's plenty of hints
For a fellow who's new in town.

History goes tickety tock,
While Reston questions the clock,
And who hasn't been gored by the singing sword
Of King Arthur Excalibur Krock?[1]

I take my Sulzberger[2] with salt,
My Krock with a chocolate malt.
If I find any jokes I don't blame Mr. Ochs,[3]
I know they're not his fault.

[1]Arthur Krock, political columnist.
[2]Arthur Ochs Sulzberger, Publisher, the *New York Times.*
[3]Adolph Simon Ochs (1858-1935), Founder of the *New York Times.*

Each day I must start with my *Times*,
I'd pay; yes, I'd part with my dimes
Since his Nibs cancelled his *Tribs*,
I've come up to the *New York Times*.

I've poured many rum and limes,
And ignored many Sunday chimes,
For I'd leave in the lurch any girl, any church,
For the *New York Times*.

☆ ☆ ☆ ☆ ☆

Oh where is my *Times*, oh where?
Will it rain today or be fair?
How would I know when each morning I go
And look . . . and the *Times* isn't there!

How long, America, how long
Must we suffer this wrong?
We're troubled, indeed, knowing what we can't read
In the *New York Times*!

Washington, DC—1962
Music: Sylvia Symington

Father and son on *Meet The Press*. NBC Studio, Washington, DC; June 20, 1971. Left to right: John W. Finney, *New York Times*; Carl Leubsdorf, Associated Press; Marquis Childs, *St. Louis Post Dispatch*; Paul Duke, NBC News; and Lawrence Spivak (Producer).

# On Romance
# And Its
# Hazards

# DISTRACTION*

After life's run

No man 'neath the sun

Can be counted as one

Whom fortune forsook,

If ever he

Could easily be

Drawn from surmise,

A task or a book

By one pair of eyes,

One look.

Washington, DC—January 1998

*Written on the occasion of our 45th wedding anniversary.

# "LET'S DO LUNCH"

She was all alone,
Waiting for a phone.
I had time to spare,
　　To stop . . .
　　To stare . . .
To pass the time of day,
And find the nerve to say,

"Let's do lunch," said to the lady,
"Let's do lunch," But says the lady,
"Thanks a bunch; I'm going steady."
"That's the crunch? Well, when you're ready,
Let's do lunch . . . someday."

"Let's break bread; the name is 'Grady' underfed."
"But," says the lady, "like I said, I'm meeting Freddy."
"Go ahead, but when you're ready,
Let's do lunch . . . someday.

　　Relationships are impatient ships
　　That sail uncharted seas.
　　If yours falls short, return to port,
　　I'll hold the fort, but please . . .

Say you'll lunch, and I'm a winner,
Play a hunch, and make it dinner . . .
A one-two punch, but for beginners,
Just a munch; I'm getting thinner . . .
Let's do lunch . . . someday!"

Washington, DC—1996
Music: Sylvia Symington

# GYPSY TOOT — (A Fantasy)

Often when I'm munchin'
My cafeteria luncheon,
Done with the dollar fight,
And keeping my collar white

I ignore the distant toot
Of a wandering gypsy flute.
Avoid the burning meaning
Of their ceaseless tambourining.

And yet if comes the chance,
I'll join that gypsy throng,
And dance a gypsy dance,
And sing a gypsy song.

I'll steal away at night,
And, like I never ran,
Run till I'm in sight
Of the gypsy caravan.

And then I'll throw my shoes
Anywhere I choose,
And doff my flannel pants,
And join the gypsy dance.

Into a sneer I'll curl
My lips at a gypsy girl,
And throatily she'll sing
This little gypsy thing:

"To be sure the lips he's
<u>Got</u> were meant for gypsies!"
I'll obey the gypsy rule,
And play the gypsy fool.

I'll flash what teeth I've got,
And slink with gypsy grace,
Pierce my ears a lot,
And muddy up my face.

We'll swirl until we're too sick
Of the strains of gypsy music,
And then, but not too loud,
We'll leave that gypsy crowd.

We'll steal into the woods,
And trade our gypsy goods,
Just a very few of us,
In fact, only the two of us.

Remaining 'til
We're very still
And too inert to be alert.
I'll find my shirt.
She'll get her skirt.
Then with no fuss,
But with a frown,
I'll take the bus
Back into town.

New York — 1952

# APRIL SKIES

April skies bring April sighs
And April lies as well.
What May will bring,
Or even June,
It's much too soon to tell.

If April sighs and April lies
Make April wise men fools.
Yet all the same
We play the game,
Can't break old April's rules.

So if one day
We come to find
We've lost our way;
Well, never mind
It won't mean a thing
Next Spring.

If April teases you with breezes
Hot instead of cool,
Don't be afraid, all men were made
To play the April fool.

Washington, DC—1965
Music: Jim Symington

*She was a junior at Sarah Lawrence College when we met. I then wired, "This sad gander's lonely honks will echo clear from here to Bronxville." During the summer of 1952 I put the question. Without commenting she embarked for Europe on an ocean liner filled with graduates of Annapolis and other suspect institutions. My father's Senate race provided a counterirritant. I penned this bon voyage:*

## HAVING JUST PHONED YOU

Having just phoned you
I'm happy as blazes,
So sweetly intoned you
Your words and your phrases.
My soul is a plant
Whose sun is your smile,
Indeed I could rant
And rave a good while.
But woe is the morn
When you take to the sea,
In a ship with men born
Of high pedigree.
Woe the newcomer
So smart in his linen,
Who courts you all summer
With his infernal grinnin'.
He with warm cloaks'll
Endeavor to lure you
Aft of the fo'c's'le.
A trick, I assure you.
When he and you stand,
And he plies you with notions,
You may toss from your hand
Little crumbs to the oceans.
I'll be with the sea birds
Who swoop to retrieve 'em,

Screaming these key words,
"Don't you believe 'im!"
I am the silvery
Flash in the sea.
Angered if pilfer he
Sylvia from me.
And if you ignore
My leaps as a porpoise,
Then what is love for
But to woof us and warp us?
Deep in Missouri
With a father much cussed,
Lost in pot pourri
Of speeches and dust,
There stands with guitar
A fellow whose spirit
Will soar very far
And so loud that you'll hear it.
In the gulls screaming,
In your sorrow and laughter,
Your waking and dreaming,
Before breakfast and after.
But if you protest, you
Just say it's too loud,
It will cease to molest you,
And hide in a cloud.

St. Louis—June 1952

With Sylvia.  St. Louis, Missouri, 1970.

# PRETEND  (A Song)

Lonely am I as the hours trickle by,
Watching the ivy climb.
The clock on the wall is not my friend at all.
Still the one thing I can bide is time.

To while away
The time of day
I play a game.
I pretend the trees are bending down to whisper
    your name.

I pretend I hear your feet
Along the rain-swept street.
Though all good things must end
That's not what I pretend.

And tell me, do
You play it, too,
This funny game?
Do you pretend the breeze is sending down
    a kiss in my name?

If you do, just thank the breeze
And tell the falling rain.
I'll hear it in my trees
And on my window pane.
And I'll follow till I find you
With a lifetime to spend,
And nevermore pretend.

St. Louis — 1953
Music:  Sylvia Symington

*January 24, 1953 marked the conclusion of an anxious courtship. A final affirmative inspired the following:*

## BONNET AND SANDALS

One evening I sat by the whispering river
Strumming my mandolin over my knee,
When out of the shadows there glided a maiden
From bonnet to sandal as fair as can be.

I watched as she knelt by the whispering river.
Her bonnet she doffed with a wave of her hand.
Then followed the sandals, she laid them all lightly,
Her bonnet and sandals upon the soft sand.

No word could I utter; my heart churned to butter,
My mandolin shuddered and fell from my hand.

Then, "Sir, if your music be over, please help me,
For carrying water it takes a strong arm."
In silence I vowed as I took up the handle
"This bonnet and sandal must not come to harm."

I asked if I mightn't be helping her often,
She smiled, and I knew she'd be down by and by.
So passed a sweet summer in moonlight and whispers
The bonnet and sandal, the river and I.

But the nights they grew colder, and me, I grew bolder
To hold her, then told her on one mighty day

"Ah, the years like the river are flowing to darkness,
Please go with me darling and lighten my way."
"My bonnet and sandals say go with you gladly.
Let's see what my mother and father will say."

Her father and mother they turned to each other.
"This young man will do, yes my young man, you'll do.
So gather her softly and go with the river.
These tears are the blessing we tender to you."

"No tempest shall harm her, no storm shall alarm her,
Her faith is my armor, the strength of my hand,
And I'll cover her over from bonnet to sandal
With love while the candle burns down to the stand."

St. Louis — 1953
Music: Jim Symington

Honeymoon. Miami, Florida, January 1953.

# HOW'S BAYOU

When I think of the sigh you sighed by the bayou,

The oath nothing loathe you did swear.

I'm rending my raiment, lamenting the payment

I made on our bungalow there.

For I wanted to buy you a bayou canoe,

And ride side by side as we'd silently glide

With pomp through the swamp that's true.


But if it's not to be I shall put out to sea

With the thought (and a whiskey or two,

Or possibly gin) of what might have been

In the fog and the bog with you.

New York—1954

# WEEKEND PASS

Who hasn't heard the whispered invitation

Of the street, or let his restless gaze,

Conscious of a certain expectation,

Be drawn along the length of darkened ways?

Who, in parting curtains for the air

Of steamy night, can instantly erase

Impressions of delight when catching there

The fleeting whiteness of an upturned face?

Who can feel so, yet follow not the course

A pounding heart prescribes, as if the pain

Of fumbling for a match could spend the force

Of urgent curiosity; again

It well could be some imperfection, say

A loveless smile that turns a glance away.


U.S.M.C., Camp Lejeune, North Carolina — 1946

# SONG OF THE LONELY SWISS GUIDE
## (A Yodel Song)

There once was a lonely Swiss guide
Who yodeled much less than he sighed.
For he was afraid that his Alpine milk maid
Would never become his Swiss bride.

Though he feared she would scoff and deride,
He swallowed his lofty Swiss pride,
And sang as he ran toward her Alpine milk can
Of the love he no longer could hide.

If I gallop up the Alps will you avalanche* with me?
I'll be as good as I can be
With my yodelayee tee.
Ah, those fillips from your chill lips,
They are kisses soft as silk
And I'll wash 'em down with . . .
Tee yodelayee
Milk.

And-if-I-sneeze in my lederhosen
It's 'cause my knees I'm afraid are frozen,
Yet for you I'd tyrolean the snow.

'Twould be no damper to my ardor,
I'd simply scamper a little harder.
No wind can blow away — my glow.

I'm dependable as a Swiss clock,
And mendable as a Swiss sock.
In fact, you will learn
That from Berne to Lucerne
There's no finer Alpine stock!

So if you gallop up the Alps you will see the Swiss chalet
Where they avalanche each day
In their yodelayee way.

St. Louis — 1957
Music: Sylvia Symington

*French for "have lunch."

*On the plight of a midwestern girl bored with her surroundings, a song:*

# I SEEK A GREEK

For a girl from Kansas,
Hunting for bonanzas,
America and Europe have run dry.
So is it any wonder
I've gone to find one under
The Mediterranean sky?

I seek a Greek, a barefoot Greek
Physique of teak.
It's chic, unique,
My clique'll shriek
When I'm dancing cheek to Greek.
I want to save my hugs and kisses,
Trade my Miss for Mrs.
Ulysses.

I want to sneak away from Topeka
To Salonika with a Greek.
He'll give my hand a squeeze
Down on his Peloponnese.
What if he's got a yacht, is that a blot
On his escutcheon? No, it's not.

I want a tonic that's Ionic,
A sandal full of scandal,
A smile, an isle, on the Aegean sea.
And if he's mean to me,
He's still Hellene to me.

My future's bleak without the Greek
I seek this week.
Here in my shift I need a lift
Bearing a little gift.

What really would be nice is,
To face the mid-life crisis
With Dionysus.
I'd even learn his credo
If I could be old Plato's
Tomato.

I've got a streak not mild or meek
That makes me seek
A Greek.
Who'll promise me the world as Euripides knew it
Before the Romans blew it,
I'm going to it.
I seek a Greek.

Washington, DC—1964<br>
Music: Sylvia Symington

# TWO  BODIES

Please pass me a brandy, a beer, or a toddy

To give me the strength and acumen

To observe the world's most deliberative body

Pondering that of a woman.

Washington, DC — January 1999

# On
# Lawyers
# And
# The Law

*In the fall of 1954, with law school and the Missouri bar exam behind me, I entered "City Hall" in St. Louis as an Assistant City Counselor. Mornings were spent prosecuting in police court; afternoons on the preparation of legal opinions for the mayor and other officials.*

*One such opinion addressed a proposed ordinance that would have outlawed "the distribution of publications which advocate un-American activities." In addition to the opinion, which dwelt drily on the First Amendment, this intriguing notion prompted the following mythical exchange:*

# A DIALOGUE WITH SOCRATES

*Socrates is standing before the Parthenon. Xenophobe approaches, breathless.*

Soc: Hold, friend. What's your hurry?

Xen: Socrates, I have here in my hand a law — an idea, that is — for a law that I wish to show at once to the elders and to the people for their approval.

Soc: May I see it, being as I am, interested in new laws?

Xen: By all means. Keep this copy. Scan it well. I think you, particularly, Socrates, do stand to benefit from a thorough understanding and observance of its provisions.

Soc: *(taking the scroll)* As of any good law. Oh, your law makes it a crime to distribute publications which advocate un-Athenian activities.

Xen: That it does. It is high time something was done.

Soc: What a marvelous concept! Yet a very difficult one at that. I believe I may be too old and my head too bony to master its subtlety and the scope of its application. Tarry, Xenophobe, and dispel the mystery of it.

Xen: Mystery! It is rather self-evident, old man. You must, indeed, be losing your faculties.

Soc: I fear so; an old mind, like an old belly, cannot readily digest the latest rich foods, but chews the cud of the remembered and the proven. It would be good to be young again and share your enthusiasm. I believe I would feel so if you could satisfy one or two questions that come to mind.

Xen: Of course, Socrates. I shall be happy to enlighten you.

Soc: You are gracious. Tell me, learned Xenophobe, is free press an Athenian or an un-Athenian activity?

Xen: Athenian, Socrates, most assuredly.

Soc: And curtailment or restriction of the press, un-Athenian?

Xen: That would follow.

Soc: Indeed. And one who would distribute a publication which advocates curtailing the press, distributes, thereby, a publication which advocates an un-Athenian activity, does he not?

Xen: From the premise, yes.

Soc: Do you now deny your premise?

Xen: Of course not.

Soc: And your law would make it a crime to distribute any publication which would advocate the un-Athenian activity of curtailing the press?

Xen: Among others, quite so.

Soc: Then, as I see it, Xenophobe, and correct me if this is not so, your law, which makes it a crime to distribute publications which advocate un-Athenian activities, makes its own distribution a crime since it advocates, if you will, the un-Athenian activity of curtailing the press. You gave me a copy of this proposed law, Xenophobe. If it is passed, it is my duty as a citizen to prosecute you. Of course, you could plead that it is not retroactive.

Xen: All nonsense, Socrates. The free press isn't an Athenian activity where it is abused.

Soc: What is it in that case?

Xen: It is, of course, un-Athenian where it is abused.

Soc: What is the test, Xenophobe, by which we may determine if it is being abused?

Xen: Socrates, you try a man's patience. It is abused where it is so exercised as to hurt Athens.

Soc: I am beginning to understand. A moment ago you told me that a free press was an Athenian activity, and curtailing it an un-Athenian activity. You would like at this time to refine those definitions, would you not?

Xen: Obviously, Socrates. It is manifest that a free press is usually an Athenian activity, but is un-Athenian where so exercised as to hurt Athens.

Soc: And, conversely, curtailing the press is usually an un-Athenian activity, but is Athenian where the press curtailed is so exercised as to hurt Athens?

Xen: That is it, very simply.

Soc: To carry it further, the Athenian activity of curtailing an allegedly abused free press may itself be abused, may it not, and is so where, in truth, the press curtailed was not hurting Athens at all? And, being thus abused, the curtailment itself hurts Athens, and becomes un-Athenian?

Xen: Possibly.

Soc: So it comes down to the question, "What hurts Athens?"

Xen: I suppose it does.

Soc: What hurts Athens, Xenophobe?

Xen: Lots of things.

Soc: Do you know, Xenophobe, what hurts Athens?

Xen: Within limits, I believe so.

Soc: You are fallible; you are not almighty?

Xen: That's not amusing, Socrates.

Soc: Are all Athenians in substantial agreement with your views on what does or does not hurt Athens?

Xen: I presume so; there are certain recognized principles.

Soc: Assuming, without admitting, that the majority do, then who applies this law of yours to the citizens so that one's freedom or fortune may ultimately be affected by it?

Xen: The judges.

Soc: Do the judges know what does or does not hurt Athens?

Xen: It is their job to know.

Soc: Well, when presented with a case wherein some activity is assailed as being un-Athenian, they may, if they cannot avoid it, rule on the question?

Xen: They may. Betimes they must.

Soc: And since they are not almighty, they are guessing?

Xen: They are deciding.

Soc: Perhaps wrongly?

Xen: In one sense, perhaps.

Soc: Then indulge me for a moment, if you will, my fancy that they are just guessing. Best guessing, perhaps, but guessing.

Xen: Very well, guessing.

Soc: But I thought it was the province of the legislators to guess what the law was, not of the judges. And that judges merely took the law as the legislators guessed it to be. And that the test of a good law was that the legislators' guess left little, if any, room for judges' guesses, one grand guess at the center being preferable to many, and perhaps, contradictory, little guesses along the periphery. Yet your law is no guess at all, but a blank parchment for the judges to scribble their guesses upon. Your law, Xenophobe, is a sort of guessing heaven, a limitless pasture for the starving imaginations of judges to graze upon till they become languid. Judges who will not all be equally honest, equally wise, nor equally conscious of what is Athenian.

Xen: I must say, Socrates, I have not been well lately, and my doctors advise me to keep out of the sun. If you will excuse me. *(leaves)*

Soc: I expect Xenophobe will withdraw his bill. If he does not, however, and it is passed, I am in a quandary. If I prosecute him under its terms for distributing it to me, some judge will guess whether or not it, in itself, advocates something un-Athenian. And if he guesses that it does not, I may be tried for engaging in the un-Athenian activity of malicious prosecution, ignorance of the law being no defense. Yet, if I say nothing, and his bill is not only not passed but exposed as seditious, and I am discovered to be one to whom he has given a copy, I may be tried for failing to do my Athenian duty of apprising the authorities of a wrongdoing. Xenophobe! Wait! Take this along with you. I have not read it, and I never saw you today.

Office of the City Counselor
St. Louis, Missouri — 1955

*Thoughts shared with the graduating class of the Missouri University School of Law:*

# RESPECT FOR THE LAWYER

Said Sam Johnson[1] of a certain acquaintance, "I hate to speak ill of anyone, but he is a lawyer."

"Is it not a lamentable thing," said the rebel Cade in Shakespeare's *Henry the Sixth*, "that of the skin of an innocent lamb should be made parchment: that parchment, being scribbled o'er, should undo a man?" "The first thing we do," said Dick "the Butcher" in the same work, "is kill all the lawyers."

Of his Utopians, Sir Thomas More[2] wrote, "They have no lawyers among them, for they consider them a sort of people whose profession it is to disguise matters."

Before recognizing the skull he held as that of, "alas, poor Yorick," Hamlet speculated, "Why may not that be the skull of a lawyer? Where be his quiddities now, his quillets, his cases, his tenures, and his tricks?"

"Washington would be better off," said Earl Butz[3] in a 1974 interview, "with a few less smart, young lawyers."

The centuries have not dealt altogether kindly with the law profession. How is it with the law itself?

"Reason," said Lord Coke,[4] "is the life of the law; nay, the common law is nothing else but reason." "Our defense," said Albert Einstein,[5] "is not in armaments, nor in science, nor in going underground. Our defense is in law and order." Or, John Locke's[6] memorable phrase, "Wherever Law ends, Tyranny begins." It is said that one early Greek tyrant posted the laws very high so the people could not read them.

Law in the abstract has certainly fared better than its practitioners in the minds and hearts of men. Inevitable, you might say. No surprise; in the nature of things. Perhaps, yet I cannot help but believe that as in every new spring, deep within every new crop of law graduates there exists a primordial strain of hope and expectation, reaching back through time to the yearnings of our earliest ancestors. "Lawyers," said Thomas Fuller,[7] "like bread, are best when they are young and new."

There is in each of you a seed of belief, partly spiritual, partly intellectual, that one day there might be just laws, just lawgivers to fashion them, just lawyers to interpret them, and just powers to enforce them. Surely this day cannot mean for you but an embarkation on a predetermined voyage on the gray seas of more-of-the-same. Surely, to you the recent history of American law and lawyers during your three-year term of study, like all history, need only be learned not to be repeated, at least in your own professional time. And to some extent and in some way, you each wish to narrow the gap in public confidence between the law and lawyers.

However, assuming you are inspired to steer clear of the shoals of avarice, deceit, and abuse of power, which have wrecked so many professional lives and so injured your society, your obligation, I would suggest, does not end there. One of your own professors brought this point home to me in a brief conversation at the Law Day luncheon two weeks ago. I had asked him if he did not find it ironic that many, including lawyers, who were privileged to serve in the highest places in government over the past half-decade, and who betrayed their trust, were now reaping rich rewards on the lecture circuit, far beyond their income as faithful practitioners of their profession. Others were preparing books and articles, either blithe accounts of the circumstances of their iniquity, or pure fiction, in reliance upon the notoriety of their name. The professor's response was immediate. "That," he said, "is the fault of society itself."

His point was that a healthy society would have the antibodies to reject these viruses; that the climate of their new blossoming would be a cold one, indeed. A society that has learned to accept the worst will eventually reward it. Your uphill task is to convince your fellow citizens that something better is possible, that goodness is a concept which can find expression in American life at all levels, beginning with the law. I say "uphill task" advisedly. For even, or perhaps, particularly among some other professions is the lawyer regarded today with suspicion. Professionals in the fields of insurance and medicine tend at times to lay at the doorstep of the law profession the prohibitive costs of malpractice premiums and excessive tort recoveries, chiefly in the auto-accident area.

Hence, the growing pressure for no-fault auto insurance and limits to malpractice recoveries. It sometimes seems as if the rest of society were drawing its wagons in a circle to fight off the lawyers. For one reason or another certain groups and individuals have come to distrust the forces that lawyers set in motion, and would prefer to see constitutional guarantees circumvented than exploited by those sworn to uphold them. Has the law entered such a dark age? Is this how the bicentennial of American law is to be marked?

Have the men and women of the law fairly or unfairly earned the condemnation of the society they are licensed to serve? Rather than spend time in a barren examination of the past, it is for us to look to the future, and to resolve that tomorrow's society will respect not only the law, but the laws, and the law profession. The demand of the sixties for "respect" for the law must be expanded to include the lawyer, too. Law and order without lawyer-made orderliness is highly unlikely. Remember Thomas More's advice to his rebellious son-in-law:

> And when the last law was down, and the Devil
> turned round on you — where would you hide, Roper,
> the laws all being flat?

> This country's planted thick with laws from coast to
> coast — man's laws, not God's — and if you cut them
> down . . . do you really think you could stand upright
> in the winds that would blow then?

In sum, the lawyer's main task today is not to be defensive, but to keep a steady eye on the truth and a steady course toward it. The law is its own defense. Man's imperfection, and the partial concealment by Providence of the precise corner where right and truth reside, warrant vigorous advocacy in an adversary system. It is by chopping through the jungle of entanglements of principle, precedent, and procedure that good lawyers make good law. I do very much hope that some of the best of you will seek careers in trial and appellate advocacy. The judges must rely in large part on the arguments brought before them.

I hope, too, that whether your practice be corporate, regulatory, or general, you will seek and maintain active professional links through bar and other associations to the great questions America must turn over in her mind. The focus of tomorrow's American lawyer must not be the small print, but the broad text, pointing and directing our future as a sane and decent society which both condemns evil and cherishes excellence, a society whose lawyers seek righteousness as naturally as they learn to say, "Your honor."

Columbia, Missouri — June 6, 1975

---

[1]Dr. Samuel Johnson (1709-84), the celebrated English man of letters and lexicographer.
[2]Sir Thomas More (1478-1535), English lawyer, statesman, and writer: executed by Henry VIII; canonized in 1935.
[3]Earl Butz, former Secretary of Agriculture under President Ford.
[4]Sir Edward Coke (1552-1634), English jurist and statesman.
[5]Albert Einstein (1879-1955), U.S. physicist (born in Germany) who formulated the theory of relativity.
[6]John Locke (1632-1704), English empirical philosopher and political theorist.
[7]Thomas Fuller, English writer.

# SUGGESTION TO THE IRS

*In 1961 I made a modest and ill-fated proposal to Mortimer Caplin, Commissioner of the Internal Revenue Service (IRS):*

Dear Mort:

It has recently been stated by a distinguished professor at Oxford that after the age of twenty-one we all lose about thirty-thousand brain cells a day throughout life. As an attorney who relies each day on the cells remaining, I was wondering if we could not deduct the value of the cells lost, presumably measurable right up to midnight of New Year's Eve. Say, ten cents a cell, or even a penny. What say?

Best,

James W. Symington

Mr. Caplin answered me fairly promptly, as I recall, in the negative.

# MODERN LAW AND LAWYERING

*The Finnish habit of diving from a sauna into the snow is a bit like leaving academe for the practice of law. Hence, this "Lawyer's Lament" in four parts.*

## A LAWYER'S LAMENT — PART I*

### As I Walked Out Of Columbia One June Day

As I walked out of Columbia one June day
A-singin' that old graduation song
I figured I'd spend all my years in the Noonday[1]
A-sippin' martinis, but, boy, was I wrong.

I bade farewell to the law books around me,
Good riddance you leather-bound tower of tears,
But they've had the last laugh, for, frankly I've found me
Not one simple question in three solid years.

Yes, this turn of events never fails to amaze me,
For now there's a term paper due every day,
And the fellow who grades them is the fellow who pays me.
I think I preferred it the opposite way.

The work of a lawyer—it hardly makes headlines.
The last minute filings, the call to Bill Maul.[2]
Yet his life is one agonized series of deadlines,
While the clients are certain he's trying to stall.

As I walked out of Columbia that summer,
A promising lawyer they said I would be.
Well it's perfectly true, but the meaning is glummer,
For I'm promising daily to earn my first fee.

---

*Tune: *Cowboy's Lament.* Performed at the St. Louis Bar Association Annual Dinner in 1957.
[1] A luncheon club in St. Louis.
[2] The court clerk.

# A LAWYER'S LAMENT — PART II

## Hush Little Barrister*

Hush little barrister, don't you bawl,
Those limping footsteps up the hall
Could be a client coming to call.
Hullverson† and Richardson† can't handle them all.

Look, his back is broken in a tricky place,
Needs a brand new car and a brand new face.
To the scene you breathless race,
Could be there's insurance in the case.

There is, indeed, but hear the worst,
The claim adjusters got there first.
Those masters of the golden fleece
Got your man to sign a complete release.

First you must get that knocked out
If persuasion fails, give a lusty shout.
Your client didn't know what he was thinking about.
He was still in shock from the terrible clout.

And if you're all prepared for trial
And your client vanishes, just smile.
And if your only witness dies,
Just you rise and claim surprise.

And when you get reversed upstairs
Just trot on home and say your prayers.
But don't you fret and don't you frown,
Cause you're still just the sweetest little lawyer in town.

St. Louis — 1957

*Tune: *Hush Little Babe.*
†James Hullverson and Orville Richardson, lead partners
  of a renowned St. Louis law firm.

# A LAWYER'S LAMENT — PART III

## Old Uncle Tom Cobbs And All*

Hey Jim, little Jim, will you come out and play?
All along, down along, out along lee . . .
No, for I fear I'll be working all day
For Bill Armstrong, Ken Teasdale, Harry Kramer, Walter
Roos 'n Ed Johnston, Henry Lamkin, Gene Dapron, Bill
Webster — old Uncle Tom Cobbs and all[†]
Old Uncle Tom Cobbs and all.

Well, how 'bout some lunch then to break up the task?
All along, down along, out along lee . . .
If you wait just a minute, I'll go in and ask
Bill Armstrong, Ken Teasdale, Harry Kramer, Walter
Roos 'n Ed Johnston, Henry Lamkin, Gene Dapron, Bill
Webster — old Uncle Tom Cobbs and all
Old Uncle Tom Cobbs and all.

Well, will you your formula for success give?
All along, down along, out along lee . . .
Certainly, boys, I must simply outlive
Bill Armstrong, Ken Teasdale, Harry Kramer, Walter
Roos 'n Ed Johnston, Henry Lamkin, Gene Dapron, Bill
Webster — old Uncle Tom Cobbs and all
Old Uncle Tom Cobbs and all.

St. Louis — 1957

*Tune: *Tam Pierce.*
[†]Senior partners of the venerable St. Louis law firm of
   Cobbs, Armstrong, Teasdale & Roos.

# A LAWYER'S LAMENT — PART IV
## The Nightmare

I dreamt one night I was ruling on a motion

With calm and dispassionate juridical devotion.

When suddenly I realized amid the grim commotion

Of the answer to the thing I didn't have the

    faintest notion.

The question, it involved an attempted interpleader

Where a woman had two husbands and neither one

    would feed her.

Morris Shenker for the plaintiff versus Charlie Shaw*

I awoke and decided to quit the law.

St. Louis — 1957

*Leading barristers of the day.

# MEDIEVAL LAW

*At Columbia Law School the immortal professor Julius Goebel's course on early English common law inspired these reflections:*

## IF*

If I held of the King[1]
I'd leave everything to you.
If your folks were bereft
I'd still be enfoeffed[2] by you.

If you'd only wait,
I'd subinfeudate,[3]
Just to share my fate — with you.

If I ran a court leet[4]
I'd be just as sweet — on you.
If I held in capite[5]
My lands would escheat[6] — to you.

I'm not such a mesne[†]
Lord[7] that I'd be seen
Venting any spleen — on you!

If I held in fee tail[8]
I'd do it in gaol[9] — for you.
If young maids to me'd flock
I'd save sac and soc[10] — for you.

You're my commonweal,[11]
My trial by ordeal,[12]
Cause I got a feel — for you.

Columbia Law School — 1951

---

*Sung at the Barristers' Ball, June 1954, to the tune Eddie Fisher made famous.
[†]Pronounced "mean."
[1]If lawful title to my land derived directly from the King.
[2]You would still be the source of my estate.
[3]I would grant you a portion of my estate.
[4]If I presided over a court of criminal jurisdiction.
[5]Same as 1.
[6]If I were to have no heirs, my land would revert to you.
[7]A mesne Lord is also the tenant of a higher lord.
[8]If my ownership derived directly from the bloodline of the original donor.
[9]Jail.
[10]The power to administer justice.
[11]Public welfare.
[12]In this oldest form of Saxon "trial," the accused was subjected to a life-threatening situation remediable only by divine intervention.

# THE IDYLLS OF A SOCAGE TENANT, or
## ROAR OF THE SERF

Oh I'd rather be a vassal

In a loosely governed castle

Than the squire of a dignified estate,

Where disintegrating morals

Provide no cause for quarrels,

But enrich the working day, and stimulate.

Where I'd be steeped in mead n' honey,

And not be needin' money

For anything from wine to romance,

And where the system while it's feudal,

Through its atmosphere and mood'll

Give creative instinct a chance.

Columbia Law School—1952

# THE CONFEDERATE CONSTITUTION
## — HINTS OF THE FUTURE —

In the film, *Back To The Future*, we saw how a young man, having ridden a time machine back to the period of his parents' troubled courtship, interceded and saved the marriage. It is, alas, only in fantasy or in Russia that we can adjust the past to serve the present.

Happily, in the case of the Constitution there is little we would change if we could. One modification, however, we all would wish to make, given the chance, would be termination of the institution of slavery. The compromise by which slavery was retained also made possible future Congressional passage of "navigation acts" and their cargo preference provisions sought by the ship-building states of New England. Those states were loathe to give up such preferences. The Southern states, for their part, would never have concluded the compact if it did not validate their "peculiar institution." Both sides gave and both got. The result: no restrictions on navigation acts, and House representation apportioned to states "according to their respective numbers" . . . including, in addition to the "whole Number of Free Persons," . . . "three-fifths of all other Persons." Thus did the framers indulge in a comforting euphemism, one which was discarded in the corresponding section of the subsequent Confederate Constitution which allocated votes and taxes in accordance with the numbers of free persons, plus "three-fifths of all Slaves."

The grand instrument we celebrate embodied the budding seed of tragedy, as we know. Its structure facilitated the peaceable management of every conflicting ambition, save one. And neither euphemism nor the Kansas-Nebraska Act could prevent that one from putting asunder what God had seemed to join. It took about two generations for the built-in centrifugal forces to reach the critical stage—the stage at which, if North and South were to live at peace with their respective views of the slavery question, they would have to live separately. This the Southern states determined to do after convening delegates and commissioners to examine the matter. Still, on the very eve of their deliberations, they indulged in the hope and expectation of peace. Inasmuch as the severance appeared to have the validity of historical precedent, it could be resolved, it seemed, both as a legal and a practical matter, without recourse to war. The decision by a majority of Southern states to secede was made in January 1861; delegates were then appointed to meet in Montgomery, Alabama to draft a constitution for a new Confederacy. A provisional constitution was adopted on February 8, 1861, and its "permanent" successor, March 11th.

In my studies, I was never introduced to the existence of a Confederate Constitution, clearly the best kept secret ever struck off by the hand of man. My exposure occurred in connection with an ancestral search of the history of my father's grandfather, Major Stuart Symington, Confederate States of America, who, after Appomattox, took the boat to Europe instead of the required oath. He and his brother Thomas, Marylanders who had fought in the Army of Northern Virginia, paid a postwar visit to Germany as guests of Jeb Stuart's friend and erstwhile comrade-in-arms, Heros von Borcke. Family lore suggested they'd attended Heidelberg University, but the Library of Congress' list of Americans who attended the university in the 1860s and 70s does not include Symingtons.

It occurred to me then that the Confederacy itself, for a brief time at least, looked forward to an immortal existence. What had been its plans? I assumed that, like the Union it sought to leave, it had adopted a constitution. But I wasn't familiar with this glimpse of the future as seen through the eyes of the delegates to the Montgomery Convention. So I looked it up. In general it tracks its durable forerunner, one which its framers considered wise and proper enough per se, but faulted in interpretation. It is chiefly in its departures from the original, however, that it merits the attention of students of contemporary political thought.

Both constitutions enjoyed the infusion of Southern political sagacity. But aside from its painful and inadmissible provisions regarding slavery, the Confederate edition incorporated intriguing modifications suggested by some three-score-and-ten years of experience with its predecessor. Some of them would enjoy broad support today. For those who would reduce the influence of re-election politics on presidential decisions, or adopt a parliamentary approach to the accountability of Cabinet officers, or make the Post Office pay for itself, or cut congressional spending generally, or remove unnecessary civil servants, the following excerpts from the Constitution of the Confederate States of America (CSA), will be of interest.

By Article 11, Section 1, the President and Vice President "shall hold their offices for the term of six years, but the President shall not be re-eligible. . . ."

By Article 1, Section 6, "Congress may, by law, grant to each of the executive departments a seat upon the floor of either House with the privilege of discussing any measures appertaining to his department."

By Article 1, Section 8, " ... the expenses of the Post Office Department . . . shall be paid out of its own revenue."

By Article 1, Section 7, "The President may approve any appropriation and disapprove any other appropriation in the same bill . . . ." This is the stuff presidential dreams are made of.

By Article 1, Section 9, "Congress shall appropriate no money from the Treasury except by two-thirds vote of both Houses, taken by Yeas and Nays unless it is submitted by a Department head with the President's approval."

By Article 11, Section 2, " . . . civil officers . . . may be removed at any time by the President . . . when their services are unnecessary, or for dishonesty, incapacity, inefficiency, misconduct, or neglect of duty."

In the Confederate Constitution states' rights enjoy a fair field over states' responsibilities. While the then-current Bill of Rights was largely incorporated into Article 1 of the Confederate text, Section 2 of that Article provides, "judicial or other federal officers resident and acting solely within the limits of any state may be impeached by a vote of two-thirds of both branches of the Legislature thereof."

There are a number of other provisions which reveal the perceptions and apprehensions of the Confederate founding fathers. The Preamble skips references to "Common Defense" and "General Welfare." And, unlike the original, it invokes "the favor and guidance of Almighty God."

Students of American political science cannot ignore the Confederate Constitution. It is more prologue than much of the past we dwell on. It presages the kind of forces that are today marshalled by States' righters; presidential-term extenders; foes of taxing, spending, and bureaucracy; and those who would keep God up front.

It has certainly never lost its relevance or importance as a guide to the conservative themes that have been in ascendance in our own time. In political wisdom, tenured committee chairmen, and a recent president, the once and future South has risen indeed. As indicated, many of its old ideas have resurfaced to claim considerable support today. Its "founding fathers" — Toombs, Howell, Rhett, Cobb, Barnwell, Chestnut, and Stephens — are hardly household words. They are lost names in American history, "gone with the wind." But the history they made is nonetheless American. As a mid-course "correction" of constitutional content and a portent of the future, the document they fashioned should be brought out of the closet of history.

An Address Before the National Association
of Retired Federal Employees
Washington, DC — September 9, 1987

# TRIALS OF OUR TIME

When race and gender "knew their place,"

Gender dominated race.

Now that "place" has lost its case

Race is trumping gender's ace.

Washington, DC—1994

☆

# On
# Congress

☆

*Running for Congress is a good, if at times painful, and definitely expensive way to discover America. In any case, Richard Nixon and I were elected on the same day, he to the Presidency, I to the Congress.*

*Later in the year I was asked by Life Magazine to review the new musical "1776" and to compare the Continental Congress to the one I had just joined (the Ninety-first).*

## A FUNDING SON LOOKS AT THE FOUNDING FATHERS

Will Rogers used to say that when he needed a laugh he just read what Congress had done that day. The Broadway musical *1776* suggests that even July 4th of that year was just another congressional day — although what was "done" was the adoption of the Declaration of Independence. A freshman congressman like myself soon learns to "doubt a little of his infallibility," as Ben Franklin counseled. But what seems to have escaped my studies — and the notice of historians I had relied on — is that the acrimonious debate over independence was also marked by good-natured raillery and impromptu barber-shop. With its cast of caricatures, *1776* is an intriguing glimpse of history as seen through an eighteenth-century laugh-in.

Poetic, or at least prosaic, license is taken with events and discourses of the period. An amiable confusion of fact, fiction, and farce characterizes this musical as it undoubtedly characterized the Congress depicted, and others since. At the opening curtain the Founding Fathers reprimand their testy, independence-minded colleague John Adams with a lusty chorus of "Sit Down, John!" I have heard this kind of suggestion whispered under the breath of my colleagues during the pronouncements of their brethren, but I've never been treated to the sight of the whole assembly bursting into song. Senator Dirksen, the choirboy of the Western world, did pirouette around his desk to question the utility of introducing dance into Head Start programs. He lost his point, but won the gallery, and the infrequency of such moments is to be mourned. We need to get back to the time, as in *1776*, when that irrepressible trio — Jefferson, Franklin, and Adams — would link arms to relieve the tensions of nation-building by engaging in light-hearted minstrelsy. Their "Egg" song, beginning "Chirp, chirp, chirp," and celebrating the hatching of the American eagle, would bring any House down.

So would Ben Franklin's hearty colloquies with Pennsylvania-loyalist delegate John Dickinson. "What's so terrible about being called an Englishman?" Dickinson asks at one point. "The English don't seem to mind." "Nor would I," says Franklin, "were I given the full rights of an Englishman. But to call me one without those rights is like calling an ox a bull—he's thankful for the honor but he'd much rather have restored what's rightfully his."

Update the cast, substitute "American" for "Englishman" and this exchange could be quite contemporary. But while matters touching on "patriotism" or judgment on grave issues still evoke earthy exchanges in Congress (read the record of the ABM* discussions), not since the Douglas-Kerr debates of the last decade has there been such robust extemporania. With press and public in the gallery, we are daily answerable—for style as well as content—to a skeptical constituency. We mute our performance accordingly.

Moreover, we have a thousand proposals to review; they had but one, independence, and they had years of experience and months of debate to savor its implications. Their mandate was clear and simple—go thou and create a nation. No lobbyists' dinners and breakfasts, staff meetings, or hometown drop-ins. No tours of the Capitol; they had the wisdom not to build one until nationhood was established, a lesson in fiscal logic for us Funding Sons.

The Continental Congress had no President to deal with, only a King, remote in time, distance, and understanding. A President with dams to offer here, airport or park construction there, defense contracts, school, job, and housing programs everywhere, has resources to divide and confuse the resolve of Congress should a near majority seek to oppose him on a major question. Nor were there political parties as such in the Continental Congress, only biases from which parties would spring, and the sectional interests of each of the thirteen colonies. This was also an advantage to an assembly with one overriding issue before it, because party loyalty could not be thrown up to any member to "keep him in line," only loyalty to conscience and country. Without presidents, parties, interviews, telegrams, telephones, news conferences, and other confusing obstacles to the rational use of time, they could actually study the issue they were called upon to decide. Legislation without contemplation was not their problem; it is ours.

It is a very big problem, which we attempt to solve by assigning each legislative proposal to a committee, with the hope that it will there receive attention, respect, and appropriate action. It is said that the sum total of human knowledge doubles every ten years. With good reason, then, members of Congress today do not consider themselves or each other to be experts in everything. The fact is that when a bill comes to the floor many vote on it without having given it extensive consideration. They look to colleagues they trust, and who ought to know, for guidance. Frequently they hope the vote will be taken in an anonymous manner, such as the voice vote, a shouting contest, or the teller vote, where members simply file by and are counted in favor of or in opposition to a proposal. A roll-call vote requires each member to answer "aye" or "nay," and is recorded. The vote on independence had to be nearly unanimous and certainly recorded. If it is true, as the play suggests, that the Pennsylvania-delegate James Wilson voted "aye" only to be identified with the majority, regardless of the consequences, we are given an insight into one weakness in man's nature which the parliamentary system could neither correct nor conceal — the desire to go with the crowd to avoid censure, or at worst, share it with good company.

The modest tensions of the play range from the delegates' vacillation to petulance and apprehension on receipt of General Washington's pessimistic messages from the field. At least one of the General's reports, "Is Anybody There? Does Anybody Care?," sounds more like a dispatch from our obedient servant Winnie the Pooh than the father of our country. The audience found such moments convincing. Could one be in Congress only eight months and already be out of touch with the people?

One raisin in this hasty pudding is the issue of whether to delete the denunciation of slavery from the first draft of the Declaration in order to secure Southern signatures. In light of current dialogue the audience recognized the question as more than something to chew on — the all-American jawbreaker, the oversized pebble in the mouth of every Demosthenes[†] who has taken the national stage these men built. Quickly enough the complicity of our Northern seafaring ancestors was brought to our attention — *our* attention, because at this point in the play we and the Founding Fathers are one, reliving the original sin of our creation. Franklin argues that a less than immaculate conception is better than none at all; the "offensive" passage is deleted and the Southern delegates sign.

*Seventeen-Seventy-Six* looks back at this point with fife and drum, and we with sadness. Thomas Jefferson's deleted passage on slavery, which says of the King: "He has waged cruel war against human nature itself . . ." should give us pause. For since that day, the King's prerogative has been our own. His sovereign power is ours, and his indifference.

Published in *Life Magazine* — September 26, 1969

---

*Anti-ballistic missile (ABM) systems were considered "destabilizing."
[†]Athenian statesman and orator (384-322 B.C.).

The author's arrival on Capitol Hill.
Washington, DC, January 1969.

*In 1973, midway through my third term in Congress, a fire broke out in the nation's largest federal building, the Federal Records Center in St. Louis, which housed the records of servicemen in four wars. The blaze owed its origin entirely to the neglect of its owner, the U.S. Government, which held the land free of local taxes. The cost of extinguishing it had to be borne by the local taxpayers, my constituents. Nevertheless, my Special Bill\* to make restitution to the fire departments was happily passed. Before the fire chiefs received the check they had to endure a rendition of:*

## THE FEDERAL RECORDS CENTER FIRE — A SPECIAL BILL

What's all this about? You're kind to inquire.
It's the Federal Records Center Fire,
Which reduced to ashes the whole sixth floor
Millions of files and a great deal more.
It wasn't as if it had to be
Were there ears to hear and eyes to see.
For years when he'd visit that glorified shed,
Chief John Gertken would shake his head.

He got a particular sinking feeling,
Seeing cardboard boxes up to the ceiling.
"Get 'em down from there," he often pled.
"And put a sprinkler there instead.
"And while you're at it, the whole place calls
For partitions, doors, and fire walls."
But the powers that were remained aloof,
And the files stayed stacked up to the roof.

In '73, one day in July
A tongue of flame caught a cyclist's eye.
He knew things shouldn't be that warm,
So he sounded the North Central County alarm.
In four minutes flat there arrived on the scene,
The Community Fire Protection Team.
A few went up but had the sense
To retreat from heat far too intense.

They pumped a powerful stream up, too,
But the stacked-up files wouldn't let it through.
Alarms went off again and again,
Forty-two Departments sent their men.
With eleven engines, six ladders, and one
Elevating platform the job was done.
But it took four long and grueling days
To bring to control this furious blaze.

There's no telling how long it'd been,
If the roof hadn't finally fallen in.
This enabled the men to loop the stream
Up into the core where it turned to steam,
It was thus they finally ended their strife,
And defeated the fire with no loss of life.
Then, counting their blessings, they added up, too,
What the whole thing cost both me and you.

Now that required another fight
Less dramatic but no less tight.
The taxpayers finally won their way
With a cranky Congress and the GSA.
There was no provision in the rules
To repay us for our time and tools,
So we changed the law, broke the hex,
Won their hearts and got the checks,
Which I will pass out one by one
To reimburse a job well done.

Records Center News Conference
Overland, Missouri — 1975

*Special bills are rare in that they target matters not covered by general legislation.

# A FAREWELL SALUTE TO SENATOR PAUL DOUGLAS

## Why Dismember That Old Senate Chamber?*

Why dismember that old Senate Chamber
Where a Dirksen[1] joke was born and christened?
Why dismember that old Senate Chamber
Where Douglas spoke and reason listened?

Why dismember that old Senate Chamber
Where Bob Kerr's[2] disclaimers made eyeballs glisten?
Try to remember it's that kind of chamber
    we're missin'.

It's nice to remember that old Senate Chamber
Where Douglas would so gladly teach us.
Nice to remember that old Senate Chamber
Where members stood and gave their own speeches.

When will each solon pour some coal on so we
    can roll on that Illinois highway?
The long, hard and sure way that ought to be your
    way and my way.

Then will the truth be uncovered forsooth
However uncouth and full of surprises,
For the Senate floor's rugless whenever
    Paul Douglas arises.

The Senate Caucus Room—1967

---

*Tune: *Try to Remember.*
[1]Senator Everett Dirksen (R-IL).
[2]Senator Robert Kerr (D-OK).

*Nineteen-sixty-nine was the year the United States stunned the world with its fulfillment of President Kennedy's promise to land men on the moon within a decade. Prior to Neil Armstrong's historic footfall, astronaut Frank Borman made the first circumnavigation of the moon, returning to describe the experience before a hushed Congress. Serving on the Space Committee, I supported the mission wholeheartedly. Still, the impending intrusion inspired a wistful reflection.*

## THE FLIP SIDE OF THE MOON

On the flip side of the moon
I'll bet the moon folk sing a tune,
Swearing by the earth above
Eternal love.

On the flip side of the moon
I'll bet they wonder as they croon
If there's life and love and mirth
Up there on earth.

Won't it be sad
To learn through our tears
We're each the dream the other had
For all these years?

Don't play the flip side of the moon,
Too dark, too empty, and too soon.
Let's dig for what it's worth
Side one of the earth.

Washington, DC —1969

The author, House Science and Astronautics Subcommittee Chairman, with Senator John McClellan of Arkansas and astronauts of the *Apollo 11* moon landing (July 20, 1969): Mike Collins (pilot) and Buzz Aldrin and Neil Armstrong (moonwalkers). Washington, DC, 1969.

# CONGRESSIONAL REMARKS

*Eight years of my Congressional Record statements fill four medium-sized books. They reveal remarkable insights into all aspects of national life in war and peace. Culling them for the essence, I chose for clarity and simplicity the two which follow: House of Representatives, May 5, 1969, "A Proposal to Eliminate Tax Inequities Concerning Wine Production for Personal Consumption"; and June 18, 1969, "The Outlook Was Not Brilliant."*

## A PROPOSAL TO ELIMINATE TAX INEQUITIES CONCERNING WINE PRODUCTION FOR PERSONAL CONSUMPTION

Mr. Symington: Mr. Speaker, today I have introduced a bill to allow individuals to produce, tax free, up to two-hundred gallons of wine per year, not for sale but for personal or family use. Heads of households already enjoy this right, and there is no reason in law or equity to deny it to single persons. Indeed, correspondence with the Internal Revenue Service reveals no intent at the outset to make such a distinction, the latter growing out of decades of regulatory interpretation of a statutory ambiguity. On September 5th last year my distinguished predecessor introduced a similar bill. I commend to my colleagues the reasoned analysis he offered on that occasion.

The Ways and Means Committee never acted on his bill because the Treasury Department, although cognizant of the inequity and sympathetic to the requested change in the law, did not assign it sufficiently high priority to submit a report. This bill is meritorious enough to deserve, and simple enough to warrant, the early preparation of such a report. It must be realized that a vintage cause like this does not die; it merely ripens. But justice must be done before the ardent spirits of an afflicted minority turn to vinegar.

Mr. MacGregor: Mr. Speaker, will the gentleman yield for a question?

Mr. Symington: Yes, indeed.

Mr. MacGregor: I wonder if the gentleman knows how many people would be benefited by the consumption of two-hundred gallons of wine produced by each person per year?

Mr. Symington: I know of at least one.

# THE OUTLOOK WAS NOT BRILLIANT

Mr. Symington: Mr. Speaker, I simply want, as an ambulatory member of the Democratic baseball team this morning, to congratulate the Republicans on their victory last night, and the fine team they fielded, Wilmer "Vinegar Bend" Mizell* and perhaps eight others.

But, Mr. Speaker, there has been progress. Last year we lost by a score of seventeen to one. This year we lost seven to two. We have cut them down to size. Even Mr. Mizell struck out only five batters, leaving open the question of what might have happened had he faced a sixth. I would like to close with three bits of advice to future Democratic batsmen, inasmuch as through trades and drafts we may lose a few.

First, on the fast ball, I suggest that if you hear the ball hit the glove, it is probably fruitless to swing.

Second, in handling the curve, do not be alarmed by the noise. It is the normal sound of the landing gear falling into place.

Finally, if you have been standing there for sixty seconds and you have not noticed anything, perhaps you should walk with dignity back to the dugout. You are out.

Mr. Joelson: Mr. Speaker, will the gentleman yield?

Mr. Symington: I am glad to yield to the gentleman from New Jersey.

Mr. Joelson: I would like to tell the gentleman that tradition changes very slowly here. The Republican congressional delegation continues to win ball games and the Democratic congressional delegation continues to win elections.

Mr. Symington: It is a consolation.

---

*Congressman Mizell had only recently retired from a distinguished career as a Major League pitcher.

Yale men in Congress. Speaker's Dining Room, U.S. House of Representatives, The Capitol; Washington, DC, 1970. Left to right: Rep. Thomas "Lud" Ashley (D-OH); Sen. J. Glenn Beall, Jr. (R-MD); Rep. Guy Vander Jagt (R-MI); Rep. George Bush (R-TX); Rep. Allard Lowenstein (D-NY); Kingman Brewster, President of Yale; Rep. William S. Moorhead (D-PA); Rep. Jonathan B. Bingham (D-NY); Rep. James W. Symington (D-MO); and Sen. William Proxmire (D-WI).

# A FAREWELL TO CONSTITUENTS

As we celebrate the Thanksgiving season I thought it appropriate to thank you for the opportunity you have given me to serve in the United States Congress. For eight years, together, we have worked on legislation to reduce unemployment, to save Lambert Field, to strengthen law enforcement, to counsel runaways, to fight drug abuse, to enhance our schools, colleges, libraries, and parks, and to carry out our responsibilities for a sound national defense and a sane foreign policy.

The popularity of Congress as an institution is not high. This is due in part to mistakes we have made here. But it is also due to the inability of government, even democratic government, to anticipate accurately and deal effectively with every problem that people often, perhaps too often, expect government to solve. I urge you not to allow your dissatisfaction with the work of any particular Congress or the behavior of any member of Congress to end your faith in an institution which at its worst is an obstacle to tyranny, and at its best can provide wise leadership in domestic and foreign affairs.

Perhaps one could say that from the Ninety-first to the Ninety-fourth Congresses, 1969 through 1977, we have seen Congress at its best (the Judiciary Committee's hearing on impeachment) and at its worst (the scandals of the past year). The main thing to remember is that Congress is what Justice Holmes described the Constitution itself to be, "a living instrument." Its character, intelligence, and drive depend on the transfusions it gets from us, the people, every two or six years. Each new Congress is thus a link in an unbroken chain that stretches back to the First Congress, and forward, we trust, without end.

In the meantime I would observe that a society which in the main tolerates and even encourages lax attitudes toward morality cannot expect automatically to elevate to offices of public trust only those who meet the highest standard. Congress and state and local assemblies are more than likely to be "representative" in every sense of the word. Moreover, citizens with a happy private life and a high personal code may tend to avoid or relinquish contact with the political world on the ground that their very presence in it creates a presumption that their code is negotiable. Public distrust of "politicians" thus can become a self-fulfilling prophecy. The only sure antidote I can see for this condition is a strenuous and continuing effort to engage our young people in civic studies and political activity.

The mail and the phone count for much, but there is no substitute for the home visit. Such schedules place a special burden on the congressional spouse. Cancelled evenings, weekends, and vacations are the rule, not the exception. Being the wife of a congressman is a full-time job. This seems an appropriate time to thank my wife, Sylvia, for her patience, understanding, and tireless efforts of her own on behalf of the second district.

Finally, it cannot be forgotten that a Missouri congressman is not called that exactly. He or she is a "x representative," and must consider the impact of congressional initiatives not only on his or her own district or neighbors, but on the nation itself. Thus, under this hat must be viewed questions in the larger context, such as aid to other countries, national defense, energy options, safe food and drugs, wage-price controls, and other problems of national scope.

To the frequently asked question, "Should the representative convey the views of his constituents or his own?," I remind the questioner that no two constituents think precisely alike on every issue, and that in some cases finding a consensus would be virtually impossible. But more importantly, as Edmund Burke* pointed out, the representative is elected not alone for his energies, but his judgment. The diligent representative, by looking, listening, and learning, may gain perspectives occasionally at variance with that of many of his constituents. I think it better to vote one's conscience on all issues, and let the people decide whether, on balance, one should be re-elected.

Final Newsletter — Washington, DC, November 1976

---

*Irish-born British statesman and Member of Parliament (1729-97).

# On
# America

# THIRTEEN STRIPES AND FIFTY STARS

Thirteen stripes and fifty stars,
What do they mean to me?
TV sets and shiny cars?
No sir, no siree!

The right to reach for the brightest rings
On life's old merry-go-round,
The right to seek and find the things
The Founding Fathers wanted found.

Yes, thirteen stripes and fifty stars,
That's what they mean to me.

Thirteen stripes and fifty stars,
What do they mean to you?
Silly gripes in local bars?
Tell me it's not true!

Oh, lift your eyes, look what you see,
It's freedom taking root.
You'll understand why your right hand
Just naturally seems to want to salute . . .

Those thirteen stripes and fifty stars
Up in the sky above,
May they wave for a million years,
Over the land, up in the sky, over the land we love.
Over — the land — we love!

Washington, DC — 1963
Music:  Sylvia Symington

# CENTENNIAL OF THE STATUE OF LIBERTY
## THE SPIRIT OF '86

Lady Liberty was the center of attention, and properly so. But a look around at one's fellow Americans was reassuring, too. They came in every garb, color, shape, and size; yet all seemed to stand a bit taller in the glow of their sentiment. They smiled at each other, at everyone, at the police. The police? Smiling, too, they joshed one another as they corrected the wayward and pointed the way. The traffic delays and waiting lines at boat, bus, and subway were of historic proportions. Yet irritation gave way to hearty greetings, jokes, and compliments between friends and strangers. The absolute perfection of the weather was severally attributed to Mayor Koch, the President, France, P.X. Kelley, and someone's "Uncle Fred."

Was it only in the eye of the beholder, or did the city become more beautiful too? Spires rising straight as a skyward glance seemed to stretch their height, like veterans on Memorial Day. Catching the sun, they returned it in flashes to the ships at anchor. Calmly centered in the midst of that bobbing flotilla were two mighty U.S. naval vessels, the carrier *John F. Kennedy*, and the battleship *Iowa*. Their combined deck areas, with a few trees, would have rivalled Central Park. When the tall ships glided by we stood with young American sailors as they returned the salute.

In each such moment past and present were linked, fused by a bond that transcends the rise and fall of nations, the immemorial mutual respect of men at sea; women, too, like the sprightly commander of our barge. As it pulled alongside the *Iowa* in choppy seas, she stood firm, giving patient and highly useful advice through a megaphone as the passengers fumbled and grabbed at railings and helping hands. Most impressive of all was the unfailing courtesy and good nature of the officers and crews. A boarding party of thousands, flourishing camera and spyglass with piratical fervor, swept across the decks, from bow to fantail, overwhelming the chow lines and consuming a year's rations of barbecue, coke, and beer.

Numberless small craft under sail or power frolicked in the waters all around. A few mavericks, straying for a too-close look at the dignitaries, were good-naturedly rounded up and returned to the herd by a tireless Coast Guard cutter. Finally, as the day drew to a close we were treated to an array of contrasts unlikely to be encountered anywhere but in America. First, as the obliging sun went to its well-earned rest, a detachment of marines, in faultless precision, performed the "Sunset Parade" drill. The flag was then lowered and folded, first to the sound of taps and then to silence but for the lapping of waves on the hull. As the marines retired, attention was invited by spotlight to the bridge where Navy Secretary John Lehman greeted the guests, thanked the crew, and introduced the durable, and still very audible Beach Boys.

In a trice we went from sundown to hoedown. The ensuing concert transformed the entire ship's company and all the guests, including a few bewildered foreign officers, into an audience of palladium responsiveness. Each marched, or rather danced, to his own beat. High brass could be found doing a discreet twist, while some able seamen demonstrated the latest dance form, which resembles a sea horse with hiccups. Neighboring cruise liners punctuated each rendition with an appreciative horn blast. Many calories later the Beach Boys bade farewell; order resumed, and all eyes turned to the spotlit Lady, now in complete control of the enveloping night. Queen of all the sparkling lights ashore and in the harbor, she seemed to give the signal for the closing celebration. Bursting rockets in transient floral patterns paid final homage to the steady glow of her torch. As others flickered out, her light followed us home, reminding us that, like our forebears, we will be measured by what we do in it.

New York — 1986

# THE GENESEE VALLEY

*Boyhood summers were spent with my brother, Stuart, Jr., on our grandad Jim Wadsworth's farm in the Genesee Valley in western New York. We forked hay into wagons, and from wagons into lofts. Combines were new to the country in the late thirties and early forties, so we drove the old "binder" and cultivator behind patient teams of draft horses. When barn cats sidled up at milking time it was fun to squirt them in the eyes. We drank milk fresh and cold as it passed over the "aerators" into the cans. We harvested feed corn and wheat and carted them to the threshing machine. We leveled the pungent "ensilage" in the silo as it poured in from the top. After lunching on sandwiches and lemonade, we would lie on the hillside and look down a valley that stretches a mosaic of green and amber westward to the blue rim of the horizon.*

## THE VALLEY

Here have I seen the tears of morning dew
Dissolve in sighs of mist, and, wondering,
Beheld the soft descent. Here clouds that wing
In silence dip a gentle greeting to
Companionships of oaks and elms that bring
Together drowsy creatures. There a string
Of blackbirds bends, alights, and bends anew.
Faultless portrait, woodland, field and pool;
And never was a painter's touch as keen
As hers, who paints with love within the rule
Of time. Her easel is the rolling green
Horizon. Nature fashions mountains cool
As galleries whence her valleys may be seen.

Geneseo, New York—1943

# THIS STAR-FILLED NIGHT

### (A Cowboy Christmas Song)

Come on, old Dan, we'll saddle up light.
We've got a watch to keep tonight.
This star-filled night's not made for sleep.
We've got a watch to keep.

See the cattle climbin' the hill,
Even the playful dogies are still.
Standin', lookin' way out far,
Watchin' the eastern star.

Why do they stand so silently?
Jackrabbit's stoppin' his hoppin' to see.
Well, old timer, we know why,
There's a new light in the sky.

A light that makes the prairie shine,
Brightenin' up these hopes of mine.
You know it, Dan, the Son of Man
Was born on this star-filled night.

This star-filled night's not made for sleep.
We've got a watch to keep.

St. Louis — 1964
Music: Jim Symington

*In 1964, two articles in the Washington Post highlighted what seemed to be an error in priorities. One heralded the U.S. commitment to take the financial lead in saving Abu Simbel, a giant Egyptian monument threatened by the waters of the Nile, which were to be redirected by the Aswan Dam project. The other depicted the rotting remains of the U.S.S. Constellation, the first man-of-war to fly the American flag. She was later rebuilt, refitted, and remains proudly at anchor in Baltimore Harbor.*

*On reading of plans to preserve an Egyptian monument (3000 B.C.) and to abandon an American ship (the U.S.S. Constellation, 1798 A.D.):*

## THE *CONSTELLATION*

America would pace
The million dollar race
To lift a pharaoh's face
As if we need him,
While steadily we've shunned
To use a federal fund
To save a ship that gunned
Our way to freedom.

So worldly we've grown,
We're propping up a stone
Ordered from the throne
When men were chattel,
While screams the lonely gull,
And weeds embrace the hull
That never knew a lull
In freedom's battle.
Unmastered and unmanned,
She sinks in sight of land

Without a helping hand
Much less a prayer.
Let's take her out to sea,
And cut the lady free,
To don a wave and be
With men who care.

Washington, DC—1964*

*Editor's Note—This poem was reprinted in the April 1996 issue of *Naval History* with an accompanying article by the former Chief of Naval Operations and President of the U.S. Naval Institute, Admiral James L. Holloway, III (retired). Admiral Holloway's article reads in part: "Chief of Protocol in the State Department, James W. Symington, undertook a one-man campaign to save the *Constellation*. He appealed to government officials, wrote to editors, and organized anyone who would listen. But Jimmie Symington's most effective weapon turned out to be an ode of his composition that was published widely in the press. This trenchant bit of poesy caught the fancy of many readers, and it aroused sentiment for saving the *U.S.S. Constellation*. Today, the *Constellation*, on the waterfront of the Baltimore Inner Harbor, still floats as a proper monument to our maritime heritage and probably the first example of historic preservation accomplished by a jingle."

*Author's Note*—Oliver Wendell Holmes' immortal lines on the *Constitution*, "Aye, tear her tattered ensign down . . . ," were much on my mind.

# MY STATE — MISSOURI

*A Missourian's proverbial demand:*

## I'M FROM MISSOURI*

I'm from Missouri
I've got to be shown
Whatever
You want
Known.

Folks in Missouri
Pay a luxury tax
On ev-
ry thing
But facts.

In case you've been there
You probably know
You can't place or win there
Unless you show!

So don't think Missouri
Has a heart of stone
It's just
We must
Be shown.

St. Louis — 1964

*Song from the musical *Schenectograd,* unpublished out of deference to sensitive negotiations between the United States and the Soviet Union, and limited resources.

*Our musical, Schenectograd, depicts the adventures in the United States of a young Russian graduate in espionage. The lad's summer job as a Moscow "Intourist" guide prepares him for his coming duties by introducing him to Americans. He comes into contact with a family from Missouri and is obliged to respond to the family's every request with the word, "Nyet." It is this attitude which occasions the Missourian's previous reminder. The songs are sung in counterpoint.*

# NYET

Nyet,
We're not wanting you should fret
But you should never not forget
The answer's nyet.
The answer's nyet.

Nyet,
Why you wanting meeting judge?
Better watch us making fudge
Or even bread
The answer's nyet.

Libraries, trials,
Homes, party files,
You want we should open?
Just keep hopin'.

Nyet
There's no book for telephone
We prefer to be unknown.
The silent set
Says nyet.

Nyet
Our decline to answer service
Covers questions that unnerve us
When it's set
To answer nyet.

Nyet,
Your not writing for permission
Helps our plan of indecision
Yes you bet
The answer's nyet.

Excuse please joke,
Ha! Ha! Ha!
We're just folk
Who can't say Da.

Nyet,
We're hail fellows and well met,
But that's exactly all you get
From Soviet,
Yes, nyet.

St. Louis and Washington, DC — 1962
Music: Sylvia Symington

*In 1964, while campaigning for my father's third term in the U.S. Senate, I visited his friend Tony Buford at his farm in Iron County. That weekend produced:*

## THE BUFORD MOUNTAIN SONG

When dogwoods bloom and red-birds sing,
And sunbeams wake the sleeping streams,
I've got to go and meet the Spring
In the Belleview Valley of my dreams.

So if you take the open road
Past Caledonia you will see
The forest slopes of Buford Mountain
Belleview Valley, and, maybe, me.

In seven days God made the world,
And His word was love as well as law
When he made old Buford Mountain
Sixty miles from Arkansas.

He must have known how men would battle
Every day and never cease,
Till brown-eyed deer and grazing cattle
Taught them how to live in peace.

Golden mornings tint the green
As roosters crow the mist away.
There's no secret, then, between
Buford Mountain and the day.

Like Ozark timber friendships grow,
Good friends not to be forgot.
All the valley folks we know,
And old Len Hall* at Possum Trot.

The summer sounds of old Missouri,
Crickets, cowbells, cooing doves,
Make a man in no big hurry
To leave the spring-fed life he loves.

So let the shadows lengthen on me,
Of life's rewards I've had my fill,
While whippoorwills at evening call me
To a richer harvest still.

These leaves will bow to autumn's fire;
These branches to the winter snow.
Like them I've only one desire,
When my season comes, to go.

For, like them, I'm just returning
To my home of long ago.
Just bury me by Buford Mountain
In Belleview Valley here below.

And when my horse and hounds can join me,
Bed them where they'll hear the streams.
Together we'll roam Buford Mountain
In the Belleview Valley of our dreams.

Missouri—1964<br>Music:  Sylvia Symington

*Missouri's favorite naturalist.

# THE MISSISSIPPI

*Missouri's history from a European perspective began in the seventeenth century. In 1673, the explorers Marquette and Joliet came ashore at what was to become St. Louis. The "voyageurs" had selected a handy thoroughfare from Canada, the Mississippi River. Three hundred years later we celebrated a re-enactment of their arrival with a song of grateful praise. (This was before the flood of '93.)*

## FATHER OF THE WATERS

Oh, Father of the Waters,
Your sons and your daughters
Are gathered here to wish you good cheer
And many a happy returning year.
We thank you for all you've done.
With the gifts that you brought us
The truths that you taught us,
Three hundred years of laughter and tears
A heaven full of hope and a flood of fears
You took us, and made us one.

You're the same wide wonder the Pawnee knew,
The Sac, Fox, the Chickasaw, the Choctaw; the Sioux
Slipped from your banks in a birch canoe.
Saw the shadow cast by the first tall mast,
Heard the creaking lanyard, the bearded Spaniard,
The robed French priest from the cold northeast.
Dios, Mon Dieu, My God, they tried
To fathom the secret of your pride.
They searched, they fought, they knelt, they died.

But the dreams that they nourished
Have risen and flourished
On the silvery heels of the paddle-boat wheels
Moving cotton and coal and the restless soul
Of a nation yearning to be.

No cargo too heavy
To load off the levee,
As the roustabout crews gave birth to the blues
Waiting in New Orleans for the St. Louis news
Of the *Natchez* and the *Robert E. Lee*.

We're going now, River,
Your promise to deliver,
To live as one in the rain and sun,
And share the navigation till the journey's done,
And it's time to meet the sea.

St. Louis — 1973
Music: Jim Symington

# THE CITY BY THE RIVER

There are cities in the mountains,
Cities by the sea,
But St. Louis on the river
Is the city calling me.

Calls me by the thunder
Of her industry;
Calls me by the wonder
Of her beauty, broad and free.

The fairest of the daughters
Born on a journey wild
Of the father of the waters,
She's the Mississippi's child.

That vagabond has brought her
Many gifts since then.
But her dowry of water
Made her beautiful to men.

Kings had looked upon her,
And hoped to win her hand,
But she had pledged her honor
To the free men of this land.

Beneath the stars above her
Their shadows long have slept,
But their children's children love her
For the promise that she kept.

Of hope for men of vision,
Whose lofty gateway beams,
"Bring me your decision,
And bring to me your dreams."

St. Louis — 1964

# ANOTHER KANSAS CITY DAY

Crown Center's smile meets the dawn half way.
It's not its style here to yawn all day.
An Indian scout on high salutes the morning sky
Beckoning the traveler to stay.

Another Kansas City Day.
You wake and see a thousand fountains' spray
Catch the colors of the sun;
Missouri's morning has begun.

You'll take a Kansas City stroll
Along old Westport to the Plaza way.
It's refreshing to the soul
To drink a Kansas City Day.

Wagon wheels once traced the trail
From here to Santa Fe.
But this old cow-town's now the now-town
U.S.A.

I met a Kansas City friend.
Her smile nearly took my breath away,
And I know I'm going to spend
Another Kansas City Day . . .

Raphael Hotel, Kansas City — 1976
Music: Sylvia Symington

# On
# Diplomacy

*My years in the Johnson Administration came to an end when I announced my candidacy for Congress, April 1, 1968. I had told the President of my plans the previous Christmas. He observed, "Well, I knew you were going to be a teacher, preacher, congressman or some fool thing! I'll campaign for or agin' you, whichever you think will help you the most." Of course, he was not only feeling the pain of Vietnam but aware of its political volatility. He asked me not to announce before April 1st. On March 31st, he stated his intention not to seek re-election. In the weeks that followed I thought about the job I had left behind.*

*In a three day "official" visit a foreign chief of state is invited to "know" America. New York, Washington, and Disneyland comprised the typical itinerary, few trips to the heartland. Yet:*

## IT TAKES TIME TO KNOW A COUNTRY

It takes time to know a country,
Time to see the land,
Time to meet the people,
And time to understand.

Time to know your neighbor
On the other side,
Time to learn to labor
In the vineyard of his pride.

Time to watch the reaping,
Tell the wheat from chaff,
Find the reaper weeping,
And learn what makes him laugh.

For this great road we're walking
Has many a pit and bend.
Who can tell for certain
Just where the road will end?

We know it's full of danger,
So walk it hand in hand.
It takes time to know a country,
And time to understand.

Washington, DC—1968*
Music: Sylvia Symington

*Performed with the Legend Singers of St. Louis at the
Presidential Prayer Breakfast, January 1975.

Among those who did make it to the "heartland" was Israeli
Ambassador, later Prime Minister, Yitzak Rabin. In this photo he is
greeted at Lambert Field by the author, then congressman.
St. Louis, Missouri, 1972.

*In 1965, Princess Margaret and her then husband, Lord Snowdon, favored us with a royal visit. Attorney General Nicholas Katzenbach and his wife, Lydia, hosted a soirée in their home, where they were regaled with sundry welcomes, including the following, published anon in the New York Times.*

## THE FAIR INVADER

On silver wings the fair invader came
And, armed with laughing glance and lilting voice,
Retook these colonies in England's name
And proved herself to be the people's choice.
Undaunted, too, along the royal whirl
Of cable car and Navajo and blintz,
That handsome husband Britons call an Earl,
But who by Yankee standards is a prince.
Alarums and excursions shook both coasts,
And traced the triumphs of the conquering pair.
The Snowdons are coming! Matrons manned their posts,
And jealous lights blew out on Herald Square.
Some corner of the hearts they touched anew
Will be forever England's and theirs too.

Washington, DC — November 16, 1965

*During President Nixon's second term, Averell Harriman, America's senior public servant, turned eighty. His service to the country had spanned a good part of the twentieth century. His distinguished tenures as Governor of New York, Undersecretary of State, Ambassador to the Soviet Union, and various roving diplomatic commissions made people think a moment before deciding how to address him. "Governor" seemed to suit him best.*

*With many happy and productive years to go, he did take a moment to mark his eightieth birthday at a dinner where he was honored for his efforts as a peacemaker by Alice Roosevelt Longworth, Franklin D. Roosevelt, Jr., Margaret Truman Daniel, Jacqueline Kennedy Onassis, and Lynda Bird Johnson-Robb. As toastmaster, I was also allowed to speak:*

## AVERELL HARRIMAN

*H – A – double R – I – M-A-N* spells Harriman. It also spells problems for the would-be autocrats of the conference tables of this world. For tenacious as they are, Ave will outlast them—because he will outlive them. And as they slowly slide under their respective square, round, or horseshoe-shaped tables, Ave quietly picks up all the unfinished business and proceeds to the next meeting.

Lengthy discussions? Three generations of old Bolsheviks have smilingly entered the panelled conference rooms of this world only to find Averell still there, seeming to grow and foliate like a Redwood out of the green baize on the American side. The result is predictable. First their smiles vanish, then their tempers, and finally their selves, as Ave benignly sips a little water and watches their departures. Then he turns to his aides and says, "Next?" And as the aides—who have also become grandfathers by now—assemble their crumbling briefcases, America's Ravi Shankar of diplomacy softly tunes his sitar for the next encounter with discord.

His manner is always engaging. At the outset he tends to say, "Let's not dwell on petty differences; let's get down to the really important things we can't agree on."

But in those rare moments of truth when men on all sides reach for their swords—Ave produces an even mightier peacemaker . . .

# LA PLUME DE DETENTE

La plume de détente
Plus forte que l'épée,
C'est la chose importante
A la recherche de la paix.

Laquelle est plus belle
Ou plus élégante
Que la plume d'Averell
La plume de détente?

Averell Harriman,
Tout le monde chantent,
Use avec élan
La plume de détente.

Les uns font la guerre
Pour éviter la honte,
Mais Ave, le sincère?
La plume de détente.

Pour Ave et sa Pam,
Travailleurs pour la paix
Monsieur et Madame,
À VOTRE SANTÉ!

Translation:

# THE PEN OF DETENTE

The pen of détente,
Mightier than the sword,
Is the important thing
In the search for peace.

What is more beautiful
Or more elegant
Than Averell's pen,
The pen of détente.

Averell Harriman,
All the world sings,
Wields with flourish
The pen of détente.

Some would make war
To avoid shame.
But Ave, the sincere?
The pen of détente.

For Ave and his Pam,
Workers for peace—
Monsieur and Madame
TO YOUR HEALTH!


Democratic Study Group Dinner for Averell Harriman
Sheraton Park Hotel, Washington, DC—May 15, 1974

*A White House reception for Latin American ambassadors was held in March 1962 to mark the first anniversary of the Alliance for Progress. The President asked me to "lighten it up" with a song I composed the previous year for the Voice of America.*

## ALIANZA PARA EL PROGRESO

Alianza para el progreso
Para cada hombre y niño,
Una gran hermandad marchando
Esperanza en cada corazon.

En libertad.

Alianza para el progreso,
Quiere decir un esfuerzo
Un esfuerzo grande y confiado
Para ayudar al debil y olvidado.

Igualdad.

Juntos conquistaremos
Los enemigos huiran muy pronto,
Ignorancia, hambre, y miedo,
Vencidos por los pueblos unidos,

Seguridad,

Applaudimos, pues, el Progreso,
Formemos la gran Alianza,
Un Alianza de esperanza,
Ejemplo para el mundo,

Alianza Para el Progreso.

# ALLIANCE FOR PROGRESS

Alliance for Progress
For every man and child.
A great brotherhood marching,
Hope in every heart.

In liberty.

Alliance for Progress
Means a force
A great and confident force,
To help the weak and the forgotten.

Equality.

Together we will conquer
Our enemies will flee quickly.
Ignorance, hunger, and fear,
Conquered by united people.

Security.

Let's cheer then this Progress.
Let's form the great Alliance.
An alliance of hope,
An example for the world.

Alliance for Progress.


Punta del Este, Uruguay—1961

White House ceremony marking the first anniversary of the
Alliance For Progress. Washington, DC; March 13, 1962.

# OUT OF THE NIGHT THAT COVERS YOU*

Out of the night that covers you,

Black as the pit from pole to pole,

You may thank whatever Gods you do

You're not the Chief of Protocol.

Washington, DC—1968

*Adapted from *Invictus* by William Ernest Henley.

128 / *James W. Symington*

Lunch *al fresco* with Canadian counterpart, Chief of Protocol
Henry Davis, during President Johnson's meeting with Canadian
Prime Minister Lester Pearson.  Campobello Island, New
Brunswick, Canada, 1966.

*Some situations are well beyond protocol. The following was written a day or two after the takeover of the Japanese Embassy grounds in Lima, Peru, by a terrorist organization. At that time, women were still numbered among the hostages, and the world looked forward to an early, benign resolution of the standoff. Long and arduous negotiations having failed, and sanctuary rejected, the subsequent decisive rescue by Peruvian troops under the direct leadership of President Fujimori brought the impasse to an end.*

## MISS ORTIZ REGRETS*

Madame, Miss Ortiz regrets she's unable to lunch today.
Madame, Miss Ortiz requests, I convey, the reason por que,
She's so sorry to be delayed,
But last evening down in Lima town she strayed—
Into the wrong reception, I'm afraid.

Señora, Miss Ortiz, your friend, simply cannot attend your almuerzo.
Señora, she is pained to explain she's detained by superior fuerzo—
In a spooky kabuki play
'Till the captive crowd will be allowed to say,
"'Sayonara, to the Tupac Amaru' today."

The saki and sushi were going down quite well.
Señora, what happened next Miss Ortiz is vexed to tell.
Each waiter put down his tray,
And from his kimono pulled out an old AK,
Shouting, "Tora, Tora, Fujimori, Olé!"

Now Miss Ortiz, Señora, has only one favor to pray—
That she's ransomed along with her handsome new attaché,
Whom she met in the nicest way,
When their hands were tied beside the café au lait.
Señora, if you set a new date, please add a new plate that day.

Washington, DC—February 1997

*Music:  An adaption of *Miss Otis Regrets* by Cole Porter.

*In the 1980s the nation's "comfort level" with its intelligence services took a dip. One who had laid that burden down before the public even knew he bore it was Archibald Bullock Roosevelt, grandson of the hero of San Juan hill.*

*"Archie Roosevelt," who had fought under General George Patton, added further distinction to an already famous name by his invaluable service to the country as an intelligence officer in the Middle East. With the same quiet whimsy that is the stuff of fictional heroes, Archie performed his delicate missions in the very real, at times surreal, world of intelligence gathering. Upon retirement he invested his skills in the Chase Manhattan Bank. For his subsequent critically acclaimed book, For Lust of Knowing, the United States Chief of Protocol, his wife Selwa, known as "Lucky," gave a reception marked by a parody of "Mandalay."*

## ON THE ROAD TO SAMARKAND*

### (An Ode to Archie Roosevelt)

By a minaret in Jidda
From Harvard many a league
Stood our honored guest amid a
Passel of intrigue.
Composing his dispatches
To his gallant little band,
Explaining where the catch is
On the road to Samarkand.

On the road to Samarkand
Where both scotch and gin are banned.
Harshly parched did Archie march
With Uncle's orders in his hand.
And though vastly undermanned
Our intelligence was grand.
It only called for Archibald
To make them understand.

Shipped him somewheres east of Groton,
Where the best was like the worst.
And where many a Yank had gotten
In trouble for his thirst.

*After Rudyard Kipling's *Road to Mandalay*.

But Arch had learned to howdy
And extend a friendly hand
To Sunni, Druze, and Saudi
On the road to Samarkand.

On the road to Samarkand,
And every nation that it spanned,
Arch was ready just like Teddy
To implant his Yankee brand.
But the gifts of every land
Were treasures rather bland
And he'll tell ya that his Selwa
Proved the *gold* of Samarkand.

Washington, DC—1988

*In 1958, anxious to learn more about the "evil empire," I travelled to Leningrad (now once again St. Petersburg), Moscow, and Kiev (now capital of Ukraine). I spent most of the time singing in parks and squares, and recorded my experiences in two articles for the St. Louis Post Dispatch entitled "Through Russia With Guitar." Thirty-eight years later, as chairman of the American-Russian Cultural Cooperation Foundation, I decided to take advantage of the 125th anniversary of the visit to America of the Grand Duke Alexis, twenty-one-year-old son of Czar Alexander II (who freed the serfs and supported our Union). As the guest of President Grant he toured some twenty cities and was enthusiastically welcomed. My thought was to replicate his visit by having young Russians who excelled in various areas take the same trip and interface with their U.S. counterparts. To stimulate interest (and contributions) we arranged — under the patronage of the Russian Ambassador to the United States, Yuli Vorontsov, and with the help of a dauntless "ladies" committee — a magnificent Tolstoyesque ball at the Russian Embassy. General Lebed and five hundred other guests endured a rendition of the commemorative song:*

## HAIL TO THE GRAND DUKE ALEXIS

Here's to the Grand Duke Alexis
Good looking, tall and polite,
Whose travels almost to Texas
Have brought us together tonight.

He arrived amidst great jubilation
In eighteen and seventy one,
And embarked on a peregrination
Historically second to none.

He was just a young Navy lieutenant,
But hardly your average tar,
For the two-headed bird on his pennant
Proclaimed him the son of the Czar.

Since his Dad liberated the serf,
This dashing yet modest gall<u>ant</u>
Set foot on American turf
As the guest of Ulysses S. Grant.[1]

After shaking the President's hand
He breasted the billowing tide
Of welcomes planned and unplanned,
And took them in nautical stride.

His manners he never forgot
At receptions, banquets, and fairs,
And believe it or not he danced the gavotte
With the daughters of all of our Mayors.

In Nebraska the Duke was unscared in
A buffalo hunt to the kill.
Led by General Phil Sheridan,[2]
George Custer[3] and Buffalo Bill.[4]

New Orleans' ears are still ringing
To that Mardi Gras voice from above.
It's Alexis in heaven still singing,
"If Ever I Cease to Love."

These events brought the Russia of Tolstoy[5]
To the nation of Whitman[6] and Twain;[7]
Dostoyevski,[8] Turgenev,[9] Mussorgsky[10] —
We welcome them all back again.

To the long-lasting bond that connects us
Pacifically coast to coast;
To partnership, peace, and Alexis,
Let's raise every glass in a toast.

As did the Brahmins of Boston
With speeches, heroics, and poems,
Especially the verse that was tossed in
By Oliver Wendell Holmes.[11]

We offer one final libation,
Not to a Duke or a Czar,
But to Russia, that grand Federation
In the light of the Northern Star.

Washington, DC — November 1996
Music: Sylvia Symington

[1]Ulysses S. Grant, 18th President of the United States (1869-1877).
[2]Philip H. Sheridan, Major General, U.S. Army (1863-1888); Union General in the Civil War.
[3]George Armstrong Custer, Lt. Colonel/General, 7th U.S. Cavalry (1866-1876), killed at Little Bighorn.
[4]William Frederick Cody ("Buffalo Bill"), U.S. plainsman and frontier scout (1846-1917).
[5]Count Leo Nikolayevich Tolstoy (1828-1910), Russian novelist and social theorist.
[6]Walt Whitman (1819-1892), U.S. poet.
[7]Mark Twain (1835-1910), U.S. author and humorist.
[8]Feodor Dostoyevski (1821-1881), Russian novelist.
[9]Ivan Turgenev (1818-1883), Russian novelist.
[10]Modest Petrovich Mussorgsky (1839-1881), Russian composer.
[11]Oliver Wendell Holmes (1809-1894), U.S. writer and physician.

# THROUGH RUSSIA WITH GUITAR

(Special Correspondent, *St. Louis Post Dispatch*; London; September 6, 1958)

You can't argue with an abacus. So I accepted the verdict, "Eighty rubles excess baggage." The impulse to reach over, flick a few beads, and say, "I make it seventy-five," is resisted like many other normal temptations in the Soviet Union. Also the return plane to London looked inviting. The excess consisted of one guitar wrapped in a wash-and-wear shirt. It spoke better Russian than I . . .

It is normal to be a little apprehensive about a trip behind the Iron Curtain, beyond the reach of habeas corpus and other extraordinary writs . . . Was guitar playing without a license a crime against the state? Would I be ignored, ridiculed, or arrested? I sat on a park bench as near the exit as I could get and gingerly tweaked out a few chords. People shuffled by glumly. Then a toddler fell down and began to cry. I asked his mother if I could sing him a song. Her stainless-steel teeth glinted in the setting sun. "Konyetchna," she smiled ("Of course"). Children lovers were then joined by song lovers, and soon the crowd swelled till I was walled in by the sweaters, pigtails, and slouch caps of curious Russians. If there was a society for the prevention of cruelty to the Russian language, it would have had me indicted, but the crowd was in a forgiving mood. Nodding and grinning they saw me through every dropped ending and misconjugated verb to a happy conclusion.

Hecklers and troublemakers were few, and only once did an Intourist guide try to break up one of these "assemblies." We were standing around an American car in the middle of the street. "Move away," he told me in English. "You're blocking traffic." It seemed a reasonable request, and I started toward the sidewalk. "Who is he, and what is he saying?" one of the Russians asked. I told him. "We stay," he said. "It is our street." . . .

Intourist cars look like middle-aged Cadillacs begging for retirement. Ignoring the protest of gears, the drivers start in second, get up to fifty as quickly as possible, and drive all through town at that speed one car's length apart. Pedestrians scatter like quail. Many of these cars had no wipers. "What if it rains?" I asked a cabby. "I put them on," he replied. Ask a silly question. . . .

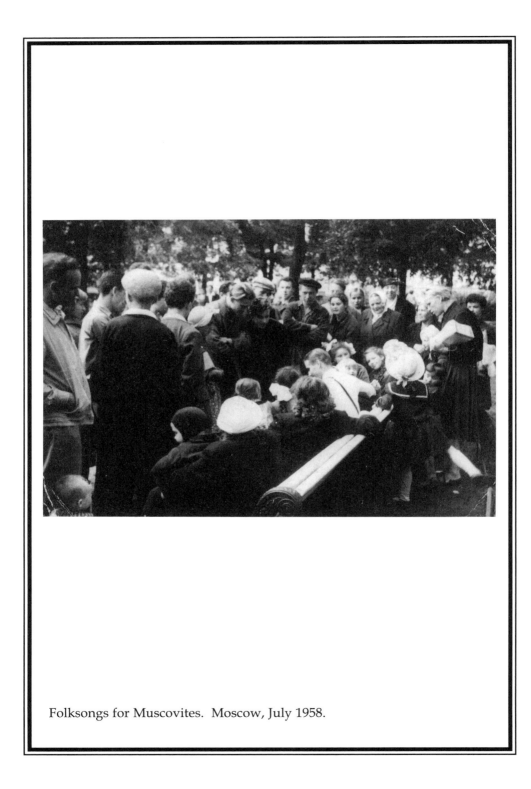

Folksongs for Muscovites.  Moscow, July 1958.

# On
# War And
# Peace

# VIETNAM, THE SONGLESS WAR

## (Let Saigons Be Saigons)

I was thinking last night of our soldiers
And the country that sent them along
We've sure put a lot on their shoulders
In their hearts not even one song.

Some ideas I was quietly filing
When suddenly, hosanna!
There was George M. Cohan[1] smiling,
"Try this on the old piana."

Let Saigons be Saigons, Uncle Ho[2]
Pack your black pajamas and go,
'Cause while you're wreckin' South Viet Nam
You gotta reckon with Uncle Sam.

Whoa, Ho, turn around and go
Let the South be free.
No more panderin' to you old mandarin,
So shove, and let 'em be.

Our bid for peace is in the mail
Tear it up, and, boy!
You'll find your famous Ho Chi trail
Leads also to Hanoi.

Let Saigons be Saigons, Uncle Ho
Pack your black pajamas and go,
'Cause while your wreckin' South Viet Nam
You gotta reckon with Uncle Sam.

Washington, DC—1967
Music: Jim Symington

[1] U.S. actor, playwright, theatrical producer, and writer of
popular songs (1878-1942).
[2] Ho Chi Minh, president of North Vietnam (1954-69).

Tennis fundraiser to provide court time and lessons for the underprivileged at the Washington International Hotel. Washington, DC, June 1971. Left to right: General William Westmoreland, Cong. Robert McClory (R-IL), Senator Jacob Javits (R-NY), Senator Claiborne Pell (D-RI), and the author (D-MO).

# FIRST POEMS

*In 1941 England no longer slept, and we were given a wake-up call by Pearl Harbor. The headlines prompted this:*

## LETTER TO HITLER
### The Thoughts of a Christian German

Friends betray we must.
Love gives way to lust.
Dreams decay to dust,
Our faith tarnished.

Is this how we must live,
Our soul to sin to give,
The truth drained through the sieve
Of falsehood varnished?

It's strange, oh Fuehrer, strange
How you our lives derange.
Wherefore this sickly change
To hate unblessed?

From our bosom borne,
A breast already torn
By war and strife we mourn
All this unrest.

Yea, quench your worldly thirst
E'er your bubble burst
Your neighbors shall yield at first,
But they are strong.

Back shall they spring and fast,
The time for mercy past,
They'll crush you to the last
For you are wrong.

# TO CARRY A SONG

Can it be wrong to carry a song

When the world about you is weeping?

Isn't it right to sing in the night

Of the fight against death on us creeping?


Some will implore we must go to war

To settle the score for a wrong.

Some with a speech would heal the breach

But I'd rather teach with a song.


Deerfield Academy, Massachusetts — December 1941

*By 1947 America could rest from the labor of containing fascism. But a new shadow loomed as big as a continent, and projected the cap and pipe of Joseph Stalin. At least that's how it looked from the cloistered halls of Yale.*

## A WARNING TO STALIN

Oh proud enigma for this restless world,
Be not so certain that the quiet soul
Of freedom rots in documents and furled
Battle flags or that a generous toll
Of meek concessions destined is to roll
From craven tongues and trembling pens, no more!
For we have come to wrestle for the soul
Of history, a goal worth fighting for,
And shoving Godless communism out the door.

## AN APPEAL TO GOD

But though the years have fruitful been in growth
Of righteousness, unconquered is the blight
Of tyranny, whose harvesters are loathe
To lay aside their instruments of might,
And ponder in sweet wonder at the sight
Of bounty, golden acreage, greening boughs
And grazing cattle. Heavenly the night
That blankets peace, and yet may God arouse
The languid swords of freedom 'ere all are beat to ploughs.

Yale University — 1948

# THE WALL

There she stands,
Her lidless eyes
Scanning the killing ground
Her tangled barbs and spikes
Striking up—at God.

What hands, what hopes, what supplicants
Have rubbed to smoothness
Her grey indifference?
What prayers impaled
On her wires?

Remember only
Every fortress
Meets its Joshua;
Every wall
Its Jericho.

Congressional visit to the Berlin Wall. Berlin, Germany, February 1970.

# WE'RE GOING TO WIN THE WORLD*

We're going to win the world
It's just a matter of time
It's been a sinful, criminal world
And the punishment fits the crime.

No need to fire a shot
Much less make a fist
For we are most surely not
Afraid to coexist.

    Hi, Hi, why die,
    When we can coexist?

Since history's on our side
We've got time to spare.
When the enemy's upped and died,
We're happy to inter.

But as we leave to roam
From town to cap'tlist town,
Don't you who remain at home
Be letting standards down.

    Hey, hee, don't be
    Letting standards down.

Utopia needs a base
Of managed news and views,
Where art and music know their place
And poets know who's muse!

*Soviet spy school pep song from the musical *Schenectograd*.

When all is done and said,
No growing boy or girl'd
Be as happy dead as red
When we've won the world.

We'll adjourn *sine die*\*
When we've won the world.
Hi-dee, di-dee, di-dee, die,
When we've won the world.

Washington, DC—1962
Music: Sylvia Symington

\*Pronounced "sy-nee-dye"; means "indefinitely."

# THE BOMB

*The successful explosion of a Soviet atomic bomb in 1948 shook the world. It seemed as if East and West were on a collision course that could well end in catastrophe. Hence:*

## STONE AGE REVISITED

A somber dawn reveals the crusted plough
For centuries transfixed and long since blown
With ploughman's dust. Another age of stone
Is born. The lofty oak is rigid now.
Awakening airs caress the reaching bough
In vain—and weep these winds for they alone
Have breached the dim abyss between the known
And the unknown to kiss the greying brow
Of earth, and grieve within the broken tower
At the lost inheritance, the final stand,
The crawling in the streets, the desperate hour
Of silent prayer, when someone's outstretched hand,
In mute defiance of its ebbing power,
Scratched, "We cannot die" upon the sand.

*Yale Literary Magazine*—1949

*The 1960s were marked by breezy discussions of first and second strike options. Hence these lines on . . .*

# CONVENTIONAL WAR

I never was much for convention
Life was too short for that.
For me a little dissension,
And an unconventional hat.

But those were the good old days
Before the atom got fractured.
Now a new hair on me greys
With each bomb that gets manufactured.

And I think that maybe convention
Has found in history its place.
It could even get honorable mention
For preserving the human race.

For as life is flimsy at most,
And we look at what may be in store,
We should raise our glass in a toast
To good old "conventional" war.

Washington, DC—1965

*Not known, perhaps, to the madding crowd was John Nef, savant, economist, Francophile, University of Chicago professor, and brilliant writer (War and Human Progress) on a quest he believed both essential and achievable, the quest for peace. An eightieth birthday salute:*

## PROPHET OF PROMISE

Three score and twenty years ago
Louisa Nef brought forth upon this continent
A new person, conceived in happiness
And dedicated to the proposition
That men might actually learn to live at peace
With one another. They called this prophet John.
And neither Harvard nor Chicago could undo
His smiling certainty in this millenium.

No idle dreamer on a dreamer's quest,
He's borne this notion through an arduous life
Of scholarship upon the vexing ways
Of economics, war and human progress.
The smoldering remains of empires others gaze upon
He sifts with gentle patience to produce
The glowing promise of a swordless future for mankind.

Washington, DC—July 13, 1979

# WAR AND PREPAREDNESS

*World War II touched the lives of all American families. In 1943, my brother, Stuart, then eighteen, enlisted in the Army and served in both Europe and the Pacific. A beloved cousin, Daniel Payson, was killed in action during the Battle of the Bulge. Turning eighteen in 1945, I checked into a well-regulated resort located at Parris Island, South Carolina. Following is the ensuing exchange of correspondence between me and my grandfather, Congressman James W. Wadsworth of Geneseo, New York. Wadsworth had served on the Military Affairs Committee of the Senate in the First World War, and was a strong proponent of preparedness.*

December 11, 1945

Dear Gramp,

Now that the smoke has cleared away, I am able to review the last three tempestuous weeks. This life is rugged. A "Boot's" day at P.I. is comparable in length and strain to the toughest I weathered on the Farm. But if I had torn up a row of corn on the cultivator, I would not have been subjected to humiliation, and extra-enforced hardship. Here such penalties are incurred daily—little things—talking in ranks, forgetting to "Sir" non-coms, tripping in drills. Dirty rifle is to the Marine as manslaughter is to the civilian. Manhandling is an unnecessary weapon in the hands of one who can, by words, inflict worse treatment—"riding the range" (that is, scrubbing a red-hot coal stove with brush and water for hours), prolonged attention, extra night watch, *less sleep*. According to authorities, the Marine's best friend is his rifle. My bunk has been a most outstanding rival for this distinction.

The Marine expresses every feature of military life in naval terms. We "hit the deck" at five minutes to 5:00. Sweep and swab down the "deck" and "bulkheads" by 5:20. Physical drill on parade grounds (now with rifles) at 5:30 for one-half hour. Very cold!

Then morning chow. Plenty to eat and good enough for me—although food is a foremost gripe. First and second weeks spent drilling intensely and marching back and forth to the dispensary for physicals, shots, and dental work. The memorable "first day," of course, succeeds in its purpose of subjugating and humiliating the "civilian" in a man. To procure equipment he goes through the "mill"—rushed through a gauntlet of hard-faced, screaming Marines—shoved, yanked, cursed, running at top speed in bare feet to myriads of unknown destinations, receiving conflicting orders in a high pitch and made very sorry for disobeying one or the other. His head is shaved clean. One look in the barber's mirror took all the "civilian" fight out of me.

Dinner is served at the many mess halls at 11:00 and 12:00. Supper at 4:00 and 5:00. We've studied and absorbed the eleven "general orders" for sentry, first aid, military discipline, the parts and function of the rifle, field sanitation, some articles of war, history of the Corps, map reading, interior guard duty, equivalent ranks and recognition of officers of the three services, and saluting (when and where). Evening lectures by the D.I. and training films have been the mediums of instruction. Each man must have complete notes on these subjects and carry his notebook with him at all times. There were three or four men (seventeen and eighteen) in this platoon who, being unable to read or write, have been sent to a post school.

One upsetting incident had to do with the use of acidic bore cleaner on our rifles, which we were ordered not to use until at the range, after firing, when the order was given. For this offense we were called before the Major, who really gave us the business, threatening everything from a setback in training to court-martial. We quaked in our shoes. Then it was uncovered by a blessedly alert armory sergeant that these rifles had been under survey before for *excessive pitting.* That got us out of the inferno of suspicion and threat. And now we are at the range in good shape one week ahead of schedule. We are to spend one week "snapping in," that is, mastering the painful firing positions, devised not for comfort but for maximum steadiness. Then one week on the twenty-two and carbine. One week on the M-1. Finally, one on the B.A.R. and hand grenade. Then back to the main area for bayonet drill and some advance stuff. This training is scheduled to last forty-eight days.

You know, Gramp, I hate to worry the folks about these things. Mom especially, but thirty-two hundred men—recruits, including platoons that *hadn't even fired the B.A.R.* —were sent to Norfolk today to ship out to China, *without furlough.* A little Oriental adventure would be a fine way to complete my service in the Corps. But let me ask. Is this nation at war or are the Marines waging battles over there on their own?

All considered—this is a good life and I'm beginning to enjoy it, even if, for dropping a fork in the knife slot, I get three days mess duty.

Private James Symington
Parris Island, South Carolina

Private First
Class, U.S.M.C.
Camp Lejeune,
North Carolina,
1945.

Author with
grandmother,
Alice Hay
Wadsworth,
on Christmas
furlough.
Washington,DC,
December 1945.

December 20, 1945

Dear Jimmy:

That was a grand letter you sent me several days ago. I would have answered it long since had I not been literally swamped with mail, visitors, committee meetings, and long, angry sessions of the House. I am beginning to catch up now and by Saturday night the desk will be pretty clean.

Sure enough, you are leading the rugged life. I do not imagine you will tear up many rows of marine corn, because I suspect that you have a knack of keeping your eye on the cultivator and can follow a straight row. What you are going through is just about what eight or ten million men have experienced during the last five years. Hike, hike, crawl, dig, squirm, let alone reporting prompt and fresh for every job. One thing, you had spent a lot of time on your feet before you went into the service. I have seen a lot of youngsters, city bred, who just could not walk two miles with anything heavier than a cigarette case. It took them a long time to build up the legs, but when that was done they could hold their own. Sergeants have to be tough.

You are learning a lot about fellers. There are all kinds of them. Scarce any two are alike. Some are quick, some are slow. Some are square, some are slick. Some want to learn and do. Others want to learn and can't. Some do not care about learning anything. But way down underneath you will find something good in pretty nearly all of them. Patience is what is needed in sizing up dependably a big gang of youngsters.

You know, I envy you. I wish I could look back on the experience you are having. When I saw that my assistance was needed to make sure that the Spaniards were defeated in 1898, I went into a field artillery outfit, supposedly on active duty in time of war, and, literally, I did not know a thing except how to ride and care for a horse. I certainly did not know how to take care of myself. Neither did anybody else in the outfit, despite the fact that four-fifths of them were college graduates. Very smart—elite. The Spaniards saw us coming and surrendered.

We spent the summer in Puerto Rico, eating and drinking everything we could get hold of. Sloppy from top to bottom. Half our horses died on the picket line and half the men were sick. I held up pretty well until, aboard the transport coming home, I insisted upon eating three rations (all at once) of spoiled beef. I lost thirty-seven pounds. Looking back on it years afterwards I realize that I had been a rotten soldier—just no good. Why? Because I had had no boot training. Nobody had in those days, except in the tiny regular Army, Marine Corps, and Navy. That's why I have been a crank about training ever since.

Take care of yourself. And write again when the spirit moves you. I like getting your letters.

Affectionately,

Grandpa

Author's grandfather, James W. Wadsworth, Jr. Member of the U.S. Senate (Republican) 1915-27, and the House of Representatives (R-NY), 1933-51.

*Following the Ribbon Creek incident at Parris Island in which a platoon sergeant's miscalculation resulted in the drowning of five recruits, the Congress contemplated new guidelines for boot training. My father, then in his first Senate term, wrote me about it. My reply:*

April 22, 1956

Dear Dad:

Your inquiry concerning my Marine training prompts these thoughts:

1. Should the U.S. have a force of men capable of fighting and winning battles in any climate, against any odds, in any part of the world at a moment's notice?

If the answer is "yes," then we must ask—

2. Is the average eighteen-year-old American such a man?

We needn't deny the courage and willingness of American boys to fight for their country to accept the fact that our pleasure-conscious youth are not, without more, a force capable of winning battles.

3. How do they become such a force of men?

4. They join and become such a force of men by enlisting in the U.S. Marines.

There, they will learn the techniques and disciplines of war. And they will learn them from their sergeants. War is the business of sergeants. Men's lives and success in battle depend on the wisdom, intuition, and resolution of their sergeants. Marine "boot" training prepares men for war by teaching them respect and obedience to sergeants. The often apparently absurd demands made of "boots" by their sergeants are but mild substitutes for the absurd demands that are made of men by war—the absurd demands of Guadalcanal and Okinawa.

If Congress believes that American boys are sufficiently prepared to meet those demands by their encounters in the drive-in theater and corner drug store, then it might consider abolishing the U.S. Marines or requiring them to provide those features as part of their program.

Parris Island, then, is a world of sergeants. As mine would say, "Listen, you guys, and don't forget it; the sun rises and sets in my beautiful face." I never actually observed that phenomenon, but I did note that when the sergeant was pleased we were pleased, and vice versa. That was the system. And the tragic miscalculation of one sergeant operating within that system of peacetime training is no justification for modifying the system; for changing methods and rules which are not made by men alone, but by war. When wars are waged by hurling rose petals at one another, then Parris Island may become an interesting relic of a brutal past. But Parris Island today is well-suited to the hard realities of the present. One of the many dilemmas of America is this: While we do not care to see free nations eaten up, nevertheless, where the consumption is marked by the latest gourmet technique of much nibbling and only an occasional and discreet clamping together of the jaws, our little friends disappear with too little fuss to justify nuclear intervention. But there is an alternative to editorial obituaries in these cases — the U.S. Marines.

And a word for Sergeant McKeon. His error consisted in his taking men into water of unknown depth. He did not err in taking them into water on a Sunday night. War respects neither sleep nor holy days. And his job was to ready his men for war. He would have undoubtedly preferred to retire early and breakfast refreshed with his wife and children. Making that march was for him a sacrifice of personal comfort to the job and trust of making soldiers. Disciplinary action may be a sop to public outrage, but will not be required to humble the heart of a man who has killed in trying to teach how to stay alive.

# On
# Technology

# REPRODUCTION

Parenthood devoid of passion

May be coming into fashion,

Generations in a neat row,

Each one fertilized in vitro.


Yet to make one's entrance in a dish

Cannot be anybody's wish—

Especially those who likely are

To make their exit in a jar.


Washington, DC—1994

# HERE COME THE CLONES

Who would have thought we'd live to see the day

When eulogists could praise a fallen friend

Without the confidence to say,

"We'll never see the likes of him again."

Washington, DC—February 1997

*The advent of the time-saving computer in our lives has been accompanied by anxiety and nostalgia; hence, these two ballads. The first acknowledges that humanity and its endeavors will perish before the last computer has its say. The second updates the legend of John Henry (the steel-drivin' man who defeated the steam drill, and then succumbed). Clearly the blue-collar worker is not alone rendered obsolete by advancing technology. It happens as well to certified public accountants, like our hero, John Smithers. Its most recent conquest over the world's greatest (human) chess player, Gary Kasparov, confirms the following thirty-five-year-old prediction:*

## COMPUTERS ARE HERE TO STAY*

Farmer Pickens counts his chickens
Before they're hatched today.
Humans are okay,
But computers are here to stay.

Galileo,[1] Dr. Mayo,[2]
They all had their say,
Humans are okay,
But computers are here to stay.

Remember all those apples,
Dropped by Isaac Newt?[3]
The old galoot
Could not compute,
Or he'd have ate
That fruit.

Now, don't you be like Noah,
Countin' two by two.
It's getting late,
So automate
Before the others do.

---

*Song from the musical *Schenectograd*.
[1]Galileo Galilei (1564-1642), Italian astronomer who advanced the untimely notion
    that the earth revolved around the sun (see footnote, p. 194).
[2]Dr. William Mayo, founder of the Mayo Clinic in Rochester, Minnesota.
[3]Sir Isaac Newton (1642-1727), English scientist and philosopher who posited the law of gravity.

What makes you think
The missing link
Is missing anyway?
It's you and me today,
So wipe that tear
And drink your beer,
Cause it's quite clear
Computers are here to stay.

Washington, DC — 1962<br>Music: Sylvia Symington

# THE BALLAD OF JOHN SMITHERS*

When John Smithers was a little feller
Sittin' on his mammy's knee,
He reached out and touched a number three pencil;
Said it's gonna be the death of me.

When Smithers he got out of college
He had a mighty fine degree
As a genuine certified public accountant
Man, he did it with a pencil number three.

When Smithers applicated to the comp'ny
What they said'd make a strong man sob
"Smithers you're neat, but you're obsolete
Cause this computer it'll do your job."

Smithers, he clutched his diploma,
And a tear dribbled out of his eye.
"Just give us a task is all that I ask
And I'll whup that computer by and by."

So the floor supervisor gave permission
Although he was a little bit annoyed.
He said, "Smithers you'll loin that you're gonna join
The ranks of the unemployed."

Smithers said, "gimme that problem
And an Eberhard Faber number three,
Cause work I don't shirk, I'm just a turk of a clerk
And no computer'll make a fool o' me."

Then he sat down beside the competition,
A twenty ton pile o' steel.
With knobs and a dial and a sinister smile
Like Smithers gonna be its next meal.

*Tune: *John Henry.*

The directors emerged with a question
That could kill a dozen men or more.
What'll be the tax on the citizens' backs
In the year twenty hundred and four?
(Assumin' just conventional war.)

They had to estimate the number of people,
And did Republicans get in yet?
And did we save face in outer space,
Without orbiting the national debt?

So Smithers he readied up his pencil,
And the computer got pluggèd in.
The information was fed while the President said
"May the best contraption win."

The computer, it groaned and it sputtered,
Flashin' red 'n yellow 'n green.
It shuddered and roared while the facts they poured
Like wheat from a threshin' machine.

But Smithers was writin' up a frenzy.
His number three whirrin' like a fan.
He scribbled and scratched like he'd come unlatched.
Oh, Lord, he was a pencil pushin' man.

The battle went on for forty hours,
And the computer was beginnin' to burst.
It came down to the wire a-spittin' smoke and fire,
But Smithers was a-gettin' there first.

Yeah, Smithers was jottin' in high cotton,
When suddenly his number three broke,
And with it the heart so strong at the start
Oh, Lord, he was a pencil pushin' bloke!

They laid old Smithers in the out box,
And filed him gently away,
Though the President tried, before he died
To tell him that maybe he could stay.

Although the computer was the winner,
Had beaten old Smithers by a hair,
It'd blown every fuse in Newport News
And all the lights on Herald Square,
(Causin' lawsuits everywhere).

Now the moral of our little story
Is lay your pencils down,
And don't blow a fuse 'cause you're gonna lose
When that computer comes to town.
   When that computer comes to town.

Washington, DC—1963

# COMMERCIAL AIRFLIGHT IN 1985

## (A Thirty-Year Projection)

New Yorker, N.A. Rush, had bought his ticket to London the previous evening through his TV set. "Where's the helicar?" he shouted to his wife as he packed his bags. "On the roof, behind the chimney," was the cheerful reply. In a few moments he was hovering over the parking lot at LaGuardia. Every spot taken. He put the vehicle down just outside the legal boundary, as he had seen others do with impunity. He then placed his bags on the conveyer belt that led from the lot to the aircraft, a wingless, cigar-shaped craft as long as a football field, and glowing at one end. As he stepped from the moving walkway through the arched entrance he saw his bags slide up into the hold.

Moving on through the aircraft he looked enviously at the first-class appointments. He was traveling in the second-class "gyroseats," which reduced vibration, while the "suspendanim" first-class accommodations removed almost entirely any sensation of motion throughout the flight. Gyroseats, now that they were equipped with personal television, were more than adequate. He had become addicted to rugby matches, and was pleased to find one in progress in Melbourne, Australia. As he settled in, the stewardess approached and asked what he would like for breakfast. "Juice, coffee, toast, and a four-minute egg," he replied. "I'm so sorry," said the stewardess. "We're landing in three minutes."

TWA Contest Entry—1955 (not the winner)

# On
# Education

# DICTIONERROR

It appears the expression, "Aye-Aye,"

Denotes, "a nocturnal lemur,"

When we thought it conveyed, bye and bye,

Assurances made on a steamer.

Now wouldn't the captain say, "Heck!"

Or complain to the mate in the least,

If an Aye-Aye encountered on deck

Was not a salute but a beast?

And consider the ensign's surprise,

If at night under threatening skies,

A chorus of hearty Aye-Ayes

Should meet not his ears but his eyes?

St. Louis—1955

# SCHOOL DAYS

*St. Bernard's School for boys occupies a time-worn brick building on Ninety-eighth Street near Central Park, New York City. In the 1930s both the curriculum and the Masters were British — the latter for the most part veterans of the Great War with eye-patches, facial scars, and limps to show for it. The school day began at 8 A.M. with the lusty singing of old Anglican hymns in the main study hall. Latin and French were introduced in the third grade. The way to find happiness there was to please the Masters, men of rare individuality who displayed ingenious and occasionally amusing ways of discouraging laziness, poor work, and, needless to say, disobedience.*

*The school still flourishes, and the "old boys" keep an eye on it. The Class of '40, assembled for its fifty-fifth, was obliged to endure a repeat of the duet from Gilbert & Sullivan's Patience as performed in 1939 by George Plimpton (Archibald) and the author (as Patience), followed by this reunion song to the tune of "Scotland the Brave":*

## "HAIL TO THE CLASS OF '40"

Hail to the Class of Forty,
Still standing tall and doughty,
Since we made our gallant sortie
On History.
　　— by heaven —

Hail to our noble Masters,
Prescient and bold forecasters,
Of the several disasters
We'd prove to be.

Our thanks for the chance to hone
Body, mind, and funny bone
Go to the one great school we've known
　　— St. Bernard's —

So before the century passes,
Let her laddies raise their glasses
To the Masters of their classes,
Griefs, pains, and joys.
　　　— And as we —

Say our ave, atque, vale,
Sing it in a spirit jolly,
Luck has made us all, by golly,
St. Bernard's Boys!

New York—1995

# SENIOR CLASS PROPHECY

(Excerpt)

"Gentlemen, in one hundred years we shall all be dead. By then we will have given what we deigned to give and gained what we were able to gain. Judging from my observations of this year's senior class, I should expect it to accept, cheerfully, its full share of gain."*

Deerfield Academy—June 5, 1945

*Editor's Note*—This approach to solemnity may have influenced Symington's classmate, journalist Michael Kernan, in his report twenty-four years later on the 1969 National Press Club dinner for newly-elected members of Congress. . . . "Senator George Murphy (the veteran actor) said he could tell which of the speakers had bothered to read his speech† in advance. Top marks went to Rep. James Symington (D-Mo.). Murphy's guess: Symington not only is a speaker of long experience but also writes his own stuff. Which seems likely, for the former protocol chief was an accomplished raconteur, writer, and doggerelist way back at Deerfield Academy."

"A Pause to Cry While Laughing"
*Washington Post*—January 17, 1969

---

†Excerpts

Your Majesty, your Worships, your Excellencies, your Honorable Mentions, your every day ordinaries, fellow bondmen, and folks:

My descent down Pennsylvania Avenue from the White House occurred as follows: As Chief of Protocol for President Johnson I had escorted an Ambassador into a broom closet, flown the British flag upside down, neglected to remind the King of Greece of an appointment with the President, and gotten lost in New York with the King of Morocco. Then six normally friendly countries broke relations with the United States. It was about this time the President asked if I ever thought of running for Congress. As he spoke Marvin Watson was removing my cummerbund and patent leather pumps. It was over. Still, reassuringly, the President put his hand on my shoulder and said, "Jim, anyone can make mistakes, but you have the satisfaction of knowing you've made them for America." . . .

# HEADMASTER

*Every age produces a few prodigious educators. By precept, example, and some indefinable power, they herd their charges to the threshold of maturity. Such a one was Frank Boyden, the Headmaster of Deerfield Academy from 1901 to 1967. The following marked his sixtieth year at the helm.*

## PAST, PRESENT, FOREVER

The game ended in the sunset. He was the first on the field to congratulate the other team and coach. And he was smiling broadly in his fur-collared coat and battered hat as he turned and raised his arms for silence and the song. The notes lifted to the quick-cooling sky as darkness made its way into the valley. Then, through green shadows, the boys went back—"back to the books," the thoughts, the plans, and the hopes that a great school is made of. Leaves scuffed in the air mixed with the ones coming down, like past and present diffused, like the values of today meeting those of yesterday and finding themselves the same; like a half-century of service joining the ages. But he stayed on the field for a moment clearing his spectacles. Was it mist or memory? For here were old touchdowns and goal-line stands, home runs and impossible catches. Here were the shouts, cheers, and stifled pain of boys becoming men.

That is what he saw, and that is how I see him, past, present, and forever. The game was over. Who won? I can't remember. The victory, in any case, was his.

*Deerfield Journal*—1962

# "OL' MISS" — A MEMOIR

In the fall of 1962 thousands of students trudged reluctantly back to welcoming schools. One willing student encountered a reluctant school. Having qualified for admission to the venerable Mississippi University at Oxford, that student, James Meredith, sought assistance from the federal government to complete his matriculation. A series of phone conversations between Attorney General Robert Kennedy and state authorities proving inconclusive, Mr. Meredith was escorted one weekend by federal marshals onto the campus and into the faculty lyceum for protection.

The President's nationwide radio appeal for calm did nothing to head off the ensuing riot. A number of marshals ringing the besieged hideaway were wounded in a fire-fight that tore up the campus and town. Leading a unit of the hurriedly nationalized State Guard, a young lieutenant named Faulkner had his arm broken by a hurled cornerstone ripped up from the street. The next day, as Administrative Assistant to the Attorney General, I was asked to fly down, join his beleaguered staff, take the community temperature, interview civic leaders, and try to initiate a reconciliation process.

Driving through Oxford with a coat over my head (at the insistence of the marshal) to deflect possibly shattering glass, I still noted overturned and smoldering cars and jeeps, the fixed bayonets of nervous soldiers no older than the jeering students they confronted, and the residual stench of tear gas, which I hadn't inhaled since boot camp. I remarked to my driver that it appeared things had gotten out of hand. Arriving at the federal bunker I joined many a good friend and colleague, including the resourceful and statesmanlike leader of the federal presence, Deputy Attorney General Nicholas Katzenbach, and the quiet-spoken, steely-nerved John Doerr, Deputy Assistant Attorney General for Civil Rights.

The following day under something like a flag of truce, the university bursar, a tall, lanky gent also named Faulkner, gained admission and asked if one of us would care to address a Lion's Club luncheon that day in Oxford. I thought it would be a good way to test the climate for "better relations," and with Katzenbach's permission, volunteered. My only condition: no television.

Oxford's Mansion Restaurant was filled to capacity with a hundred or more husky, shirt-sleeved representatives of the town's male population.

My host was the Mayor, Richard Elliot. Political appearances on behalf of hapless candidates had inured me to scowls, but my appetite was curtailed nevertheless. As luck would have it, I was saved by an odd recollection stored in my usually vacant data bank. Mayor Elliot introduced me with very little flourish as, "the gentleman from the Justice Department who is here to explain what's going on."

"Thank you, Mr. Mayor, but before I speak, there's something I'd like to say — or at least recount. It is the story of one of Nero's visits to the colosseum to gratify his artistic temperament by watching Christians being thrown to the lions. All was going well, except for one Christian. Every time a lion would approach him he would deftly step aside and whisper in the beast's ear. Tail between his legs, the lion would slink away. Frustrated, Nero ordered the young fellow to be brought before him. 'What have you got with my lions!?' he demanded. 'I simply remind them, sire,' replied the lad, 'that after they've eaten, they'll be asked to speak.' Gentlemen," I said, "you may have noticed I've hardly touched my lunch."

I then pointed out that being from Missouri, where there had never been a proven infraction of law, I appeared before them with a pretty clean conscience. I suggested that they all probably looked forward to the day when friend meeting friend on the street would say, "What's new?" In the meantime, to answer the Mayor's introductory challenge, "Why are you here?," I began with the well-worn excuse that everybody has to be somewhere. In any case we were not there to harass fellow citizens we were sworn to protect — but rather to ensure that laws to which all citizens were now subject not be circumvented by a few who were in disagreement. I then went through a portion, at least, of the laws, decisions, and court orders, resistance to which occasioned our visit. What did we find? A concerned community of good Americans struggling to accommodate to change and frustrated in their efforts to do so by a few home-grown and a great many outside agitators.

For example, trucks and cars with out-of-state license plates and filled with very burly individuals were being stopped and inspected by the troops. In this connection I told them my suggestion that the soldiers examining the vehicles for weapons, also check the tires, oil, and gas, and wipe the windshields. This idea was summarily rejected at the platoon level. A stuffy lot, the army. Weapons were, indeed, found and confiscated. "We're goin' sqwirl huntin'," was the standard explanation. I said I could not conceal my admiration for anyone who could dispatch a squirrel with a machete or a baseball bat with a nail driven through DiMaggio's signature. Well, onward and upward.

At the conclusion of my treatise, the Mayor rose and thanked me, as I recall, as follows: "Well, suh, we didn't much want you people down here, but even less did we need or want the violence and destruction which was tearing up our town, so, I guess I'd have to say we're grateful." A confirming murmur led to handshakes, and escape, followed by some young Lions who collared me at the door and asked me to join them that night for dinner. I recall walking the dark and quiet streets of Oxford, guitar in hand, wondering how safe it was for a "fed" to leave his encampment.

Arriving at the little frame house of my host I was met by same with a large tumbler of bourbon in hand. "How 'bout some ice?" I asked. "We don't water our drinks," was his quiet response. "Now, would you like to see what you're havin' to eat?" "Certainly," I assured him, and was conveyed to the kitchen. There on the kitchen table, neatly flayed, were the up-staring carcasses of a number of luckless squirrels. Drawing heavily on the now-welcome tumbler I was escorted into the parlor to face my accusers. Some twenty were gathered, each equipped with equivalent refreshment. A tumbler or so later dinner was served.

As I prepared to make a half-hearted incision, my host intervened. "Yankee," he began. "Just a minute," I remonstrated. "I'm from Missouri, a border state. Even though I lost a Union ancestor in the Battle of the Wilderness, my dad's grandpa was a captain on Pickett's staff. His horse fell on him and saved his life." "Alright then," continued my patient host. "What I got to tell ya is how to eat squirrel." "I'd be grateful if you would," I said. "Well then," said he, "you see that there li'l blob o' white just behind the eyes." "Yes I do," I confessed. "What you suppose that is?" said my interlocutor. "I think it might be the brain," I ventured. Confirming my worst fears, my young host went on, "Now, you take this little here foke [fork] and poke it right in that little blob, fetch it out, an' eat it! It's the fust thing you gotta eat." "Well," said I, bargaining for time, "there's no other way?" "Not for squirrel." The die was cast. I speared the glutinous mass and plunged it well past my taste buds, so I can report no flavor, only a faintly slimy consistency. "He did it," shouted my tormenters in unison. "The Yankee did it!" Clearly, geography and history lessons had not taken. In any event the rest of the squirrel was very good.

After another tumbler of un-iced bourbon everything seemed good. I sang some folksongs, including Southern lullabies. Then we touched on the subject: the difference between "loving" certain peoples, which they claimed to do, and "schooling" with them, for which they professed a disinclination. I told them I was reassured by the "loving" part, as it might even lead to "schooling." One tumbler later, with a tearful farewell of abrazos, I staggered out into the night, found my way back to headquarters, fell fully clothed on my army cot, and slept effortlessly past dawn.

The next day, charged with contacting local ministers, I found the way barred to most of the churches. We were meddlers, and fear abounded, with one exception. I was welcomed vigorously into one temple of fundamentalist persuasion. The pastor sat me down and with a minimum of ceremony declared, "You, suh, represent a tyranny!" Still heavily sedated, I was only able to inquire, "What does the minority think of your government?" The simplicity of his answer still wakes me up at night. "It's better," he thundered, "to have a lot o' little tyrannies than one big one!"

This interesting constitutional theory helped me understand the reasons some youngsters gave for their participation in the riot. "My poppa told me," said one. "My preacher told me," said another. A third said he had telephoned his father to tell him he was okay and not involved. "What?" said his father. "Not involved? You get out there and defend your university!"

That night I went to the college auditorium to see Hal Holbrook give his legendary impersonation of Mark Twain. Events of the week did not diminish audience enthusiasm, laughter, and generous applause for his acid comments on racism.

Next day I returned to the Justice Department. The phone rang. It was Mississippi Senator John Stennis, who said "You come down heah, I want to see ya." "Yes sir." That's it, I thought, I've offended an elder statesman. Later, seated on the edge of the chair he offered, I heard him say, "I just want to thank you for the way you spoke to my people."

The Attorney General was curious to know the reason for my summons. When I told him his eyes flickered with incredulity. "And what did you *say* to the people?" he asked. "Most of it," I answered, "doesn't bear repeating."

Oxford, Mississippi—fall of 1962

# LATIN

*Letter to daughter, Julia Symington-Rucker, on learning Latin was to be dropped from her children's school curriculum:*

September 21, 1992

Dear Julie,

You have asked for thoughts about the importance of Latin. Latin may well be an unnecessary burden to any young American who by the age of five or six has clearly demonstrated that he or she is unfit, or otherwise unlikely, to pursue a career in law, medicine, science, literature, the arts, horticulture, religion, philosophy, linguistics, theatre, and the teaching of any of the foregoing plus history and government. Since the most clairvoyant educator might find it difficult to arrive at any such determination, the safest policy would be to make Latin abundantly available to every child throughout primary and secondary school years, and a requirement for at least four of those years.

Ab initio, and in re the curriculum (Latin being sub judice at your school), I am acting merely as amicus curiae whose opinions are admittedly ad hoc, ex parte, ultra vires, and certainly neither de jure nor ex cathedra, inasmuch as I graduated neither magna, nor summa cum laude, and am certainly not a member of the curia of the literati. So my judgment may be questioned, but not my bona fides. I don't claim the status of deus ex machina; nolo contendere on that point. Nor would I want my views to provide a pedagogical* casus belli. If I, or you as my alter ego, were to make ad absurdum much less ad hominem arguments, we could well become persona non grata. Mea culpa if I were to contribute any impedimenta, inter alia, to your magnum opus, et cetera.

Mirabile dictu, I have concluded my observations in persona without one drink, in vino veritas notwithstanding. I tender them to you in camera, in situ, and in nomine Domini, trusting those into whose care they are committed will agree, "humanum est errare."

Ave, atque, vale,

Dad

---

*Forgive this Greek derivative.

# On
# The Family

*Recent interest in overnight accommodations at the White House reminded me of a young college graduate who spent four turbulent years in the residence as Private Secretary to President Lincoln. He was John Hay of Illinois, a graduate of Brown University and subsequently Secretary of State and great-grandad of the author. His impressions of Lincoln, the man and the President, are revealed in:*

# A HAYRIDE WITH LINCOLN

How Lincoln would have enjoyed reminiscing on the Civil War before this distinguished gathering of citizens of America's first state—a state which gave such a proportionately high share of blood and treasure to achieve the outcome! The same Lincoln who, after receiving a series of despatches from General Pope during the latter's retreat, each signed, "Pope, Headquarters in the saddle," was moved to observe, "That's the trouble with Pope; his headquarters is where his hindquarters ought to be"—the same Lincoln who once sent a wistful message to the hesitant McClellan, "General, may I borrow your army?"—or who responded to the dark intelligence that Grant was drinking by exclaiming, "Find out what he is drinking, and give it to my other generals."

The Civil War was an all-American family affair. The trail that led to your Lincoln Club this evening began at some intersections of that struggle which my father's people might have styled, "the war of Northern aggression." His grandad, Captain Stuart Symington, at the age of twenty-one, and described as a "refugee from Maryland," enlisted in the Army of Northern Virginia and was eventually detailed staff aide to Major General George Pickett. My mother's great-grandad was General James Wadsworth of Geneseo, New York. Wadsworth had run for Governor in 1862 but remained that year in Washington in charge of the city's defenses. He lost the election by fifteen-thousand votes to Horatio Seymour, Mayor of New York City. It was said the Republicans went south to fight and the Democrats stayed north to vote.

According to the chief archivist who wrote my father on the subject, Wadsworth and Symington had fought against each other in almost every major engagement east of the Mississippi until Wadsworth's death at Wilderness, upon news of which his son, Jim, left his sophomore year from Yale to enlist in the Union cause. He was later breveted Major for gallantry at Five Forks, Virginia. Fort Wadsworth on Staten Island is named for the old general. Gettysburg had brought the elder Wadsworth, a brigade commander, face to face with Symington, who was in the charge to the end with his horse killed under him.

At a White House meeting after Gettysburg someone asked, "Why did Lee escape?" According to young John Hay, Lincoln's twenty-two-year-old private secretary, General Wadsworth replied, "Because no one stopped him. Northern generals have not gotten over the idea of Southern superiority they learned at West Point, and this accounts for an otherwise unaccountable slowness of attack." Little did Hay or Wadsworth, who was approaching sixty, know that the latter's grandson, Senator Jim Wadsworth of New York, Yale '98, would marry Hay's daughter, Alice, or that their daughter, Eve, would marry the grandson of a confederate officer, W. Stuart Symington, of Baltimore. A footnote to Gettysburg—the reading copy of the subsequent address the battle occasioned might have perished from this earth had not John Hay retrieved it from its author, as the latter, disappointed in the crowd's seeming indifference, was about to discard it. My grandmother, Hay's daughter Alice Wadsworth, donated it to the government in 1913.

In 1865, Captain Symington carried despatches between Lee and Grant just prior to Appomattox. At the surrender Southern officers were given three choices: sign the loyalty oath, go to jail, or leave the country. So Symington embarked with his brother Tom on a boat for Europe and eventually Germany, where they were guests of the adventurous Prussian, Heros von Borcke. Von Borcke had fought with Jeb Stuart as the Inspector General of the Confederate army, and is said to have wielded the largest sabre in either army. The boys returned in about a year to take up their lives in the changed South. Hay also survived, as will be seen, into the next century.

It is impossible, in the strict time-frame allotted, to detail the life and character of Abe Lincoln; his pioneering boyhood, his physical courage and prowess, his hesitant romances, his martyrdom in marriage, his law practice, his brief military service when his closest brush with action was arriving at the scene of an engagement with the Blackhawk, as he said, "just in time to bury the dead," his campaigns, his dreams, his moods, his mysticism, and the hold he had on men, crowds, and history. Moreover, this has been done. So it is a personal pleasure to give you just a few glimpses of the "Tycoon"— as he was dubbed and seen by his young secretary, great-grandpa Hay. What kind of a fellow was Hay that his views of Lincoln should have any claim on our indulgence? He was a whimsical man. He saw the humor in things. Let me move the clock up a notch.

In 1890 during the Chinese Boxer Rebellion, a tense time for all governments with legations in Peking, Secretary of State Hay commented to his daughter Alice, "Minister Wu came by this morning and stayed for two hours, at the conclusion of which Wu was hazy, and Hay was woozy."

In 1898 after the "splendid little war," as he called it, with Spain had placed the infant Cuba on our doorstep, Hay gave voice to a durable insight about that new country. "Dealing with Cuba," he wrote, "is like trying to carry on a polite conversation with a squirrel in your lap."

Hay's gifts of proportion and balance, equity and judgment, which made his advice so welcome to presidents, and his diplomacy so enduring, were really the by-product of a nature given to smiling at the follies and vanities of the world; a tolerance, if not a genuine affection for the absurd. In 1901, after the untimely death of his eldest son, an aging and careworn Hay, pierced with grief, wrote his friend and *New York Tribune* colleague, Whitelaw Reid:

> "Moral integrity and a sense of humor will carry you a long way; but when your sense of humor fails—woe unto you! Mine, I fear, is on the wane. There can be few things funnier than sixteen Senators wrangling over a two-thousand-dollar consulate. But it has ceased to be funny to me—and that is a bad symptom."

Even in sorrow, Hay cannot rid himself of the impulse to share a laugh. It came upon him early. After graduating from Brown University where he delivered the class oration, Hay was urged, as he said, "by his pious friends," to enter the ministry. Of this he wrote, "I would not do for a Methodist preacher, for I am a poor horseman. I would not suit the Baptists, for I dislike water. And I would fail as an Episcopalian for I am no ladies man."

Accordingly, he joined his uncle, Milton Hay, in a Springfield law office adjacent to that of a fifty-year-old lawyer-politician, Abraham Lincoln. Like many a youngster since, he campaigned for a conveniently located candidate and served as assistant to the campaign secretary, John Nicolay. When Nicolay was named secretary to the President-elect, he suggested the duties of his office would exceed his industry and capacity and that Hay would be a great help. "We can't take all Illinois with us down to Washington," said Lincoln—and then, after a pause—"Well, let Hay come." Hay went. Then there were two. Of course, improvements since that time in the technology of communication have enabled the White House to trim its personnel—down to twelve hundred at the latest count.

In his biography of Hay, William Roscoe Thayer described the division of responsibility as follows:

> "Nicolay had charge of official correspondence; Hay, who shared part of this task, wrote letters, saw callers, went on errands to the Departments, kept in touch with personages political, military, and social, and in case of need, escorted Mrs. Lincoln when she drove out, or amused

the Lincoln boys on a rainy day. He made himself very quickly a member of the family; and Lincoln, the most unconventional of men, welcomed his young, versatile, and trustworthy assistant, whose willingness and common sense would always be depended upon."

Lincoln's patience with visitors first caught Hay's attention as per this entry of April 1861:

"Three Indians of the Pottawatomies called today upon their Great Father. The Spokesman's English was exceptional; the other two were mute. The Tycoon amused them immensely by airing the two or three Indian words he knew and his awkward efforts to make himself understood by saying, 'Where live now?' 'When go back Iowa?'"

Then again in September 1863, this entry:

"Today came to the Executive Mansion an assembly of cold water men and women to make a temperance speech at the Tycoon. They filed into the East Room looking blue and thin in the keen autumnal air. Three blue-skinned damsels did Love, Purity, and Fidelity in Red, White, and Blue gowns. A few invalid soldiers stumped along in the dismal procession. They made a long speech at the Tycoon in which they called Intemperance the cause of our defeats. The President could not see it, as he said, 'for the rebels drink more and worse than we do.' At this they filed off drearily to a collation of cold water and green apples."

The *compassion* of Lincoln, who never hunted or shot anything but a wild turkey, is evidenced by his review of court martials. In July 1863, Hay commented on the eagerness with which the President caught at any fact that would justify him in saving the life of a condemned soldier. Cases of cowardice he was especially averse to punishing with death. He said it would "frighten the poor fellows too terribly to shoot them." One fellow, who had deserted and escaped into Mexico after conviction, he sentenced saying, "We will condemn him as they used to sell hogs in Indiana — as they run."

An insight into the importance Lincoln assigned to reasonable conduct in all circumstances was provided by Hay's Uncle Milton, who recalled a day in 1857 when some boys were bedeviling a goat to make for people and butt them off their feet. Lincoln, lost in thought, was about to be tried in this manner, but according to the elder Hay, he got "aholt" of the goat's horns, stooped down with his face up to the goat's and slowly drawled:

"Now there isn't any good reason why you should want to harm me, and there isn't any good reason why I should want to harm you. The world is big enough for both of us to live in. If you behave yourself as you ought to, and if I behave myself like I ought to, well, we'll get along without a cross word or action and we'll live in peace and harmony like good neighbors."

Then, according to Uncle Milt, he lifted the goat by the horns, dropped it over a high fence, and walked on.

Lincoln's forgiving nature and wishful belief in the good intentions of his foes is captured in many a diary entry of his young Boswell. In late 1864 as the war ground uncertainly on, Lincoln was urged to question the bona fides of certain opposition members in the House and Senate. As Hay recalls, "The President declined, saying 'it is much better not to be led from the region of reason into that of hot blood by imputing to public men motives which *they* do not avow.'" On a like occasion Lincoln rejected retaliatory measures, saying:

"You have more of that feeling of personal resentment than I. Perhaps I may have too little of it. But I never thought it paid. A man has not time to spend half his life in quarrels. If any man ceases to attack me I never remember the past against him."

From Hay's close-up view it is clear that the President found relief from the tensions of war both by brief immersions in other facets of national life and the ever-present inspiration of great literature. On August 23, 1863 Hay writes:

"Last night we went to the Observatory. The President took a look at the moon and Arcturus. I went with him to the Soldier's home, and he read Shakespeare to me and the end of *Henry the VI* and the beginning of *Richard III* until my heavy eyelids caught his considerable notice, and he sent me to bed."

Again, in a subsequent entry, Hay records a conversation with the President as the latter examined the moon through a telescope propped between "his toes sublime."

In December of '63 Lincoln took both his secretaries to Ford's Theatre to see *Henry the Fourth*, Hay remarking, "the President showed a very intimate knowledge of those plays of Shakespeare where Falstaff figures." Earlier Lincoln himself had written to one Hacket, a famed actor:

"I think nothing equals *Macbeth*—also the King's soliloquy in *Hamlet*. 'Oh, my offense is rank,' it surpasses Hamlet's own 'to be or not to be.'"

Yet he was hardly chained to classics as per Hay's entry of May 1864, shortly after the Battle of the Wilderness.

"A little after midnight the President came into the office laughing, with a volume of Hood's works in his hand, seemingly utterly unconscious that he with his shirt tail hanging above his long legs and setting out behind like the tail feathers of an enormous ostrich was infinitely funnier than anything in the book he was laughing at. What a man it is! Occupied all day with matters of vast moment, deeply anxious about the fate of the greatest army of the world, with his own fame and fortune hanging on the balance, he exhibits such simple bonhommie and good fellowship that he gets out of bed and perambulates the house in his shirt to find us that we may share with him a bit of fun."

Lincoln was wont to pace the White House halls in the small hours in his nightshirt to share an impulse, thought, or joke. On one such occasion Hay made bold to comment on the "considerable underpinning" which Lincoln had retained. The President responded that his weight was even at 180 pounds, which Hay found reassuring. But it was on August 7, 1863, a month after Gettysburg, that Hay's diary entry summed up for all time the man he served. "The Tycoon is in fine whack," Hay wrote.

"I have rarely seen him more serene and busy. He is managing this war, the draft, foreign relations, and planning a reconstruction of the Union, all at once. I never knew with what a tyrannous authority he rules the Cabinet till now. The most important things *he* decides, and there is no cavil. I am growing more convinced that the good of the country absolutely demands that he should be kept where he is till this thing is over. There is no man in the country so wise, so gentle and so firm."

Two years later Hay was chatting with Robert Lincoln in the White House when word came of the tragedy. They rushed to the little room across from the theatre where Lincoln lay. Hay watched at the bedstead throughout the night. Gradually the slow and regular beat grew fainter, and as Hay describes it, the "automatic moaning" ceased, and, "a look of unspeakable peace came upon his worn features. It was Secretary of War Stanton who broke the silence by saying, 'Now he belongs to the ages.'"

Hay's life went on through diplomatic services in Paris, Vienna, and Madrid, the editorship of the *New York Tribune*, authorships, and appointments as Assistant Secretary of State under Garfield, and Ambassador to Great Britain and Secretary of State under McKinley and Roosevelt. "What a strange and tragic fate it has been of mine," an aging Hay wrote a friend, "to stand by the bier of three of my dearest friends, Lincoln, Garfield, and McKinley, three of the gentlest of men, all done to death by assassins." But of course it was Lincoln whose claim on his mind and heart never diminished.

In 1905, to the despair of his family, associates, and dear friends Henry Adams and Mark Twain, Hay's health declined. Near the end he records in his diary, "I dreamed last night that I was in Washington, and that I went to the White House to report to the President, who turned out to be Lincoln. He was very kind and considerate, and sympathetic about my illness. I was pleased that what he asked was in my power to obey."

The century Hay entered as a careworn diplomat of the old school is about to close. We don't know what Lincoln asked of him in his last dream. We do know what he's asked of us, *his* dream, as it were. And we surely have both the power and the responsibility to obey.

Remarks before the Lincoln Club of Delaware*
Wilmington, Delaware—February 10, 1994

---

*These recollections were known to my old friend, David McCullough, historian and narrator of Public Television's "Civil War." He suggested to Ken Burns, producer of the series, that I share them with him.

Right: John Hay, Private Secretary to President Lincoln, 1861–65; later, Secretary of State under Presidents McKinley and Theodore Roosevelt.

Left: Brigadier General James S. Wadsworth, United States Army. Killed at the Battle of the Wilderness, Spotsylvania, Virginia, 1864.

Right: Captain W. Stuart Symington of Baltimore, Maryland. Aide-de-camp to General George Pickett, Confederate States of America, 1863.

*Co-descendants of discovery and colonialism, the Americas, North and South, constitute an extended, inter-dependent family. This was brought home to me in my first assignment in the Kennedy Administration as Deputy Director of Food for Peace under George McGovern. The program was designed to provide surplus farm products to the world's hungry, including millions south of the border. My visits with them gave rise to this song:*

## A CHILD CAN GROW

When a child wakes in a far-off land
And his mother takes him by the hand,
Glad the day if mother knows
The child grows
In that far-off land.

From hunger's chains can come release
With food for progress, food for peace.
America would have it so
A child can grow
In a far-off land.

And grow he will, the child until
He leads his people up the hill,
Knowing they are not so far
From friends who are
In a far-off land.

Recorded in English and Spanish
for the Voice of America—1961
Music: Jim Symington

Author and "Noble Regent" (the cow) with Food For Peace staples: milk, corn, and wheat. Beltsville, Maryland, Agricultural Station, 1961.

Deputy Director, Food For Peace, singing with Peruvian families at
a school-lunch opening. Lima, Peru, 1961.

*A continuing source of anxiety for the heads of average households is, of course:*

# THE BILLS*

Hear the tolling of the bills,
Monthly bills.
What a world of solemn thought each envelope instills.
In the silence of the night
How I shiver with affright
At the melancholy menace of the mail,
For fear of an announcement
Of some irrevocable bouncement
And a jail.
Eyelids barely close
Before financial woes
Prevail.
Painfully recalling
In lamentable detail
Some galling act of falling
For a sale.
And for all of their acumen
Creditors aren't human,
They are ghouls,
Whose curses track the hearses
Of poor non-reimbursers,
Though mercilessly worse is
That their automation kills
With frills, and gaily-colored bills,
Bills of many hues,
Reds and blues.
Ah, would I were astuter
Than that evidently neuter
IBM computer
With its tinted tabulation of these bills, bills, bills,
Bills, bills, bills.
Oh, the moaning and the groaning
Of the bills.

Washington, DC—1963

*Adapted from *The Bells* by Edgar Allan Poe.

# A FIFTH WEDDING ANNIVERSARY LETTER TO MIAMI'S KENILWORTH HOTEL

January 24, 1958

The Management
The Kenilworth Hotel
Miami Beach, Florida

Gentlemen:

I have a suggestion for promotion of your fine hotel. It is simply this: Your public relations office should circulate the information that newly-weds choosing the Kenilworth as their honeymoon spot would receive an invitation from the Kenilworth to spend a fifth anniversary honeymoon *at* the Kenilworth and *on* the Kenilworth; that is, with all ordinary expenses paid *by* the Kenilworth, including room and meals, but no bar, gifts, or travel expenses. I think, however, a rental car should be thrown in for best results.

By entering upon such a program you would not only induce hundreds of undecided wedding planners to select your fine hotel, but you would also be making a contribution of social importance by reducing the divorce rate among couples during the first five years of marriage.

This is all very well, you might say, but how are we going to get this thing started? Where, for instance, are we going to find a couple for whom we can inaugurate this excellent idea without waiting five years? Again, I think I can be of assistance. Although reluctant to inject personal factors into business proposals, nevertheless, in fairness to you, I should point out that my wife, Sylvia, and myself, were married five years ago today. At this time in 1953, I was adjusting, with very good humor under the circumstances, a faulty collar button which I have since disposed of. We then winged to Miami and the Kenilworth, where we had an enjoyable time for the next five days, drinking orange juice and so forth.

Accordingly, it is with humility and respect that I would consent to interrupt my busy schedule and volunteer to be, retroactively to be sure, your first guest under this plan.

Awaiting your reply, and glad to be of service, I am . . .

Yours sincerely,

James W. Symington

*A Muse 'N Washington / 193*

# POSTSCRIPT TO THE KENILWORTH LETTER*

The hotel politely declined. On the eve of our tenth anniversary, in 1963, I sent the hotel another note, asking if they would like to reconsider their original response, pointing out that ten years was a more impressive and less onerous figure to work with. The hotel replied, rather curtly this time, that it had not changed its view. In January 1968 I wrote again suggesting that time might have softened their attitude, and that, moreover, fifteen years was not a bad place to start. There was no answer to this letter.

Undiscouraged, I was preparing to write once more on the eve of our twentieth when my attention was drawn to a television advertisement for a carpet manufacturer. The picture showed a wrecking ball smashing a building from top to bottom. When the rubble, which tumbled onto the lobby floor, was cleared away, it left the carpet unscathed. My joy at the resilience of the carpet was tempered by the revelation that the demolished building was the Kenilworth Hotel.

---

*In early 1996, Club Med extended a promotional offer to couples married five or more years: If couples would celebrate their anniversary aboard the *Club Med 2* sailing ship, they would receive a discount off the price equal to the number of years married. Proof of Hadrian's observation that, "A man who is ahead of his time is wrong."

# TWENTY-FIFTH WEDDING ANNIVERSARY

### Lord Byron's[1] Challenge:

"Think you if Laura had been Petrarch's[2] wife
He would have written sonnets all his life?"[†]

Lord Byron flings a challenge to all men
That best be met, if we would skip the pain
Of having to our loving wives explain
Why sonnets haven't poured from every pen.
Here's a poor Petrarchan sonnet then,
Concocted in the often muddled brain
Of one who for his Sylvia would strain
To beard that chauvinist Byron in his den.
That leaves six lines to tell you what I know
Of the blue-eyed gal who pinned me to the mat
Two dozen and a couple years ago.
She makes me eat my greens, also my hat,
Two children and myself she's caused to grow
And I'd like to raise my glass in thanks for that.


### Postscript

Let every husband turn his hand to verse
Lest wife believe some lurking Laura's tease
Will serve to lure her man from bed to worse.
Now utter it as naturally as you sneeze.
Compliment it with an open purse,
And spend some fervent moments on your knees.

Washington, DC—January 24, 1978

---

[1]George Gordon, 6th Baron Byron (1788-1824), English poet.
[2]Petrarch (1304-74), Italian lyric poet and scholar.
[†]*Don Juan*, canto 111.

# REMARKS AT SERVICES FOR
# SENATOR STUART SYMINGTON

In St. Paul's Cathedral is the epitaph of its great architect, Sir Christopher Wren. It reads, "If you would see the man's monument, look around." My father might well say the same, not of this glorious cathedral, per se, though he served it well, but the people in it—loving friends—the truest monument to any life.

Born eighty-seven years ago, he came with the century, and in every walk, or rather giant stride, of that life gave back to his country the best his country could produce. He was graceful in manner, keen in competition, resourceful in business, caring and just to laboring men and women, compassionate and fair to minorities and the less fortunate, and ever so proud of his peers and colleagues in the Air Force, the Senate, and the wide worlds of public and private endeavor.

Formidable in a fight, philosophic in the outcome, forgiving of his adversary, but most of all devoted to each and every friend, his joy was in their achievement more than his own. There was something about him that drew others to him. What was it? The eyes? What the journalists called, "the look of eagles"? It's the same look in all the old photos. The judgmental infant; the solemn towhead with bangs; the eleven-year-old paperboy who emerged from the 1912 Democratic convention in Baltimore exclaiming, as reported, "It's Woodrow Wilson, <u>unaminimously</u>"; the seventeen-year-old lieutenant of field artillery; the impatient industrialist; the Air Force Secretary; the Senator; the great-grandfather. Those constant blue eyes were windows to a light that burned to be seen and felt, and not eclipsed. He was tall and built to move. But as Emerson said of Hercules, he needed no contest. He conquered where he stood.

At this point he is undoubtedly standing up there looking down and saying, "Make it short, Jim, these are busy people. My old friend Dean Walker[1] has a long day ahead, and anyway, I want to hear Dave Acheson,[2] Hollings,[3] and Clifford.[4] By the way, thank them for me." Well, Pa, I'm used to the five-minute rule, and in your presence the ten-second rule, but reflection is the order of the day.

So, first a few other illustrative strictures. Chronologically: 'Sit up. Hit those books. Don't drop your racquet head; get that math down. Be on time. You can't learn what you already know; the greatest fool is the fool who fools himself. The greatest thrill in politics is to make a friend out of an enemy. There's nothing older than yesterday's newspaper.'

Whence these principles and perceptions? What confluence of genes and experience produced them? His great-grandpa quarried the cornerstone of the Washington Monument. His grandad was a captain in the Army of Northern Virginia and went up the hill at Gettysburg. His father abandoned a low-paid professorship in romance languages to study law and become a judge in his hometown of Baltimore. His mother campaigned for women's suffrage, and ran a shelter for homeless black families.

Stuart Symington was a Southerner, with that admixture of charm, remembered pain, and lofty spirit that could carry the ramparts of Northern institutions and national respect. A Missourian by choice, he brought to government a "show me" mindset as well as a concept of public service that stands like a Doric column against the gray Washington sky. With that "look of the eagles" he saw beyond most—and lived to see much that he'd foreseen: Western democracies ill prepared to meet a ruthless enemy, a separate and more effective air arm and an academy to nourish it, a faulted and futile war in Asia, the debts and deficits of an unbalanced economy, a brighter future for Missouri, and a changing world where hope would one day outpace fear.

In 1946 as my brother and I headed for college, he counseled, "Take Russian. We'll either be fighting or doing business with them in the next half century."

Like the Spartans at Thermopylae his wounds were all in front. And honorably earned in just causes—"I'm not afraid of you," he said to Joe McCarthy.[5] "I'll meet you any time, any place, anywhere." "I believe you," he said to the falsely-accused Annie Lee Moss.[6] Yet he appeared to stand above the very conflicts that engaged his energies in a way that led friend and foe alike to consider him trustworthy. This was true of Harry, Ike, Jack, Lyndon, Jerry Ford, and all his colleagues on both sides of the aisle. Yet the essence of Stuart Symington, what was it?

"The best portion of a man's life," wrote Wordsworth,[7] "is his little, nameless, unremembered acts of kindness and of love." But my father's are remembered.* For I've read them in your letters and in your faces. As Longfellow[8] said:

> When a great man dies
> For years beyond our ken,
> The light he leaves behind him lies
> Upon the paths of men.

So, to the well-intentioned gentleman who observed, "It must be tough for you and your brother, living in your father's shadow," I say, "Correction, sir. We live as we always have, and always will, not in his shadow, but his light."

Washington National Cathedral—Tuesday, January 10, 1989

[1]John Walker, Dean, Washington Cathedral, Washington, DC.
[2]David Acheson, Attorney, Washington, DC.
[3]Senator Ernest "Fritz" Hollings (D-SC).
[4]Clark M. Clifford, Washington DC lawyer, Presidential Adviser, and former Secretary of Defense.
[5]Senator Joseph McCarthy (R-WI).
[6]Annie Lee Moss, witness before Senator McCarthy's Committee on Un-American Activities.
[7]William Wordsworth (1770-1850), English poet; poet laureate (1843-50).
[8]Henry Wadsworth Longfellow (1807-82), U.S. poet.
*As are my mother's. For a tribute to her legacy, see the following pages.

Father and son on a stroll.  Washington, DC, 1985.

At home in Washington, DC, 1985.

# SELECTIONS FROM THE POEMS
# OF EVE SYMINGTON

*My mother, Evelyn Wadsworth Symington, left many enduring legacies for her children, grandchildren, family, and friends. Among these were her glorious voice, her captivating songs, and her verses. Perhaps these few selections will tell more of her than the books we would all wish to write.*

## THE DISMANTLED HEART

There were flowers at the windows of my heart
All the long winter, while the pointed stars
Through the deep cold scratched at the frosty pane
In vain.

It was a warm room curtained against the dark:
Your words the books, your fancy painted on the walls,
And always music in the firelit air
Was there.
Now it is swept, and through the naked glass
The public sun examines and displays
The indestructible pattern, and the thing
Past comforting.

Strange voices echo in the empty heart,
Strange boots may stamp and mar the polished floor;
The newcomer will want to decorate —
It can wait.

## PERMISSION

Here is the high earth, here the wind-swept hill.
Lie here, dig a hollow for your hip in the hard ground,
Look through the grass as through a grove of trees.
Here is the polished lady-bird upon a stalk,
Behold the ant's castle built of slipping sand,
The pearly highway where the snail has walked; —
All tiny mysteries made plain. See them,
But never bring your eye so close to mine.

# KINDLY STEP TO THE REAR OF THE CAVE, PLEASE

I waked at dawn and cried your name.
Never in the long, wide world —
World without end,
Shall I turn on the bed of thorns
And find you there.
Each lies alone. And walks alone,
With treasures tied in a handkerchief;
Look, word, note — the thin and brittle rose
Of memory as talismans against the dark.
There is no mercy underneath the sun;
Change and decay, the ripe fruit in the dust,
No shade along the way,
No friend, — but hooded truth
Stands at the entrance of the heart's deep cave
Where ever burns the Fire and the Word.

## BEAUTY

I have loved Beauty for her own sake —
Not for the strangeness in her:
Rose-pale cockatoo in the black room,
The feather mantle, or the carved bone.
Nor for her age: gold flaking from the wood,
Church colors strained through glass —
Tap of the fan, tap on the tortoise box,
Stiff satins — dancing in candle-light.
Not for her purity: for the white nuns
Rustling in prayer behind the grille,
Nor the silver cup in the mossy spring,
For all of these and none; but now
For just one voice — that turns the heart
As the leaves of the poplar tree are turned
And lifted on the rim of the breeze.

# IN THE MUSEUM AT BAGHDAD

The golden leaves of laurel lie

In a fringe above the painted eye —

The thousand years are shifted, like a stone,

And the sleep meant for eternity

Is here revealed. Here in the jewelled dust

Lies the frail armature of love —

This is the one who leaned above

The flowery pool. The hand opens,

And the last petal falls.

Evelyn W. Symington (1903–1972)

Mother, Eve Symington. New York City, 1938, and St. Louis, 1942.

Family outing in second-hand pedicab purchased in Kuala
Lumpur, Malaysia, 1967. Author, his wife Sylvia, Julie, Jeremy, and
Brandy (retriever).

☆
# On
# Music
☆

# BEETHOVEN*

Music's immortal colossus,
With power to lift us and toss us,
Is Ludwig van B.
Whom all will agree,
Symphonically speaking, the boss is.

Undismayed by eighty-eight keys
Ludwig arranged them with ease
Into his kleine
5th in C minor
Plus cantatas, sonatas and glees.

For Beethoven, God had in mind
Immortality pure, unrefined.
For even when deaf
He could brandish a clef
Like a thunderbolt over mankind.

Washington, DC — 1981

*Prepared for the WETA Limerick Contest to mark the 200th anniversary of his birth.

Music and words—Sylvia and Jim. New York City, 1953.

*At a 1962 benefit for the National Society of Arts and Letters I was asked by NBC hostess, Deena Clark, to "defend" music in a debate over the relative merits of the arts. The contestants were told to take only two minutes and not to be serious. Hence:*

# DEBATE ON THE ARTS

The evidence is clear. Music—the most beautiful way of saying what cannot be said—is the pre-eminent form of human expression. The arts were conveyed to us by the nine muses who gave their precious collegial name to the one they esteemed the most. Moreover, the only mortal ever to get on the wrong side of the fearsome nine was one Thyrssis, who tried to outsing them. For this effrontery he was terminated with a blow to the head from his own lyre. The muses must have considered music their exclusive province, and mortals engaged in it at their peril. Later they were let in on the secret. Poor Thyrssis missed the cut.

Again, as I understand it, the purpose of this exercise is to identify the art which has elevated humanity above all others. Let's look at the others. Without meaning any disparagement, it is clear that lower forms of life have proven competitive in every art but music, birds aside. It is pretty well established that a monkey given a typewriter and plenty of time, ribbon, and paper, will eventually write all of Shakespeare's plays. So much for literature, poetry, and drama. Painting? Chimpanzees have been winning art contests worldwide.

Very well—surely this distinguished panel will wish its decision to encourage the winner to compete with other human beings, rather than apes. In this genetically uncertain time this court will prove whether it has faith in the future of man.

NBC Studios, Washington, DC—May 26, 1962

*Editor's Note*—The following news article covered the happy event in a framework that carries the flavor and spirit of "Camelot," in which academics, politicians, diplomats, and Cabinet and White House officials and their families found time to enjoy each other's company in good causes.

# EVEN MONKEYS MUSE ON MUSIC

The "most beautiful way to say what cannot be said," music, won an eloquent defense and a prize-winning speaker Saturday night.

He was James Wadsworth Symington, youthful Administrative Assistant to Attorney General Robert F. Kennedy, who took the honors in an unusual televised panel show, Arts and Letters TV Spectacular, sponsored by the National Society of Arts and Letters, to determine which of the arts should receive the Society's annual $1,000 scholarship.

Competing against such veterans as Louis Untermeyer, consultant in poetry at the Library of Congress, speaking for poetry; the Rev. Gilbert Hartke, Head of the Speech and Drama Department of Catholic University, for drama; and the Australian Ambassador, Sir Howard Beale, for art, Symington made a spirited defense of his chosen muse.

Inferring that anybody could be taught to write or paint, even monkeys and chimpanzees, he closed his speech with ringing words that would have done justice to another persuasive defender of the arts, the Elizabethan Sir Phillip Sidney:

> "In this genetically uncertain time, this court will prove whether it has faith in the future of man."

After the performance, Symington confessed that chimpanzees in the St. Louis Zoo have also been taught to play "Yankee Doodle," and he was quite worried that Untermeyer, who followed him, might bring up the point. "They may play it, but I am sure they don't feel it," Symington added, …. The spectacular, which was performed to a capacity audience of diplomats and socialites, will be telecast at 6 P.M. June 9th on the WRC-NBC program, *A Moment With* ….

Sen. Kenneth Keating of New York won a few unofficial laurels for himself with his graceful and witty introductions Saturday of the speakers, the four young women who represented the muses, and the three judges, Associate Justice Potter Stewart, Secretary of the Army Elvis J. Stahr, Jr., and Mrs. Samuel J. (Scottie) Lanahan. He introduced Symington as the son of Sen. Stuart Symington, who sits on the Space Committee and is "intimately concerned with the music of the spheres."

Jane Ribicoff, daughter of the Secretary of Health, Education and Welfare, was described as a "muse with portfolio." Kinga Perrone-Capano, daughter of the Minister of Italy, was "an Italian work of art on temporary loan to America," Keating said, and the White House was one of culture's "best known addresses" in Washington. Anne Mansfield, representing the muse of music, was crowned with a garland of flowers by Dr. Leonard Carmichael, Secretary of the Smithsonian Institution.

A battery of elegantly dressed men and women paid $15 a ticket to see the spectacular, which was also a benefit for the Society's Scholarship Fund. Among the guests were the Ambassador of Israel and Mrs. Harmon, the Ambassador of Liberia and Mrs. Peal, the Ambassador of Norway and Mme. Koht, the Ambassador of Iceland and Mme. Thors, the Ambassador of India and Mme. Nehru, the Chief Justice of India, the Ambassador of Pakistan, and the retiring Ambassador of Costa Rica and Señora de Oreamuno.

Also, the Ambassador of Tunisia and Mme. Bourguiba; the Netherlands Cultural Attaché, D.J. van Wijnen; the South African Cultural Attaché, William Wilson; the U.S. Military Representative to the President, Gen. Maxwell D. Taylor, and Mrs. Taylor; the Air Force Aide to the President, Gen. Godfrey T. McHugh; the Administrative Assistant to the President and Mrs. Mike Manatos; Sen. and Mrs. Clinton Anderson; Sen. and Mrs. Estes Kefauver; Mrs. Abraham Ribicoff; Mme. Platzer, wife of the Austrian Ambassador; and Mrs. J. Borden Harriman.

*Washington Post* — May 28, 1962

# NOSTALGIA FROM RADIOLAND

*In days of yore there was a genre of ballads called "cowboy songs." Performed by gentle folks like Gene Autry and the Sons of the Pioneers, their focus was on the job at hand ("When The Work Is All Done This Fall"); the essential companion, the horse ("Old Paint," "Strawberry Roan"); the perils of thirst ("Cool Water"); empathy for the land ("Tumblin' Tumbleweeds"); nostalgia for days gone by ("Empty Saddles"); and acceptance of mortality ("Bury Me Out On The Lone Prairie"). But for their occasional re-emergence in "bluegrass" themes, these soothing and instructive sounds and thoughts receded into rural American memory, making way for "country" and "rock-and-roll." Of the two, one extends the flavor of nostalgia to human relationships, while the other conveys its message of male dominance from the midsection, prompting the following parody of "Ragtime Cowboy Joe":*

## ROCKTIME COWBOY JOE

Way out West where the music is the best
There's one cowpuncher who's a menace to the rest,
That bowlegged, glassy-eyed, pathetic little pest,
Rocktime Cowboy Joe.

He'd always rock — rock, rock, rock around the stock,
Put the heifers in a state of shock,
With his gruntin' and his groanin'
And his syncopated moanin'
He had everybody phonin'
The police.

When they hear the fellas gunnin'
The Western folks all know,
It's that goofy-gaited, addle-pated, son-of-a-gun
The over-rated Rocktime Cowboy Joe.

St. Louis — 1956

# On
# Sports And
# Fitness

# SKIPPING — ON THE ROAD TO FITNESS

Quaint and quixotic is a report that comes to us out of the little hamlet of Gurgl, Austria. Located roughly midway between the illustrious resort towns of Obergurgl and Untergurgl, Gurgl would have preserved its anonymity were it not for recent revelations concerning its most noteworthy resident, Dr. Hans Fuerstenklas. Dr. Fuerstenklas, a forty-year-old orthopedic surgeon with a thriving practice during the skiing season, had devoted his leisure time to research on conditioning exercises for the leg. Knee injuries are the most common affliction with which he has had to deal, followed closely by damage to the ankle and tendons of the foot. And in 1985, after ten years of careful study, data compilation, and analysis, he became convinced that neither running nor walking were as dependably beneficial to the relevant muscles and ligaments as skipping, "springen" in German.

In a paper delivered at the 1986 Vienna Conference on Orthopedics he reviewed his findings and with the aid of films, working models, and the testimony of a dozen patients, presented his conclusion that the serious athlete should make "shkipping" a major part of his daily routine. Moreover, the weight watcher or middle-aged person desiring to keep fit would greatly benefit, in his judgment, both aerobically and with respect to the conditioning of vital joints and muscles, were he or she to skip regularly. The non-athlete could meet daily requirements, he said, by "shkipping" about the house and on the street, as well as to and from, and on, the job.

By means of x-ray films, enlarged and in slow motion, he demonstrated the advantage of "shkipping," as he puts it, over running, jogging, and walking, to such delicate human machinery as the "extensor hallucis longus," the "flexor digit," and the other "gastrocnemius," which extends the foot at the ankle and is known to us as the "Achilles tendon." To the conferees, Dr. Fuerstenklas's conclusions were both startling and compelling; startling because it had never been thought that skipping, normally considered a harmless expression of joy, could produce orthopedic benefits; compelling because both in theory and evident results, the scientist had made a clear-cut case for skipping as a conditioning exercise. Historically, Dr. Fuerstenklas conceded that as a form of collective locomotion, skipping had been discarded in ancient times by military leaders whose armies required stealthier modes of advance and speedier modes of retreat.

Withal, his paper was in the last stages of being accepted as the conclusions of the Conference itself when it was subjected to one of those interventions which the world's press is inclined to visit upon ideas and personages about to be crowned with the laurel. On the final day of the conference (June 20, 1986), it was disclosed in an article in the *Nieu Osterreich Zeitung* that Dr. Fuerstenklas's costly research had been funded over the previous five years by Hielentoh, Inc., one of Austria's largest manufacturers of footwear, especially dress and work shoes for the average citizen. Further press inquiries produced the minutes of a meeting of the company's Board at which approval of the project was voted. The key argument in favor of the proposal was that the skipping citizen would probably require new shoes and/or resoling at about three times the existing rate. This disclosure, in and of itself, did not disturb Dr. Fuerstenklas's findings nor, indeed, his conclusions. Nonetheless, it created a climate which made it imprudent for the Conference Committee to incorporate his paper in the plenary report.

Dr. Fuerstenklas himself has resumed his surgical practice, undismayed by a turn of events which in his judgment merely defers inevitable recognition of "shkipping" as a vital adjunct to daily fitness. A copy of his report is available to any who may wish to write him at 62 Neinstrasse, Gurgl, Austria, R6-402.

Gurgl, Austria — July 1, 1986

*On the day of the below-referenced contest a cabby told me he was, "for the white guy; who're you for?" "The American," I said.*

# BOXING

## THE JOHANNSEN-PATTERSON BOUT

Ingomar Johannsen
We were duly told,
Even with his pants on,
Was impressive to behold.

The European title
Bore his Nordic stamp.
One more little fight'll
Make him world champ.

Blithely did this latter son
Of the mighty Thor
Declare that Mr. Patterson
Would wind up on the floor.

America went frantic.
Wild went the press.
As he sailed the Atlantic
After Patterson said, "Yes."

With both names on the card, 'n
"Ivory versus teak,"
The Madison Square Garden
Was sold out in a week.

Indeed, it would amaze ya
Him bein', well, a for'gner,
To see all of caucasia
Gathered in his corner.

Some, still hoarse from yelling,
"Heil" to Maxie Schmeling,
Had thought it meet and right
For the champion to be white.

The world's breath was baited,
As in awe and wonder,
It anxiously awaited
The lightning and the "tunder."

And anyone could tell
The devastating roar
That drowned the opening bell
Was for this son of Thor.

What happened next is blurred.
Fans called it a rooking.
It seems to have occurred
When nobody was looking.

Reporters noted Floyd,
Mild and gently bred,
Was apparently annoyed
By something Ingy said.

It must have been a blunder
For with lefts and rights
Floyd silenced all the "tunder,"
And doused the Northern Lights.

New York—June 20, 1960

# SOCCER LESSONS OF '74

I am proud and grateful to receive the Soccer Coaches' Award in a year that marks a symbolic transition from the Roman-circus values of the football stadium to the simple, steadfast virtues of the soccer field. How well I remember the bracing sensation of taking the field in the soccer games that preceded the so-called "football classics" that took place in the adjacent Yale Bowl. Soccer was actually denominated a "minor sport" in Yale parlance. We played our games in a kind of lonely splendor, watched perhaps by some parents, and a few curious early arrivals for the "big" game. After the final whistle, we would shower, dress, and disappear ourselves into the yawning arena of pageantry, pomp, and peanuts, cleansed and refreshed by sixty minutes of unvarnished and unnoticed action. That was 1949.

Now as we draw near to reliving the Spirit of '76—what can be said of the Spirit of '73? Nineteen-seventy-three was the "year of the huddle"—where time and again men of higher station than standards made vital decisions in determined secrecy while presenting their backsides to the people they served. It must be admitted that the huddle itself is not an evil institution regardless of the mayhem that is planned there. It is undoubtedly a very necessary opportunity to refresh memories capable of retaining but one play at a time. It also provides regular periods of relaxation. It would be more reassuring, however, if after returning to the line, the players would not continue to stoop in the manner of their tree-climbing forebears. The soccer player, much to his credit, walks erect and seldom falls down on purpose. His feet are on the ground, not on the other players. His habitat is the open field—not the jungle of the hand-off, the reverse, the delayed buck, and the bootleg. Recently our President was invited to call a play at a Washington Redskins practice. The play he recommended was a screen pass—very much in the spirit of '73 and preceding years of secret plans, secret wars, secret deals, and secret funds.

Soccer offers a different perspective and requires different disciplines. The soccer player must be independent, resourceful, and creative. His only huddle is with himself. The product of his perception, vitality, and skill will be openly displayed and openly judged by his team, the opposition, the spectator, and the coach! He well remembers patterns of play, the habits and talents of his teammates, but he relies in the end on the intuition of the moment. And he can hide nothing except those split-second options he selects to move the ball downfield. Personal accountability for error is clear in the game of soccer. It isn't muffled by pileups, downfield flags, musical and cheesecake diversions, excuses, or the pious comments of the sportscaster. Moreover, the man of soccer takes the field pretty much as God made him—plus a few wisps of cotton and a pair of shoes—better equipped certainly to respond to the demands of the energy crisis than those centurions who depend on heavy supplies of plastic for helmets and pads. Perhaps the word "dribble" has been an impediment to a proper understanding and respect for one of the soccer player's principal occupations. Could a more majestic word define this delicate enterprise? Coax, prod, thread, inveigle, perambulate? "Dribble" will do if for no other reason than its fundamental honesty.

And what of the kick? The kick has come back to football, and now that the foot has been rediscovered by the tycoons of that well-financed sport, where do they go for the feet? To the world of soccer! How amused the former soccer player must be to be paid so handsomely for suiting up and with a simple swing of his leg, sending thousands of football fans into paroxysms of joy, sorrow, or indebtedness.

The contrasting foreign-policy lessons of the two sports is clear. Football was well-suited to the period of clash and conflict, crunches into the line all over the world, accompanied by the threat of massive retaliation. Now, in the climate of détente, mutual force reduction, arms control, and a generation of peace, there seems to be something out of place in a national pastime that works its viewers into the frenzied chant, "Throw the bomb!" Soccer does not tolerate, much less encourage, such an abdication of reason. We leave that bleak alternative to a less imaginative age and sports that reflect it.

For soccer, like the game of life, is dynamic, flexible, fast-paced, and ever-changing. Its laurels go to the heads-up teams and the coaches that train them. It both honors and fosters the necessary discipline, conditioning, drill, experience, and buoyant spirit of true play.

Now the last is not the least. Of course, motivation for the great games embraces a desire to win — because to win is to demonstrate a certain superiority that day, at least, with lady luck neutral if not generous with her favors — but to win fair and square by the rules and with the sportsmanship that maintains humility in the presence of victory. To win in any other way or in any other spirit is a mockery of the players, the spectators, and the game itself — whether the prize is the soap box derby or high public office.

If the rules of the other games we play are insufficiently precise to provide for such victories, then the lesson of soccer is that they should be made so. If a great national decision is to become a political football — let it be your kind of football — in the open field where the instant replay is unnecessary because for better or worse we all saw the play.

Remarks at the National Convention of the
National Soccer Coaches Association — January 12, 1974

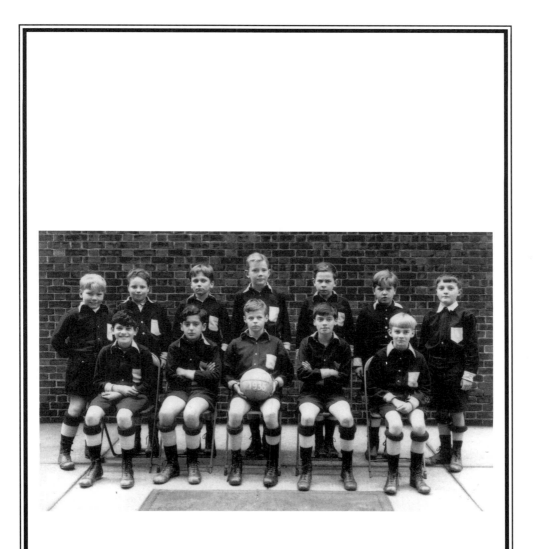

Arthur ("Punch") Sulzberger, front row left, and author, front row
right, equally amused by Captain George Plimpton's deadpan expression.
Undefeated "Giants" of St. Bernard's School, New York City, 1936.

Juggling for girls softball team, the "Symington Patriots," in the Kirkwood Bicentennial Parade. St. Louis County, Missouri; May 29, 1976.

# On
# The Passing
# Of Time

# RUNNERS TO COME

Historians tend to belittle,
And from Gibbon[1] to Toynbee[2] we've heard
That fame is fleeting and brittle.
What now that we've gotten the word?

Do we quit because history forgets
And buries the pride of today?
Or cover all visible bets,
And take them on anyway?

It's said that societies languish,
And rest to death on their oars,
But I say they live on the anguish
Of boatmen who seek better shores.

Ahead are new patterns of giving,
New works of the hand and the mind.
And for every traveler living
There's an Atlantis to find.

So take your local historian
To lunch, and ask how he's been,
And whether his views are euphorian,
Despairing, or something between.

Then ask, in your manner of speaking,
What's the "it" we "together" must "get"?
What is that something we're seeking,
And will the deadline be met?

The historian parries the question,
The priest has a pious reply.
The cynic a silly suggestion,
The politician a lie.

---

[1]Edward Gibbon (1737-94), English historian.
[2]Arnold Toynbee (1889-1975), English social reformer,
   economist, and historian.

But the child unthinking might know,
And doesn't the answer lie there?
For given his season to grow
His secrets in season he'll share.

Clearly whatever the strife,
Our highest duty in sum
Is to pass on the baton of life
To the wondrous runners to come.

Miami Beach—July 1972

With Julie and Jeremy at home.  Washington, DC, 1962.

Escorting young guest at a benefit performance for the United
Planning Organization (UPO). Washington, DC, 1962.

# TIME

Time is the thief that will take all I own

The faces, the choices, the voices I've known,

The dust I become and my mossy stone

Will belong in time to time alone.

Vandal, old vandal, have patience for soon

This candle, slim candle, that burns in its noon,

Will flutter and fade and bow to the shade,

And sink in the ivory pool it made.

If the wick be still and the wax be chill

You may take and gather them up if you will.

But silver will spill from the pocket you fill,

And laughter will trickle out over the hill,

For the texture you trouble, the prize you probe,

Will be but the robe, the empty robe

Of a dream released, and you'll know you stole

No more than the mantle of my soul.

London—1959

# FIFTIETH BIRTHDAY SALUTE*
## THE FIRST FIFTY YEARS

The first fifty years of laughter and tears,
Were only a test on the way to the best fifty years.

Still in our prime, we'll take 'em one at a time
We'll depart from the text and get smart for the
   next fifty years.

We've struggled for world peace; we've raised a
   family, too.
We've supported our local police, and made democracy
   safe for you.

It's not our careers, but our friends it appears,
Who've brightened the past, and lightened the last
   fifty years.

And if we're in arrears, it's in women and beers;
We'll make up for a lot, though we haven't quite got
   fifty years.

Washington, DC—September 28, 1977
Music:  Jim Symington

---

*Duet sung by the author and his cousin, Timothy Wadsworth Stanley (Washington economist),
  who was born on the same day, September 28, 1927.

# THE APPLE TREE

Woven into the high branches

two arms, two legs, and

there, the boy face

With a "watchme" look.

Yes, I see you,

Now come down!

That memory, kodak-ambered,

for me to guess

Why he stands

Now, upward looking,

touching an arthritic hand

to the gnarled trunk.

No more climbing, and

The apples

Are gone.

The Plains, Virginia—Summer 1995

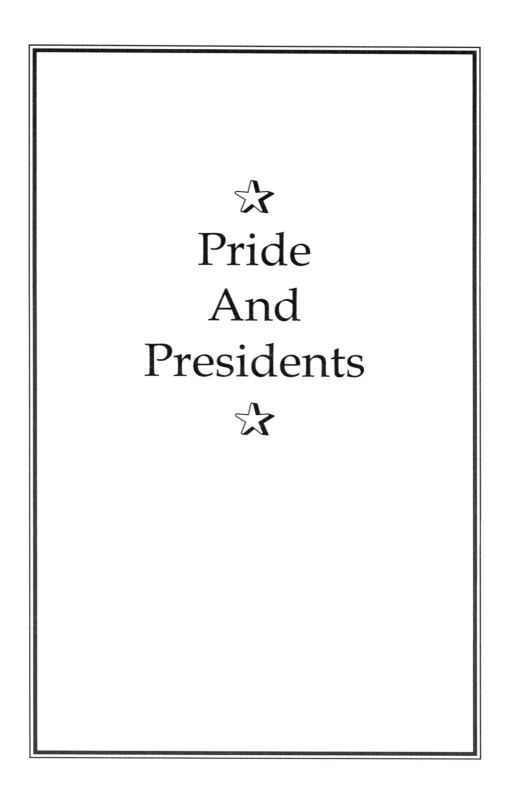

# Pride
# And
# Presidents

# ☆☆ TRUMAN ☆☆

*A retrospective on the Truman years:*

## WHISTLE STOP

(Excerpts from a Letter to Sylvia)

The President's train eased into St. Jo amidst much cheering and waving and clanging of the "Pony Express Band." Bobbysoxers climbed up on fire engines to take snapshots. Shouts of "Give 'em Hell, Harry!" went up all about, and "Doin' a great job!," et cetera. One lady held aloft a wilted "Ike" sign. We went up the little steps into the observation car, and there was Mr. T. himself, the first to greet us; I fumbling with my camera, all the coats, and Dad's briefcase.

Margaret was the graceful hostess, full of homey talk. She seems to have soured slightly on being the people's choice. She makes wry faces and remarks when the clamor goes up for "Maggie!" One young girl pounded on the window to get her attention, and Pop turned and pointed to himself as if to say, "How about me?" The girl grimaced and held her nose, much to our dismay.

The President was very relaxed and little-boyish about his train trip, wearing his hat askew and saying, "What's wrong with my hat?" He was ruddy-faced and a bit pudgier than I remember him two years ago at the Army-Navy game. Margaret is thinner. When the President thinks it's time to bring her on, he turns and says, "C'mon, Skinny, they wantcha."

Hotel Muehlebach, Kansas City — October 10, 1952

## HARRY'S WAY

Problems never bothered Harry
He faced them with determination,
A disposition not to tarry
And a tough Administration.

For political neuralgia his
Prize would go to Alger Hiss,[1]
Of whose activities the baring
Proved fishier than herring.

'Twas no simple country bumpkin
Put those papers in a pumpkin.
But Harry garnered some disfavor
By acts that made the nervous quaver.

Some resentment he still gleans
From his denouncement of Marines,
And that note to David Hume[2] n'
Other things distinctly Truman.

Many folks are in the dark
About appointing General Clark.[3]
Perhaps to tell us that he can
Get on with the Vatican.

Or to combat communism,
Yet it nearly caused a schism
Here at home. We learned at best
That Protestants can still protest.

Stalin tested him for certain
By bringing down his iron curtain.
But Harry calmly took the dare
And fed Berliners from the air.

Then with no whimper but a bang
He gonged the gang from Pyongyang.
His severest test began
When he brusquely wired Japan,

Summoned home, and spanked the hero
North Korea couldn't zero.
The general who had led a million
Answered to just one civilian.

And what today may seem a mystery
Will prove to be confirmed by history.
But when McCarthy joined the fray,
It was enough to spoil his day.

Meanwhile he had to flush the geezers
Who presented him with freezers.
As other men were forced to think
Just how their wives came by their mink.

In crime New Yorkers led the nation,
So it was without elation
That Tobey,[4] Halley,[5] and Kefauver[6]
Met to look the matter over.

When they op'ed Pandora's box,
They found Costello's[7] dirty socks.
Immediately this grim committee
Subpoena'd him to learn the bit he

Had in running all the rackets
Through underlings in cashmere jackets.
He then immortalized the phrase,
"I don't quite recall them days."

Committees roamed between the oceans,
And raising hackles and emotions,
Plied the underworld with queries
Sufficient to confirm their theories.

City cops with modest salaries
Stammered to the crowded galleries
That one plus one must equal three,
And that's how they got their TV.

Yes, a number of our rookies
Succumbed to glib and wealthy bookies.
Though sad, our duty was, of course,
To dismiss them from the force.

Sadly, too, crime's easy path leads
To the doorstep of our athletes.
These incipient T. Lamars[8]
Now face the world through iron bars.

And though Sollazio[9] gets eight years,
Who will dry their mother's tears?
Meanwhile we must start upon a
War on dope and marijuana.
We should clearly zero in
On them that pushes heroin.
Take them that sells that laudanum,
And put the fear of Gawd in 'em.

I guess I've ranted ad absurdum
But the people, they has got to gird 'em
Selves against the foul crimes
That's perpetrated in our times.

Harry's scalpel, sponge and suture
Mended old wounds; now the future
Must be handled Harry's way
Lest we learn to our dismay
A pound of cure don't have the bounce
To sub for old prevention's ounce.
Meanwhile, our heartiest farewell
To the man who loved to "give 'em hell!"

St. Louis—1952

[1]Alger Hiss, U.S. lawyer-diplomat convicted of perjury.
[2]David Hume, music critic for the *Washington Post*.
[3]Mark Clark, U.S. General nominated as Ambassador to the Vatican.
[4]Senator Charles W. Tobey (R-NH), ranking Republican member of the "Kefauver Committee."
[5]Rudolph Halley, Chief Counsel, "Kefauver Committee."
[6]Senator Estes Kefauver (D-TN), Chairman, Special Committee on Organized Crime
    in Interstate Commerce Committee.
[7]Frank Costello, target of Kefauver Committee inquiry.
[8]T. Lamar Caudle, indicted IRS Commissioner.
[9]Louis Sollazio, gambling tycoon.

1960 Democratic Presidential contenders rally around Harry S. Truman. Washington, DC, spring 1960. Left to right: Gov. Robert Meyner (NJ), Sen. Hubert Humphrey (MN), Gov. Leroy Collins (FL), Gov. G. Mennen "Soapy" Williams (MI), Sen. Stuart Symington (MO), Sen. John Kennedy (MA), Gov. Edmund "Pat" Brown (CA). Missing—Sen. Lyndon Johnson (TX).

# JOE McCARTHY

*When American scapegoats for Stalin's successes were sought, Senator Joseph McCarthy of Wisconsin, self-appointed leader of the search party, terrorized the landscape until he, himself, was brought to ground. The U.S. Army, with its Congressional champions, proved a more durable foe than academe and the foreign service. By Christmas (1954), the McCarthy "era" had drawn to a close. But he did not go gently into the night, the Army-McCarthy hearings of that year providing scope for all his rage and rancor. Thus, the nation's Christmas reprieve seemed a very blessing from the North Pole and its most distinguished resident, unless his powers were usurped by:*

## THE KNIGHT BEHIND CHRISTMAS

Not long before Christmas 'twas heard through the land
  That Joseph McCarthy's bottom got tanned.

Windows and chimneys were opened with glee
  And files on the children for Santa to see.

Up to that time all houses were locked
  For fear it was Joe and not Santa who knocked.

The report of the Utah Senator's[1] parley,
  However, made Joe think of Indian Charlie,[2]

And raised in his breast such an ache of self-pity,
  That he kneed every groin in the capital city.

You'd find anywhere all along the Potomac
  Many a patriot clutching his stomach.

For Joe's part, he termed it a communist shame
  To have questioned his motives and sullied his name.

The most cowardly, senile, dishonest, obscene
  Event in our history, completely unclean.

Then he sought out some folks who recited his credo,
  And waited in line to massage his libido.

Yet he paced in his hideaway rubbing his sinuses,
  Not sure that his plusses outnumbered his minuses.

---

[1]Senator Arthur V. Watkins (R-UT).
[2]A mythical figure who assaulted anyone who looked askance at him.

"Who engineered this circus, this derby,
Was it Alger,[3] or Adlai,[4] or Harry,[5] or Herby?[6]

Or Robert,[7] or Cabot,[8] or Sherman,[9] or Hoover?[10]
Any one of those reds could have been the prime-mover."

He pushed on the side of his nose with his pencil,
"Maybe Rogers,[11] John Adams,[12] or Clifford,[13] or Hensel.[14]

I'll get sick if I find that the cowardly crew
Took their cue from sanctimonious Stu.[15]

What to be; who to knee, those are the questions.
Even Sokolsky's[16] run out of suggestions.

I've got it," he grunted, "Santa's a red!
I'll expose his design and be Santa instead!"

Pleased with himself, he tried the idea
On a female typist-clerk volunteer.

"You don't love little children," she playfully teased.
"A fantastic lie!" he retorted, displeased.

"Little children? A blessing—so trusting and weak."
A pudgy fist brushed at a tear on his cheek.

"So respectful, believing, submissive, the dears."
His jowls collapsed from the weight of his tears.

"I've faith in the young," he muttered along.
"It's when they grow up that they start to go wrong.

Time and again experience has taught me
That rather than follow and praise me, they've fought me.

[3]Alger Hiss, lawyer-diplomat convicted of perjury.
[4]Adlai Stevenson, 1952 Democratic candidate for President.
[5]Former President Harry Truman.
[6]Attorney General Herbert Brownell.
[7]Senator Robert Taft (R-OH).
[8]Senator Henry Cabot Lodge (R-MA).
[9]Sherman Adams, Assistant to President Eisenhower.
[10]FBI Director, J. Edgar Hoover.
[11]Attorney General William Rogers.
[12]Army Counsel, John Adams.
[13]Clark Clifford, former Special Counsel to President Truman.
[14]H. Struve Hensel, Counsel, Army-McCarthy hearings.
[15]Senator Stuart Symington (D-MO).
[16]*Chicago Tribune* columnist, George Sokolsky.

It's history's most foul and senile disgrace
    The way they will argue a point to my face."

She laughed, "Do you think any kid would believe
    There was something subversive up Santa's sleeve?"

"An irrelevant thought, but you know if I can't
    I'll go for the elves that work in his plant.

That gullible Claus is a threat to our homes,
    Being blind to the treasonous bent of his gnomes.

And, believe me, I don't give the damn of a Tinker
    What man, high or low, might call me a stinker.

I'll fix the grin on that jolly old soul
    When I've cut off his aid and blockaded the Pole."

"But you haven't the dough to make up for his toys,
    Having gone through Lustron's,[17] David's,[18] and Roy's."[19]

"That's a senile remark, but for a few fins
    I can fill a whole satchel with loyalty pins.

When I've mailed them out on my Senator's frank,
    There'll be no one but Santa McCarthy to thank."

The lady looked in his malevolent face,
    And said, "Santa Joe, this may seem out of place,

But from what you've been huffing and muttering tonight
    I can't help but wonder if Stu[20] wasn't right.

And whether you think it unruly or not of me,
    I suggest you submit to a frontal lobotomy."

His brooding eyes flicked as he smothered a laugh
    Like a vulture will blink at a motherless calf.

[17]Lustron Corporation, corporate supporter of Senator McCarthy.
[18]David Schine, investigator for the McCarthy Committee.
[19]Roy Cohn, counsel to Senator McCarthy.
[20]Senator Stuart Symington (D-MO).

He grinned at the irony—served by a traitor
    Was America's number one communist baiter.

"That does it," he nasaled, "you never were pretty;
    You're subpoenaed tomorrow before my committee."

Then up to and out on the rooftop he clambered,
    And burping and puffing and shivering, stammered,

"Who can rejoice in this 'holiday' season,
    When there is not one but two parties of treason!

Fly over the country I must, just to warn it
    Once and for all that I'm virtue incarnate.

Come, fellows, come Welker,[21] now Butler[22] and Mundt,[23]
    With a homer in sight don't ask me to bunt.

Knowland's[24] in harness, come Jenner[25] and Nixon[26]
    By Christmas morning we'll all have our licks in.

Sokolsky[27] and Lawrence[28] await in the sleigh,
    Now Hearst,[29] now McCormack,[30] up, up and away!

Let this be our slogan and rallying call,
    'Justice for none and malice for all.'"

By now his reflections had made him so avid, he
    Jumped, but struggled in vain against gravity.

Crying, "Malice for all and to all a bad night!"
    He plopped in a snowdrift and sank out of sight.

St. Louis—Christmas, 1954

[21]Senator Herman Welker (R-ID).
[22]Senator John M. Butler (R-MD).
[23]Senator Carl E. Mundt (R-SD).
[24]Senator William Knowland (R-CA).
[25]Senator William E. Jenner (R-IN).
[26]Vice President Richard M. Nixon.
[27]George Sokolsky, columnist, *Chicago Tribune*.
[28]William H. Lawrence, columnist, *New York Times*.
[29]William Randolph Hearst, Publisher, *San Francisco Examiner*.
[30]Robert R. McCormack, Publisher, *Chicago Tribune*.

The Army-McCarthy hearings (May 1954) interfered with preparation for final exams at Columbia Law School. My attention was riveted by my father's combative participation. At the outset he advised Army Secretary Robert Stevens that Joe "would not fight by the Marquis of Queensberry rules." And he didn't. Nor did his staff, headed by the industrious and wily Roy Cohn. One of the Army's initiatives that annoyed Messrs. McCarthy and Cohn was the transfer outside of New York of Cohn's friend and fellow investigator, David Schine. That dust-up provided some fodder for the Barristers' Ball.

## SCHINE*

Just because my hair is curly
Just because my stick pin's pearly,
Just because I pal around with Roy,
That don't make me such a naughty boy.
Although I miss that night life,
Except through Roy I never whine,
Cause I love to fight left wingers
Half as much as sippin' stingers.
That's why they call me Schine.

Cause I drive a caddy
I owe it all to Daddy.
Just because I never try KP
Why, when my old man can buy JP?
We hate to be alone
Don't like to have to use the phone
So if I don't get New York assignment
The Army'll know what Cohn and Schine meant,
Or else you can call me Schone.

Columbia Law School—June 1954

*Melody: *Shine.*

# ☆☆ EISENHOWER ☆☆

*One pledge of the Eisenhower re-election campaign was to award states with "tidelands" (offshore) oil reserves all the revenue therefrom, to the exclusion of the federal government. This comment gave rise to —*

## PRIDELANDS
### A Sad Tale Concerning A Simple Farmer
### And Some Great Decisions

Perhaps you've heard of Joshua Brown,
Who hated all commotion;
Who worked a farm far out of town,
And miles from the ocean.

His native state I needn't name,
So call it what you may,
In most respects it is the same
As many are today.

That is to say an inland one,
Living off its soil,
With its share of rain and sun
But not of offshore oil.

A bill was passed some years ago
By them that legislates,
Which gave the stuff as we all know
To the offshore oil states.

A cry rose up as cries will do
Whenever Congress acts.
No need at present to review
The "huzzahs" and "alacks."

Scholars for both sides did look
For possible solutions
In Grotius,[1] Kant,[2] and Bynkershoek[3]
And several constitutions.

States' Righters cheered and rang a bell
For Laissez fairer laws.
Others sighed a fare-thee-well
To the "necessary-proper" clause.

Years went by, and with issues,
Forgotten were results.
Except for their sporadic misuse
By schools and other curious cults.

And if you'd asked old Joshua Brown
What was up and what was down,
He'd only stroke his chin and frown,
He lived so far from town.

Fact is old Brown was quite content
With raising corn and stock,
And only blinked the day he bent
His hayrake on a rock.

Inquisitive as he was stout,
Down he dug and got it out,
And took it home; without a doubt
The strangest rock he'd seen about.

In a day or so word got around,
And squads of gaunt professors
Appeared and poked in Joshua's ground
To substantiate their guesses.

[1]Hugo Grotius (1583-1645), Dutch scholar, jurist, and statesman.
[2]Immanuel Kant (1724-1804), German philosopher.
[3]Cornelius van Bynkershoek, 18th century Dutch legal philosopher.

Within a week the Brown menage
Was host to men of science,
And bulging was the Brown garage
With geigerish appliance.

At last the leader of the bunch
Announced in whispered tones
The answer to his fondest hunch
Lay there in Joshua's stones.

What the answer, what the hunch?
Reporters strained to catch.
The elder mumbled through his lunch,
"Atomic power, natch."

Joshua's minerals, of course
Would satisfy the craving
Of all America for force,
And at a cozy saving.

Dear me, he sighed, I talk a lot
But, briefly, it's a fuel.
Enough to make Alaska hot,
And Argentina cool.

Josh's minerals would feed
Engines great and small.
Indeed, we'd have no further need
Of petroleum at all.

For since we've nearly conquered friction,
It remains for grease to dare,
According to a harmless fiction,
The plague of falling hair.

"Brownite," they called the precious stuff
They found on Josh's place.
In quantities, ample enough
To serve the human race.

"Why that's exactly what we're doin',"
The raging oilers cried.
While those with cash awaited ruin,
Those with stock just died.

Their lawyers were a little shot.
For years they'd been quite glad,
To languish on the dough they got
For the last idea they had.

Finally, they grinned at doom,
And said, "the rocks belong to
Precisely Sirs, the ones to whom
They do the greatest wrong to."

In reply to this verbosity
The head of Josh's state
Promised generosity
To the entire forty-eight.

"But, legally, you offshore birds
Have made our inland nest.
Our highest court in ringing words
Affirmed that you know best."*

Once again we students learn
When the case went up to court
It couldn't lightly overturn
Precedent, in short.

A sad decision you might say,
And one that called for frowns.
Some states dried up and blew away
While others looked to Brown's.

The matters Josh's find affected
Are too lengthy to relate,
But every President elected
Was a native of his state.

*In United States v. California (1950) the Supreme Court obviated this implausible scenario by ruling in favor of national sovereignty over the disputed submerged lands and thus their mineral content (oil).

And when these men proposed a bill,
And Congress took a vote,
An amazing singleness of will
One could not fail to note.

And citizens quite deep in debt
By plane and boat and rail,
Made many a pilgrimage to get
Old Josh to go their bail.

So Josh's state became right then
A haven for the needy;
Among them: barefoot oilmen,
And tideland waifs quite seedy.

At home and wading in their yards,
They all together voiced,
"Upon our own sublime petards,
We are unjustly hoist."

Thinking back, they rued a lot
Those high judicial lamas',
Approval of the deal they got
From that ancient campaign promise.

St. Louis—1956

Men and machines, sharing a laugh. Overland, Missouri, July 1968.

*An undeclared neutral in the McCarthy wars, President Eisenhower easily won re-election in 1956. Missouri was the only state in the Union that had voted for him in 1952 but switched to Adlai Stevenson. Since we stood out in this way, Republicans referred to us as the "sore-thumb" state. Ike was too popular for strident criticism to find an audience, but gentle chiding was acceptable. Hence the following parodies performed for Eleanor Roosevelt and two thousand others at St. Louis's Kiel Auditorium on October 1, 1956.*

## EISENHOWER*

Eisenhower,

Every night my honey lamb and me

Sit alone and gawk at the way you talk

In lazy circles on TV.

We know you belong to the land,

And the land down here could be grand.

So when we say, "Hey!"

It's just our little way

Of saying you're doing fine, Eisenhower,

But you're miles away.

*Music: Oklahoma.*

# IVORY TOWER*

Come down, come down, from your ivory tower,

Eisenhower, come down.

He's so far above it all, he just can't hear us call,

So let's help the dear fellow down.

Haven't seen it; haven't read it;

Didn't mean it if he said it.

I love Foster,[1] and Dick[2] is a dream.

And if Charlie[3] makes you yell, just remember I'm swell,

And try not to think of the team.

Come down, come down, from your ivory tower,

Ike, we don't mean no harm.

But the Ike that we like oughta strike for the pike

That leads to that Gettysburg farm.

*Music: *Ivory Tower.*
[1]John Foster Dulles, Secretary of State.
[2]Richard M. Nixon, Vice President.
[3]Charles Wilson, Secretary of Defense.

# ☆☆ KENNEDY ☆☆

*In the 1960 Presidential primaries Senator Hubert Humphrey (D-MN) was a leading contender. Having left a pharmaceutical career for politics, he observed that the Kennedy clan at work made him feel like a "sole proprietor running against the chain." His comment inspired a sympathetic echo from Gilbert & Sullivan's Pinafore:*

## THE PLAINT OF JFK

I fear my youth will be ill spent,

Unless you make me President,

And so say my sisters and my brothers and my Dad,

My sisters and my brothers, whom I reckon

　　share my druthers,

Plus my in-laws, and their Mothers and my Dad.

Washington, DC — 1960

With "the Master," Senator Hubert H. Humphrey, endorsing author's Senate candidacy. St. Louis, Missouri; July 23, 1976.

*As a post-convention volunteer for the Kennedy-Johnson ticket, I campaigned for a history professor, George McGovern, against the Republican incumbent in South Dakota, Senator Carl Mundt. Senator Mundt had chaired, with an uncertain hand, the Army-McCarthy hearings. The old tune, "Sweet Betsy From Pike," provided the model for this brief observation . . .*

## McGOVERN

For years South Dakota has borne the whole brunt

Of sliding farm income and Carl E. Mundt,

So vote for McGovern and bring them to gaff

With a man who can tell the wheat from the chaff.*

Sioux Falls, South Dakota — 1960

---

*McGovern lost this race but went to the Senate two years later to succeed the late Senator Francis Case.

*Mr. Nixon's campaign speeches, press conferences, and off-the-cuff remarks prompted the following parody of "Tiptoe Through the Tulips," which was recorded for the campaign in the Kennedys' Georgetown home:*

## TIPTOE THROUGH THE ISSUES

My name is Richard Milhous Nixon,

And I hope that you're all fixin'

To just tiptoe through the issues with me.

I don't want to analyze; I'd rather generalize

So please don't penalize, simply close your eyes

And tiptoe through the issues with me.

Washington, DC—1960

# JOHN FITZGERALD THE SECOND

*After his election, and before he took office, President-elect Kennedy welcomed his second child, a son, into the world. Having returned from his campaign to law practice with the Washington law firm of Arnold, Fortas & Porter, I penned this congratulatory note to him:*

## TO PRESIDENT-ELECT AND JACQUELINE KENNEDY

No man could live the prophets said,
Nay of the best or the worst,
Who could sit at his leisure and take the measure
Of John Fitzgerald the First.

But brief is the glimmer of fortune
Fleeting the flicker of fame.
Even Prexy's Elect may be suddenly checked
By the pitiless rules of the game.

And now it has happened to him.
For when John Fitzgerald was beckoned
He opened the latch and there met his match,
John Fitzgerald the Second.

Washington, DC — December 17, 1960

*Affairs of state notwithstanding, the President-elect responded in kind through the good offices of his friend, Chuck Spalding:*

## AFFECTIONATE REPLY TO
## JIM AND SYLVIA SYMINGTON

(Lines in lieu of formal dictation)

Thanks for your spirited rhyme.
You're right and you know it this time.
There's a way to take those who traffic in power
Campaign from a crib, be a diapered flower.

Hubert was tough, Ditto your father.
You fight for dear life and take what you gather.
But what do you do 'gainst a gurgle and howl?
I'll tell you. I did it. You throw in the towel.

Response is courtesy Charles Spalding,
Poet Laureate for the occasion.
Best to you both,

JOHN KENNEDY

With Jacqueline Kennedy Onassis at Averell Harriman's
Testimonial Dinner.  Washington, DC; May 15, 1974.
(See pages 122-24 for author's remarks at this dinner.)

*In 1961, Nikita Kruschev, still smarting from the effrontery of the U-2, displayed his bellicose veins to President Kennedy in Vienna, prompting the latter's dry remark that we were in for a "long winter." It was certainly the end of a summer.*

# BETHANY BEACH

### Morning

The surf recedes and the summer, too,
Carrying out the cares I knew,
As I read a book and chew a peach
On the sun-white sands of Bethany Beach.

I let my thoughts drift out to sea
To the never, the maybe, the used-to-be,
Then to lift on the frivolous breeze
And go with the gulls wherever they please.

This is what the world needs
Say I as the sibilant surf recedes,
A book to read and a golden peach,
And time for both on Bethany Beach.

### Afternoon

But the sun drops low and the waves return,
Lesson enough for any to learn.
It's time to finish the golden peach,
And close the book on Bethany Beach.

Lesson enough in the spray and din
That a tide more fateful still is in
That can't be faced with a book and a peach
In a terry cloth robe on Bethany Beach.

Yet as I rise and brush the sand,
I feel I should for a moment stand
And give thanks for the day, the sun, the peach
And the page I turned on Bethany Beach.

Bethany Beach, Delaware—September 1961

*Some months later, in April 1962, the Shah of Iran paid a State Visit to Washington. So . . .*

## APRIL SHAHS*

When April Shahs
They come our way.
They bring Farrahs
Who bloom like May.
But when it's Iranian
Have some regret.
It isn't really raining rain,
It's the Iranian national debt.

And when we see Shahs
Up on the Hill
We'll soon receive the Shah's
Imperial bill.
So keep looking for the budget,
And listening for the gong!
Whenever April Shahs come along.

Washington, DC — April 1962

*Tune: *April Showers*.

*By 1963, the Kennedy Administration had guided the ship of state through major crises, foreign and domestic, including the showdown over the Russian missiles in Cuba, and the admission of the first Black student, James Meredith, to the University of Mississippi. The period also marked the emergence of key aides, including White House historian Arthur Schlesinger. By turns profound, genial, scathing, and witty, he was withal the only Arthur since the King of that name who could not comfortably be called "Art." Hence, this salutation:*

## OH, ARTHUR SCHLESINGER

Oh, Arthur Schlesinger,
Ask we with verve,
Since when such a messenger
Did fate deserve?
For us it's euphorian,
Heady and rare,
To know a historian
Who was ready and there!
Actually there!
Actually, factually there!
A seer in residence
Without any hesitance
Counseling Presidents
As to what lay in store,
'Cause it happened before.

Passingly odd it is
For Presidents all
To have at their call
Their own Herodotus*
Right down the hall.
Critics dissected you;
Took you apart,
Yet always respected you;
Did not call you, "Art."
"Arthur," not "Art,"
Music and poetry, yes, but not "Art."
And any who'd say
Your power has diminished
Might well their words weigh
At least till you're finished.

Washington, DC — 1963

*Greek historian (485-425 B.C.), called the *Father of History*.

*Laughter and hope went hand in hand until the news broadcast from Dallas on November 22nd, which stopped the world's heart. I walked to our church, St. John's on Lafayette Square. As I passed the old Hay Adams Hotel across from the church I was reminded of the letter my great-grandfather, Secretary of State John Hay, had written a friend after the death of President McKinley. "What a strange and tragic fate it has been of mine," he wrote, "to stand by the bier of three of my dearest friends, Lincoln, Garfield, and McKinley, three of the gentlest of men, all done to death by assassins."*

*John Kennedy was the fourth of thirty-five Presidents to be taken from the people this way. There have been narrow escapes for others, and a ratio of eleven percent is hardly reassuring.*

## THE YOUNG CHAMPION

He came out of his corner
Like the young champion
He was.
With practiced eye and Irish smile
For a challenger
He knew,
Had beaten before.
In the Pacific
Wrestled him under a wave,
And came up spitting
Jokes, face shimmering
With destiny.
He seldom wore a hat
To shield us from his sunlight,
His blazing thought,
And the radiant challenge
Of his spirit.
They'd been locked
Like this, too,
Etherized, but straining,
Till the Challenger
Was shoved away,
Good-naturedly,
Like a dull-witted
Sparring partner,
When the young champ

Suddenly remembered
An appointment.
Still, this rematch
Came too soon.
Granted, the Promoter
Thought it time,
The Promoter,
Who was Trainer besides,
And Referee,
Timekeeper,
And finally, Announcer,
That this was a dream,
And the record would show
The title really passed
A generation ago
On a beach near Rendova
Where the old challenger
Forever lost,
And failing to pin him then,
And snuff out that spark
So far from our notice,
Cannot now, or ever,
Expect the mantle of years,
To contain the radiance,
Much less the flame.
So we file from the arena
Comforted.
This was truly a dream.
And his heart, his voice,
His hatless glory,
The reality.

Washington, DC—November 26, 1963

# ☆☆ JOHNSON ☆☆

## THE JOHNSON YEARS
### (1964–1969)

The first part of the Johnson years I spent as Executive Director of the President's Committee on Juvenile Delinquency. The Committee consisted of three titans: Attorney General Nicholas Katzenbach, chairman; the Secretary of Labor, Willard Wirtz; and the Secretary of Health, Education and Welfare, John Gardner. My principal achievement was getting it to meet, which it did once in Katzenbach's office. It was a great moment in bureaucracy.

Of course, I was no match for the subsequent centrifugal forces which agencies of government employ to avoid outside interference. Rather, I was comforted by my former law-boss Paul Porter's description of a coordinator, which I will reveal on an as needed basis. Delinquency persevered. In any event, I was removed from this absorbing task by a telephone call from President Johnson asking me to serve as his Chief of Protocol. I accepted before having time to look up the word. At my swearing-in Secretary of State Dean Rusk observed, "You have now graduated from the world of juvenile delinquency to the world of adult delinquency."

At one time or another during the next two years I managed to conduct an ambassador into a broom closet, fly the British flag upside down, walk the King of Morocco into a blind alley, get lost in Seoul, fail to anticipate a gift exchange with the President of Mexico, escort the King of Greece to the airport instead of the White House, and arrange a welcoming motorcade for the President and his visitor, King Faisal of Saudia Arabia, through the emptiest streets ever recorded in our nation's capital.* Finally, as the Marine Band struck up "Hail to the Chief," I turned to the President and said, "Mr. President, our song." It was about this time that the President asked me if I had ever thought about running for Congress.

*As noted in excerpts on p. 172.

Serenading President and Mrs. Johnson at the LBJ Ranch on the Pedernales (near Austin, Texas). An evening for Israeli Prime Minister and Mrs. Levi Eshkol, December 1967.

*The abrupt transfer of White House prerogative and access from Brahmins to Longhorns made me think of its consequences to some of the best and brightest. And what became of Arthur Schlesinger? No longer did he haunt the family rooms and share his visions of the future with the First Family. With other New Frontiersmen, he graciously removed to the Sans Souci restaurant, a stone's throw, as it were, from the White House.*

*He was there, according to reports, hunched over a dubonnet, when word came that LBJ had ordered White House "lights out" at 10:00 P.M., ostensibly to save energy. Recalling the Kennedy Administration's disinclination to slumber, Arthur rallied his considerable powers to oppose the initiative.*

## EXILE

At the Sans Souci,
His chosen Elba,
He spread his brie
On toast of melba.
Silver trumpets,
Silent now.
Munching crumpets
Furrowed brow.
Mutely wondered
How 'twas sundered
From 1600,
The new domains
Of Luci Baines.
O' tempora!
O' mores!
What Emperor,
What glories,
What stories
Lay ahead
To be read?
With anguished yen
And languished pen
He viewed the mystery,
The end of history.

But then some news
Awoke the muse:
To save on frills
And Pepco* bills
The new-crowned King wished
Lights extinguished
At tick or tock
Of ten o'clock!
To quit so early
The hurly burly?
Douse each light
In House of White?
The world's cop?
Oh, that's terrific!
The world's prop
A soporific!
Time to toughen!
Finish muffin
Fix the ribbon
(That's a Gibbon)
Then place a call.
And put a stamp here,
"Decline and fall
Of the American Ampere."

Washington, DC — 1964

*Potomac Electric Power Company.

The high point of the Johnson diplomatic years must have been the seven-nation summit conference in Manila, with prior visits to each of the seven. The rituals of welcome were imaginative and varied.* One national anthem lasted five minutes in one-hundred-degree heat, as the President, head lowered, fixed me with a baleful look. At another capital the two anthems were played simultaneously. At a third, a very portly and scantily-clad chieftain, covered with paint from head to toe, rushed up and hurled a small stick to the ground. I advised the President that he was to pick it up and return it as a sign of peace. "You pick the dang thing up," was his measured response. I did so, explaining to the gentleman that I was the President's "peace-stick lifter." On still another occasion I had to present the President's arrival gift (an Acutron watch) to his royal host on a velvet pillow, exiting backward between two rows of immensely satisfied presidential assistants.

These experiences I distilled and, in a short hop from reality to fantasy, presented as a memoir during the long return flight. White House aides Liz Carpenter, Bess Abell, and others joined in performing it on Air Force One to Secretary of State Dean Rusk's astonishment and a few chuckles from our Chief of State. Herewith the libretto of "On The Road With LBJ" (to the tune of "Mandalay"):

## ON THE ROAD WITH LBJ

In an old Moulmein Pagoda
Lookin' eastward to the sea
There's some potentate or other
And I know he thinks of me.
Yes, a stir is in the palace
And the ministers they pray
Won't you leave the Pedernales
And sidle out our way,
Sidle out our way?

On the road with LBJ
Guess we'll find a place to stay.
They don't dock it from our pocket cause
    Bill Crockett[1] has to pay

On the road with LBJ
From the ranch to Mandalay
Where the Nabobs have no day jobs
    but to bill the USA.

Ship me somewheres west of Austin
Where a man can raise a thirst,
And the pills of Dr. Burkley[2]
Will help prevent the worst;
Where the wind is in the speeches
And the temple bells they say
Come you back you Texas Ranger
Come you back you LBJ.

Come you back you LBJ
Bring Clark Clifford,[3] that's okay.
Bring Bill Moyers,[4] bring your lawyers
Bring your own communiqué!
Cause we're with you all the way,
And we've gathered here to say
If the dawn comes up like thunder,
    it's no wonder, LBJ!—

*Air Force One*, over Alaska—1966

*For an imaginary briefing aboard *Air Force One* on the rituals of a mythical empire, see the following pages.
[1]State Department escort.
[2]Dr. George Burkley, White House physician.
[3]Washington, DC attorney, Presidential Adviser, and former Secretary of Defense.
[4]Former Peace Corps Director and White House Press Secretary under President Johnson.

Performing "On The Road With LBJ" aboard *Air Force One*, somewhere over Alaska, October 1966. Left to right behind the President: Liz Carpenter (Presidential Aide), John Roche (Foreign Policy Consultant), Bess Abell (White House Social Secretary), the author (Chief of Protocol), and Connie Gerard (Secretary to the President).

# WE'RE LANDING, MR. PRESIDENT

## A Briefing While Taxiing Up The Runway
## Of A Mythical Empire

We're landing, Mr. President.

No sir, we did Bumtoy yesterday. This is our last stop—Bhurdoo—capital of Sen-Sen. What, sir?

Friendly, sir. Mr. Rusk[1] says a "quasi-constitutional empire." Contenders for the royal crown draw straws—the loser is King—the others are flogged and sent out as ambassadors.

You will be met at the foot of the ramp by His Majesty, King Kumquat, and the Crown Prince, His Royal Highness, Spitin Imaj.

No sir, you're not to deplane by the rear exit. No sir, not the forward exit either. By the emergency exit, sir.

Didn't Watson[2] tell you?

On the inaugural flight of their national airline—Air Sampan—the aircraft carrying the King became lodged between two rubber trees, and His Majesty was obliged to leave by the emergency exit. Since that time, in deference to His Majesty's experience, all Heads of State are requested to deplane in the same manner.

Mr. President—the moment you set foot on Sen-Sen soil five thousand pigeons will be released overhead. A parasol bearer is assigned to you.

Also, a herd of goats will be driven toward you. You are not to touch the goats as this is against their religion. Okie[3] would like to get your picture dodging them.

In addition, five high-spirited water buffaloes will be drawn up and each member of your official party is requested to ride one by the reviewing stand. Actually, we'll have to double up—Rusk and Bundy,[4] Watson and Valenti,[5] McPherson[6] and Rostow.[7] Dr. Burkley[8] gets his own with saddlebags. During this traditional procession they will be pelted with native fruits in a gesture of good will.

The King then takes you to the platform for the national anthems, which will be played simultaneously on native instruments. They regret there will be no twenty-one guns. They were overloaded during the last State Visit and blew up, collapsing the pavilion. McNamara[9] is reviewing their request for replacements.

Following the rendering of anthems there will be a moment's silence during which the Grand Chamberlain takes three slow steps forward and breaks an egg on your head. That's good luck, and you are to smile.

The King will then take you along the line of dignitaries. Here they do not shake hands. Their form of greeting is to step up smartly and dig their elbow into your ribs. Your response is simply to smile and say, "Proy," which means "ouch."

You will know the diplomatic corps. They will be in shackles.

After doing Proy with the receiving line you will be carried to your car with the King. Please don't refer to the car as your "bubbletop" because this happens to be His Royal Majesty's pet name for the Queen.

Mrs. Johnson—you deplane with the President, and are greeted by Queen Woesme. Together you follow the President and the King throughout, except the Proy greeting. Instead of proy, each lady hands you a bouquet. There are approximately fifty ladies, so when you deplane you will be immediately fitted with a traditional native wicker basket, which is strapped on your back by six schoolgirls singing their national song.

Don't wear blue, Mrs. Johnson. It is the mourning color for women. No, ma'am—white is the mourning color for men. Greens, reds, and yellows are permitted only on holy days. How about a nice mud color—it's permissible everywhere but in the palace, and you can change in the car.

[1]Dean Rusk, Secretary of State.
[2]Marvin Watson, Appointments Secretary.
[3]Yoshi Okamoto, Presidential photographer.
[4]William Bundy, Assistant Secretary of State for Asian Affairs.
[5]Jack Valenti, Assistant to the President (currently President of the Motion Picture Association of America).
[6]Harry McPherson, Counsel to the President.
[7]Walt Rostow, National Security Advisor.
[8]Dr. George Burkley, the President's physician.
[9]Robert McNamara, Secretary of Defense.

# SUGGESTED ARRIVAL STATEMENT FOR SEN-SEN

Your Royal Majesty, Your Worships, Your Excellencies, Your Every Day Ordinaries, and Folks.

This is a great day for Mrs. Johnson and myself. Like all Americans, we cherish the relationship of good will that has existed between us since the founding of your great nation—last month. Moreover, there is no reason in the world why this happy association should not continue on and on—for another month.

Your Majesty—I've met your Prime Minister; your Deputy Prime Minister; your Foreign Minister; your ministers of defense, labor, commerce, and agriculture; and I'm deeply impressed, particularly to find them one and the same person, your son.

Twenty years ago—with the help of young American boys—foreign imperialism was wiped away from this jungle paradise, and the work of eliminating imperialism at home began. You authored a new page of history. Some say it is still blank. But as your own proverb goes . . . "A wise man swallows before he chokes."

This, then, is the wisdom of Sen-Sen, a country rich in potential.

If you are a have-not nation, then we are too, for we have not the tranquil spirit of a people who have uncomplainingly endured for two thousand years the lack of an alphabet. But that has proven no impediment to communication. When you enlarged your jail cells so our missionaries could stand up, that was a language we could understand.

Sir, under your inspired leadership many old institutions have been toppled. Most of them will have to be rebuilt. But progress has been made.

For example, unbelievably rampant inflation has been reduced to mere rampant inflation. Your currency—the poon—owing to the vigorous measures you have initiated under the prodding of your general staff, has been pegged at forty-five thousand to the dollar.

Finally, Your Majesty, I know you are in the Week of the Wallaby. Indeed, it's a heartwarming thing to see a whole nation hopping up and down for seven days. But more than this you should always carry with you in your pouch of pouches the fact that America's hops go with you toward a brighter future for both our peoples and both of yours.

*Air Force One*, over the Pacific—1966

President and Mrs. Johnson's arrival at a Royal Airport reception
(with Marvin Watson, White House Chief of Staff, and the author).
October 1966.

Another song conveyed the imagined state of mind of the President's Press Secretary, Bill Moyers. Moyers, a former Director of the Peace Corps, knew no peace on this trip. Bearing the burden of securing favorable press coverage, he knew neither sleep nor respite for the duration. The entire White House Press Corps was on hand throughout — restive, querulous, and unsympathetic. Hence, "Moyers' Lament" (to the tune of "Sit Right Down and Write Myself a Letter"):

## MOYERS' LAMENT

I wanna sit right down and write myself a column,
And make believe it came from you.
I'm gonna write words oh so fine,
And sign with your by-line,
With kudos in the copy
That'll please our Poppy.

I'm gonna write and tell how LBJ has conquered,
And Asia's eating out of his hand,
I'm gonna sit right down and write myself a column
That the whole darn world will understand.

Gonna ask old Elie Abel[1] to the table.
Gonna thank ol' Frankel[2] for his *Times*;
Gonna open up the door
To Peter Lisagore,[3]
And try to be much dearer
To Bailey[4] and Ray Sherer.[5]

Gonna hide my dander from Miss Alexander;[6]
Try that trick with Kilpatrick,[7] too.
I'm gonna take Mark Childs[8] and treat him like a grown up.
I'm gonna press the flesh of all the press I know.

[1]Elie Abel, *New York Times*.
[2]Max Frankel, *New York Times*.
[3]Peter Lisagore, *Chicago Daily News*.
[4]Chuck Bailey, *Minneapolis Star and Tribune*.
[5]Ray Sherer, NBC.
[6]Shana Alexander, *Life Magazine*.
[7]James J. Kilpatrick, *Richmond Times Dispatch* and the *Washington Star*.
[8]Marquis Childs, *St. Louis Post Dispatch*.

I'm gonna sit right down and write an editorial
That wraps the trip in colors true,
'Cause I get no afterglow
From Bonnie Angelo,[9]
And I'd really like to tidy
Up those comments of Hugh Sidey.[10]

If only Merry Smith[11] would be a pard
I'd get him a state dinner diner's card.
I'm gonna sit right down and write about our fame
And sign each doggone stringer's name.

                                   *Air Force One*, over Alaska—1966

[9]Bonnie Angelo, *Time Magazine.*
[10]Hugh Sidey, *Life* and *Time Magazines.*
[11]Merriman Smith, United Press International.

*After a few tempestuous years before the mast of public service, Billy Don Moyers went quietly ashore to take the helm of a Long Island newspaper. He deserved both congratulations and a hearty farewell as he assumed a task that seemed improbable at the time, but undoubtedly propelled him on the enviable journalistic career he pursues today.*

## QUIET FLOWS THE BILLY DON*

### (A Farewell To Bill Moyers)

Quiet flows the Billy Don
Through many a crisis-laden night
In Corps of Peace and House of White,
Hither, yes, and also yon
Flows the Billy Don.

Unpolluted was this tide,
And never turbulent at crest,
Giving journalists a ride,
And brushing bureaucrats aside
With a gentle zest.

What estuary waits to fold
The Billy Don in its embrace?
Will it be a pleasant place?
Is there one for waters bold,
Before they get too cold?

No idle friend with feet of clay
But grew and flourished all the more
For having stood beside the shore
This river touched along its way,
And wanted it to stay.

Meanwhile, no levee can contain
A stream, which, full, should well resound
With more than a mere Long Island sound.
Then quietly, like needed rain,
The Billy Don will flow again.

Washington, DC—1966

*Adapted from *And Quiet Flows The Don,* by M.A. Sholokhov.

The author with President Johnson on the Truman balcony.
The White House, January 13, 1967.

*Other starbursts illuminated this period. One such was the marriage of the President's daughter, Lynda, to a young Marine Corps captain assigned to the White House. He patrolled the Rose Garden just long enough to secure its most glorious blossom before his requested transfer to the less congenial horticulture of Vietnam. His bachelor dinner was attended by no one unfamiliar with the Marine Corps Hymn. A brief review of his courtship provided a new lyric for the flexibility of that martial strain.*

## THE SAGA OF CHARLES ROBB

From the Halls of old Milwaukee
To the grand North Portico —
With a minimum of talk, he
Stole the whole darn show.

Alert as any eagle
Yet not devoid of soul,
He befriended every beagle,
And moved on toward his goal.

He stalked the rosy garden
With firm and steady pace,
He even begged her pardon
When they met face to face.

Although the goal was far away,
He determined to pursue it.
A true Marine, he'd never say,
"Why not let George* do it."

So, like Caesar this young captain came
And conquered what he saw.
Now he's proud to claim the titled fame
Of United Son in Law.

Fort Myers, Virginia — 1967

*George Hamilton, actor and former escort.

Receiving line at the White House wedding reception for
Charles and Lynda Robb. Washington, DC; December 9, 1967.

# ☆☆ NIXON ☆☆

## ON NIXON
### (Letter to Parents)

It was interesting to see Nixon in action . . . he moves about easily; chats with people; handles the press as the *Observer* notes, like a "player" (professional) "versus the gentlemen." As a speaker, he is both glib and sincere-seeming, not powerful. He had some fine things to say—but while his voice is pleasant, low and modulated—it does not convey conviction, the compelling urgency of leadership. He seems to me like a nice young man who would deserve and manage competently a Cabinet post. But in watching his boyish, dark face, the furrowed brow, the quick smile, I wonder if I do not understand why he appears "tricky."

I feel he lacks the deep springs of imagination that give strength and substance to an analysis. It's hard to tell if the analysis is his, or if he has memorized the notes of advisers, and rephrased them through a technique of translation that is purely superficial. Consistency is not likely to be the mark of such a man. And it is the same lack of comprehension of his own present and past words that, perhaps, makes it so surprisingly easy for him on occasion to charmingly admit having been wrong at such and such a time, and having been corrected.

He denies the emergence of a "new Nixon"—and I would agree. His dilemma may consist of his never having known himself very well, and, therefore, never having a fixed reference point for analyzing the world about him. This weakness, if I am right about it, is poor company for ambition. Because it makes him prey to what others, who support his ambitions for one reason or another, would have him do or say. It is dangerous for a country to be guided by a man who is not himself guided by the well-springs of his own intuition.

On another level, would his choice of advisers be sound? I'm not sure. He has lived most of his productive life as a politician. Politicians tend to befriend—and to trust—men who have befriended them, and to be blind to their faults. They feel beholden to old friends, and make allowances for them—to a fault. A man's judgment in such things can be measured by the character and calibre of any persons he permits to speak for him and to be near him.

And a Cabinet minister is no more important to the Head of State than his personal aides. Less in a way, because a minister's official mistakes are public, and these others are hidden. . . .

James W. Symington—Attaché, U.S. Embassy
London—November 30, 1959

*As President Nixon's first term drew to a close, the nation had yet to learn his "secret plan to end the war." On the contrary, the Cambodian invasion of 1970, unrevealed even to our Secretary of State, Bill Rogers, amounted to a secret war to end the plan. In any event, Rogers' successor, Henry Kissinger, once and future architect of Nixon's war strategy, was determined to extricate the President before his second term. He was certainly well-equipped to do so, having provided valuable counsel to thirty-six Presidents, seven in their lifetime and the remainder posthumously. By October 1972 he was pleased to report that peace was "at hand," but by Christmas it had unaccountably slipped from his grip. Hence this borrowing from the carol, "O Tannenbaum" ("Oh Christmas Tree"):*

## OH, CHRISTMAS PEACE!

Oh, Christmas peace we understand
October last you were at hand.
To us the deal was never known
For Henry liked to work alone.
But, fleeting joy, our wonder boy
Convinced them all except Hanoi.
Except Hanoi and General Thieu,[1]
Admittedly, a very few.

How proud we watched our Henry go
To and fro 'tween Thieu and Tho.[2]
How could they both verstehe nicht
The stern command of Richard's wish?
Let neither Congress nor the press
Presume to wildly second guess . . .
The grand accord we're moving toward
To the music Henry scored.

The citizens November seven
Seemed to voice the will of heaven.
Lock-step we grouped and pollward trouped,
Never dreaming we'd been duped
What shock to hear from Henry K.
Hanoi indulged in foul play.
Oh Metternich,[3] our Metternich
Did they play a better trick?

The Teutonic tones of Henry's groans
Sent reporters to their phones.
His heavy sighs and drooping eyes,
Told more than words his own surprise.
What right has history to sour
His aphrodisiac of power?
Tears will well in all our eyes
Until the fates apologize.

[1]General Nguyen Van Thieu, Prime Minister, South Vietnam.
[2]Le Duc Tho, Prime Minister, North Vietnam.
[3]Clemens Wenzel Lothar von Metternich (1773-1859), Austrian statesman and diplomat.

# THE WATERGATE PERIOD

Fate was busy in the fall of 1972. Dr. Kissinger's hopeful announcement competed for attention with a "minor burglary"—the break-in at the Democratic National Committee Headquarters in the Watergate Hotel. Campaigning for my third election to Congress I conjectured,

> "We don't have the facts, but one thing is certain. Any Administration that would employ such tactics to gain power will certainly use them to keep it."

I suppose, in retrospect, it was both to gain and keep power that those tactics were used. And as the nation slowly came to realize what was done, all of us in public life were called upon to react. I was inundated with "suggestions." Some White House supporters sent me small pebbles with the note,

> "He who is without sin among you, let him cast the first stone. John 8:7"

These I returned with a disavowal,

> "I regret that I must return the enclosed stone, as I do not feel qualified to cast it. Your confidence in me, however, is greatly appreciated."

More serious signals were received back home, including one steady-eyed pledge to shoot me down if I voted to impeach. I pointed out that one could get ten days for killing a congressman.

Sylvia Symington's dinner partner speaks. Washington, DC, 1970.

*The growing national preoccupation with "Watergate" irritated our Chief of State. He urged the country to get on with its business and stop "wallowing in Watergate." Indeed, we were,*

## WALLOWIN' IN WATERGATE TONIGHT

Across this land of honey, grain and plenty,
Between old Key Biscayne and San Clemente,
There's no serenity for the likes of you and me
But enough apparently for el Presidente.

Some are born to lead and some to follow,
Some to mix the feed and some to swallow,
Some to do the deed and some to wallow,
So we're wallowin' in Watergate tonight.

Yes, we're wallowin' in Watergate tonight,
Hopin' everythings a gonna come out right.
The truth was never meant to annoy this President,
So we're wallowin' in Watergate tonight.

Best not to raise your voice or shine your light.
He's put it out of mind and out of sight.
Too busy to be bothered by the scandals that he fathered,
So we're wallowin' in Watergate tonight.

Our leader and his dedicated crew
Have so many big and better things to do.
We'll try not to be jealous of that happiest of fellas,
As we go to fix the leak in our canoe.

Wallow left—Wallow right
Till we've run all out of plumbers to indict.
Ignoring little factors like the principal contractors
While we're wallowin' in Watergate tonight.

One simple little message in this song,
Addressed to any folks who come along,
It's only to remind that the world is gonna find
Two hundred million wallowers can't be wrong!

Washington, DC—1973

*In that summer of '73, various White House operatives were under the shadow of indictment. It seemed they could trace their predicament to their personable and newly-loquacious colleague, John Dean. Hence, with apologies to Rudyard Kipling and his Gungha Din:**

# JOHNNY DEAN

### (Lines Penned Awaiting Indictment)

No Presidential tear
Disturbs your gin or beer
Much less the woes that plague the man who weeps it.
While we, foregoing violence,
Just pray for simple silence,
And would kiss the boots of any man that keeps it.

Down in marbled Washington
Where my staffer's spurs were won,
A-serving of His Righteousness, I mean.
Of all his faceless crew
The most innocent I knew
Was the regimental houseboy, Johnny Dean.

He was Dean, Dean, Dean,
Our cool, collegiate colleague, Johnny Dean.
He could write a note or burn it,
Remember or unlearn it,
That accommodatin', grinnin' Johnny Dean.

The uniform he wore
Was gray flannel to the core,
And was cut for ivy leaguers on the go.
His mouth was like a wreath
Around a set o' teeth
Like chicklets standin' upright in a row.

Ah, that dimpled little devil, Johnny Dean,
The most conscientious cog in the machine.
He could take a file and hide it,

---

*Who also "blew the whistle" on his captors.

And never look inside it,
And you'd never think to ask where he had been.

Now, at governing the land
The firmest mortal hand
I ever saw belonged to the incumbent.
To ensure things that folks missed
Stayed curled in that fist
Our mission was to keep the press recumbent.

So when affairs of state
Broke loose at Watergate
We rallied 'round the standard we all shared.
'Tween honesty and face
The former must give place,
And blessings on the soul that isn't bared.

So 'twas Dean, Dean, Dean
That muddied up his mates by comin' clean.
Who'd a'thought the truth would out
From the boyish little pout
Of our faithful, fawnin' fixer, Johnny Dean.

Yes, it's Dean, Dean, Dean,
No matter how carefully we'd screen,
We had to hire a spy
That couldn't live a lie,
A dishonest little guy, like Johnny Dean.

Washington, DC—Summer 1973

*We were then advised by the President that the tactics of his opponents should be held responsible for any departures from propriety on the part of his government, a novel notion.*

## THE DOCTRINE OF EXECUTIVE PILFERAGE*

What others choke upon before they say,
He says with ease, leaving naught to chance.
Thus his hint: Dissenters showed the way;
Authority, reluctant, learned the dance.
"Le loi, c'est moi," a maxim coined in France?
No, here at home, at least by inference,
When White House curiosity holds sway.
Will "privilege and immunity" win out,
And truth be silently to slaughter led?
Or will there be a giant turn about,
More momentous than the price of bread,
When America will see beyond all doubt,
The Constitution meant just what it said?

Washington, DC—September 1973

*For a sporting view of Watergate, see pages 219-220.

# 1973-74: THE IMPEACHMENT YEARS

*These were very difficult years for the country and those of us under oath to guide it. Not until some point in July 1974 did I decide; could I bring myself to decide to vote to impeach our President. A year earlier, engulfed as I was by doubts and imaginings of the dangers in such a course, I wrote my friend, Meg Greenfield, that perhaps it was as unnecessary as it was dangerous, and that somehow we could navigate with a crippled helmsman until we could make a landfall — through an election — two years hence. I wrote the letter on a beach where I had gone for a moment to think.*

Dear Meg:

Perspective, so hard to come by in the verbal wrestling matches, with all holds barred, between the President's critics, his apologists, and himself, comes more easily here. Intuitive as a man may think he is, the ocean has a way of putting him in his place. And the Gulf of Mexico is ocean enough for that purpose. Its message, as a novel as eternity, is that this, too, will pass. It deposits this reminder with every tumbling cache of broken shells it leaves at our feet — remnants each of a sometime struggle to exist.

The American experience, fed by two centuries of outpourings of the human spirit, is now akin to a sea, wherein old truths run deep, undisturbed by the life cycles of lesser ideas. These it casts up in time, and in its own inexorable way. It does not require unnatural upheavals to purify itself. It relies on the steady rhythms of the electoral process. In the meantime, like the micro-organisms that alternately feed and digest oceanic living matter, maintaining a kind of dynamic balance, so the multiplicity of impressions, discussions, and choices of the American people preserve, in their interaction, the ecology of their political environment. The excesses of demagogues, militants, assassins, and even of Presidents are in this way broken down and rendered harmless. Sensing this, the people are but rarely inclined to coalesce into a giant interruption of the rhythm, so as to dash against the rocks things they consider uncongenial to the harmony of their life. They can wait. And they do wait, apprehensive but nonetheless confident in the digestive cycles established by their organic law.

To emerge, before going down for the third time in that metaphor, I would say that if there is any corrective we are nostalgic for at this time, it is an election. We are denied that cathartic at present. Yet we look upon the alternative, impeachment, with proper caution. Because tidal waves can result in the untimely destruction of things dear as well as of things not so dear. They are not discriminating. So we live, as it were, in a political atmosphere which is somewhat polluted. The polluting element is mistrust, which once one-sided (the President's trust in the people has never been pronounced) is now mutual, thereby in a way, more bearable. It is the unknown which poses the greatest danger in the ocean and in organized human society. For it can be exploited by those who favor it, and either under or overestimated by those who do not. The President's "role" in at least the aftermath of Watergate is now, for all practical purposes, known. And what is known, or at least fairly well understood, need not be feared. For it can be managed. And it is to the Congress, the courts, and the general collective common sense of their fellow citizens in public and private life, that the American people entrust the management of their relationship with the Chief Executive. They are conscious that such management may even entail earnest cooperation, particularly with respect to international affairs and negotiations. Whether or not they agree with the President's priorities of expenditure or other domestic policies, they hold the Congress and the Courts to proper vigilance in this area. They sense that the President, himself, suffers from no apparent pangs of conscience, and that he owes to this want of remorse his useful imperturbability and capacity to respond to the normal challenges of his office.

An observant student of political practicality, he will move about the remainder of his term like an earnest apprentice of the new ethic. They see him as a now willing and perhaps even enthusiastic prisoner of the new vigilance. In sum, they see no need to trade the rolling rhythm of their political process for a volcanic eruption which can engulf progress and draw into their midst other and perhaps greater dangers. As inheritors of the legacies of 1776 they would like to believe, and they do believe, that in the next three years the American experience can dissolve this foreign material so effectively that there won't even be enough left to poison the birthday cake.

Boca Grande, Florida — August 20, 1973

# ☆☆ REAGAN — BUSH ☆☆

*Almost unnoticed during the Reagan years was the growing power and prominence of women. Women figured on the "supply side" of everything the country needed.*

*In his Democracy in America, de Tocqueville put it this way: "If I were asked to what the singular prosperity and growing strength of that people ought to be attributed, I should reply: to the superiority of their women." His perceptive view remains uncontested. Hence this hymn commissioned as the preface to an essay on "Women of Achievement" by Gaetana Enders, published in the Courrier Diplomatique, June 1983:*

## BATTLE HYMN TO THE REPUBLIC OF AMERICAN WOMEN
### (Washington Division)

Preface

When Alex Pope,* no bosom buddy,
Asserted that the proper study
Of mankind was man, the fuddy duddy
Went contented to his tomb n'
Never knew he'd slighted woman.
So glad am I if in some small way
I can help light history's hallway
With a verse as terse as possible,
Yet laden with a later gospel.

Mine eyes have seen the glory of emerging womankind.
They are trampling down the barriers of habit and of mind
That for centuries stood firmly in a world man designed
As time went marching on.

Glory, glory to Her Honor,
Justice Sandra Day O'Connor.[1]
Transports of glory heart and soul
To Secretary Betty Dole.[2]
To the S.E.C. whose highest llamas
Listen now to Barbara Thomas.[3]

To the senatorial lebensraum
Prepared for Nancy Kassebaum.[4]
Glory, rah, and boola boola
To Sweden's Goddess, Willy's Ulla,[5]
As time goes marching on.

In the beauty of the Corcoran Mrs. Livingston[6] I presume
Has made for Sheila Isham's[7] art considerable room.
Her works and those of Polly Kraft[7] dispel the city's gloom,
As time goes shimmering on.

Glory to the A.F.I.
Under Ginsberg's[8] steady eye,
To Jeanne F. Beggs'[9] enduring fealty,
To the principles of realty,
To needy folks no longer nervous
With Peggy Heckler[10] at their service.
To Mayor Barry, worlds smarter
Since he hired Carlyn Carter.[11]
To all of those refreshing pauses
The work of Gloria Lemos[12] causes.
To Peggy Cooper's[13] high ambition
For the D.C. Arts Commission.
To producers who won't do it
Without the help of Frankie Hewitt,[14]
As time goes dancing on.

Lucky now for Protocol that a Roosevelt[15] is Chief,
For cultural direction with Istomin in relief,
For litigants with Carla Hills[16] working on their brief
As time goes sternly on.

A Posty toast to the enduring fame
Of the winsome, lose none, Katherine Graham.[17]
Glory, glory, plain and fancy
To Ms. Reynolds (Nancy's Nancy).[18]
Glory, sanctus and te deum
To Billie Holiday's[19] museum.

To projects saved from being narrower
By the hand of Tina Harrower.[20]
To Ms. Poussaint, you know, Renee,[21]
Whose anchor we would never weigh.
To all the above whom we can tell
Are dressed by Val Cook's[22] Saks Jandel.
Add one more for ease of life
A dear achiever, mine own wife,
As tempus tip-toes on.

Postlude:

This was writ with furrowed brow
And the help of Julia Ward (that's Howe)[23]
Having lifted history's blot,
Further deponent saith not.

Washington, DC — 1983

*Alexander Pope (1688-1744), English poet.
[1]First woman Justice, United States Supreme Court.
[2]Secretary of Transportation.
[3]S.E.C. Commissioner.
[4]United States Senator (Rep.) from Kansas.
[5]Countess Ulla Wachtmeister, Painter; wife of Swedish Ambassador to the United States,
    Count Willy Wachtmeister.
[6]Jane Livingston, Director, Corcoran Art Gallery.
[7]Painter.
[8]Ina Ginsberg, Director, American Film Institute.
[9]Real Estate Executive.
[10]Margaret Heckler, Secretary of Health and Human Services.
[11]Executive Assistant to the Mayor of Washington, DC.
[12]Vice President, Coca Cola Company.
[13]Director, D.C. Arts Commission.
[14]Director, Ford's Theatre.
[15]Selwa ("Lucky") Roosevelt, United States Chief of Protocol.
[16]Attorney (former U.S. Trade Representative).
[17]Publisher, the *Washington Post*.
[18]Nancy Reynolds, Chief of Staff for First Lady Nancy Reagan.
[19]Wilhelmina Holiday, Founder and Director, National Museum of Women in the Arts.
[20]Public Relations Chief Executive.
[21]Renee Pouissant, TV Anchorwoman.
[22]Fashion Executive.
[23]Julia Ward Howe, Authoress, *Battle Hymn of the Republic*.

*294 / James W. Symington*

*Washington Post* Book-and-Author Luncheon—Bill Moyers,
Katherine Graham, and the author. Washington, DC, 1970.

# QUESTIONS FOR GRANDPA

## (2000 A.D.)

I've got some questions for you, Gramp.
Fire away, you little scamp.
They have to do with the Middle East.
For that I'll need a drink, or priest.
Well, when Iraq took on Iran
Were we pro or were we con?
Who did we rock around the clock?
Was it Iran or just Iraq?
Look, with our hostages in hock,
We surely had to help Iraq.
Okay, but didn't weapons sales
To Iran reverse the scales?
Well that was just to get some dough
To help the Contras fight the foe.
You mean our chosen leaders fleeced us
Just to beat the Sandanistas?
No, indeed, the <u>un</u>elected
Were the only ones suspected.
The Ayatollah took the cake
From Bud McFarlane,[1] for pete's sake.
While Hussein (no relation to the King
Of Jordan) never took a thing,
Except control and then Kuwait.
That is when we kept our date
With honor (a convenient foil
For another thing called oil).
But where were Bush and Reagan at
When mighty Casey[2] came to bat?
Well, as the situation warmed
They were never quite informed.
Their focus was containing cults
Plus Mullahs, Communists and Shultz.[3]

The fault for our strategic follies
Was Secord's,[4] Poindexter's[5] and Ollie's.[6]
When he learned of their adventures
Reagan nearly dropped his dentures.
Congress went into a funk,
And Bush retired to Kennebunk.
What and when he ever knew
Are two ingredients in the brew
Of history, which you'd better salt
Before deciding who's at fault.
Now run along and let me think
But first I'll have another drink.

Washington, DC — 1994

[1]Robert C. ("Bud") McFarlane, U.S. National Security Adviser (1983-85).
[2]William Casey, Director, Central Intelligence Agency.
[3]George P. Shultz, U.S. Secretary of State.
[4]Richard Secord, retired Air Force Major General.
[5]Rear Admiral John Poindexter, U.S. National Security Adviser (1985-87).
[6]Lt. Colonel Oliver North, Deputy Director, National Security Council (NSC)
   Division of Political-Military Affairs.

*The emergence of Saddam Hussein dusted off this muse. His brief absorption of Kuwait, in the "War of the Gulp," would have inspired a genuine racket from Tin-Pan-Alley had he not been forced to leave before the songwriters could get to their pianos. In the immediate aftermath of his uninvited sojourn in Kuwait the world pondered its, which is to say our, next move. In that uneasy calm before Desert Storm it seemed reasonable to address the aggressor as follows:*

## MAKING A MESOPOTAMIA

Saddam Hussein it's a shame ya
Made such a Mesopotamia.
History's certain to blame ya
For stompin' on little Kuwait.

You thought by a stroke of your pen you
Could broaden your sovereign venue,
But milk Sheiks aren't on the menu,
And that's why you're getting the gate.

Consider why Russia and Syria,
Who once could admire and cheer ya,
Have joined us all waiting to hear ya,
Say you'll pull out and the date.

You've even made Momar Qaddafi
Look like he'd rather pull taffy
Than join your miniature mafi-
a in your adventure of late.

True, you're a petty aggressor,
And at times a pretty sharp dresser,
But you ain't no Nebuchadnezzar,
Whatever you pontificate.

From the Tigris to the Euphrates,
You can still be a wow with the ladies,
If you cash in your ticket to Hades,
And return to your natural state.

The alternative's not sweet to ponder.
We love peace but of justice are fonder,
To avoid being transported yonder,
Put the food back on the plate.

Washington, DC—September 4, 1990

*As Christmas approached Saddam Hussein thought it good public relations to release various captives in a gesture of good will and peaceful intent. This display of holiday spirit brought to mind the old carol, "The Twelve Days of Christmas."*

## CHRISTMAS IN IRAQ

On the First Day of Christmas Great Saddam will release
    An American in a wheel chair . . .

On the Twelfth Day of Christmas Great Saddam will release
        Twelve Danish dancers
        Eleven Lebanesers
        Ten Russian teachers
        Nine German doctors
        Eight British bankers
        Seven Saudi sinners
        Six sick Kuwaitis
        FIVE JAPANESE
        Four Italian cooks
        Three French nuns
        Two touring Turks
        And an American in a wheel chair.

Washington, DC — Christmas 1990

*Hussein ignored President Bush's kind and gentle ultimatum. Thus it appeared by January that we were going in. Troops arrived and pitched their tents. One could not help but think of their frustration during liberty hours when two of the greatest yearnings (sex and drink) were out of reach, bounds, and the question. Since most great wars produce a rose song, why not one depicting the plight of a GI on the sands of Araby?*

## RIYADH ROSE*

Riyadh Rose
GI Joes
Wonder why
Nothing shows
From your toes
To your eye.

Yet one look at your clothes
Makes me suppose
There's a girl there,
Somewhere by and by.

Riyadh Rose
Please disclose
Goodness knows
If there's any way
In poetry or prose
To howdy a Saudi
Without being rowdy
Now that I've taken on her foes?

It makes me sad
To hear your Dad
Selects your beaux.
If that's the case
I think my case
Is closed.

So's not to start a jihad
I'd best forget my Riyadh,
My tantalizin', mesmerizin', lost horizon
RIYADH ROSE.

Washington, DC—1991

*Music written by Judge William Hungate, former
  Congressman (Dem.) from Hannibal, Missouri.

*The world's press, in constant search of the "big story," finally happened upon one: President Bush's antipathy for broccoli.*

## BROCCOLI

Hickory Dickory Doccoli

The Prexy won't eat his broccoli.

It seems since his teens

He's resented these greens,

But never could say it so cockily.

Washington, DC — 1991

# THE CHUTE FITS*

Why the mighty fall

Is fodder for conjecture,

Sermons biblical

And professorial lecture.

Some received a push.

Others simply crumped.

But GHW Bush

Fell because he jumped.

Who'd have ever reckoned

A descent more swift

Than thirty-feet-per-second

Would give us such a lift!

Washington, DC—March 1997

---

*Dateline*—March 25, 1997, Yuma, Arizona—At approximately noon on this day, George H.W. Bush, sometime President of the United States, stepped out of a moving plane for the second time in his life. Unlike the first such instance his act was not prompted by enemy fire. He just felt like it. Hence the above lines.

# ☆☆ CLINTON ☆☆

*By 1992 Republicans had taken up residence in the White House for all but four of the preceding twenty-four years, a fact which produced these reflections:*

## A SONNET TO THE 1992 ELECTION

How can we win thee, let me count the ways.

First we choose the candidate from Hope,

Whose heart and mind are tethered to the days

Ahead, not those behind; who has the scope

To grasp the nettles of our discontent,

Endure the cuts, and, holding high the shards

Of broken dreams, and promises unmeant,

Calls us to the strength that ever guards

Our fate: belief in self, combined with care

For others, plus respect for every right

And lawful preference; yes, that all might share

The nation's work and bounty and the sight

Of children proving every day anew

"We can do better" happens to be true.

Washington, DC—June 1992

# THE FIRST HUNDRED DAYS

The ship of state pulled proudly from the pier

Quivering with hope along her keel.

Nothing lay ahead to fear but fear,

With Captain Clinton smiling at the wheel.

A few weeks out he noticed that his course

Was not responding to the wheel's spin.

He asked the crew below to check the source.

What condition was the rudder in?

What they discovered deep within the hold,

Was just what mate Panetta[1] had suspected.

The rudder had been wholly Robert Doled,[2]

Which is to say completely disconnected.

With winds of opposition blowing free

We've spent the first one hundred days at sea.

Washington, DC — 1993

[1] Leon Panetta, former Director, Office of Management and Budget
(1993-94), and White House Chief of Staff (1994-97).
[2] Senator Robert J. Dole (R-KA), Majority Leader of the Senate.

# PRESIDENTIAL BYPASS

When he wanted to prop up the peso

Congress wouldn't obey, so

He said, "Never mind,

If you must be unkind,

I'll just do it on my own say-so."

Washington, DC—1995

# REPUBLICAN REVERIE*

Oh, there's bound to be a link

So let's have another drink

From that old Whitewater Fountain.


Cause it's anybody's guess

Who's included in the mess

On that Little Rock Candy Mountain.

Washington, DC — 1996

*Tune: *Big Rock Candy Mountain*.

# ON THE TRUMAN BALCONY[†]

Here beside the grieving man from Hope
We mourn our own lost innocence.
Like him we scan with inward gaze
What might have been.
Monuments to virtue and achievement
Stretch in vain before us in the unforgiving sun.
Heaven help us heal one another,
And, all together, put our precious House in order.

Washington, DC—September 10, 1998

[†]The Truman Balcony is the south-facing White House second-floor balcony erected by President Truman.

*Consider His plan.*
*Conclude, perhaps oddly,*
*His great gift to man*
*Was the chance to be godly.*

# About The Author

In *A Muse 'N Washington*, Missouri Congressman James Wadsworth Symington, Marine private, lawyer, legislator, diplomat, writer and singer, has compiled nearly sixty years of verse, articles, speeches, and letters on the passing scene. Footnotes, often in jest, to history range from the personal to the political, bringing into stop-shutter focus events and personalities that define each decade since the outbreak of the Second World War.

Graduating from Yale (1950) where he boxed, sang, and played soccer, he earned his law degree from Columbia University, paying his tuition from his balladeering fees at New York's Sherry-Netherland Hotel and other nightspots.

Subsequently, as Assistant City Counselor, and City Court Prosecutor in St. Louis, foreign service officer in London, Deputy Director of Food For Peace in the White House, Administrative Assistant to Attorney General Robert F. Kennedy, Director of the President's Committee on Juvenile Delinquency, United States Chief of Protocol, four-term member of Congress from Missouri, and chairman of the Fund for the Improvement of Post-Secondary Education, Jim Symington has followed a public career path blazed by ancestors on both sides of his family. Among others they include his father, Senator Stuart Symington of Missouri; his grandfather, Senator James Wadsworth of New York; and his great-grandfather, John Hay of Illinois, who served as Private Secretary to President Lincoln, Ambassador to Great Britain, and Secretary of State under Presidents McKinley and T.R. Roosevelt.

During his years in public service and following as a Washington lawyer, Jim, like his ancestor Hay, has enjoyed recording his reflections in essays, verse, and song, including parodies and songs set to music by himself, and more frequently by his wife, the former Sylvia Caroline Schlapp, a Sarah Lawrence graduate who earned her Masters in Composition at Washington University in St. Louis. For forty years they have performed for the good causes of Washington, New York, Missouri, and other communities around the country. In England they played and sang at embassy soirées for the Royal Family, government officials, and the diplomatic community, as well as schools, orphanages, prisons, and the BBC. His 1958 tour of Leningrad (now St. Petersburg), Kiev, and Moscow as a free-lance folk singer in Russian and English was described in his two-part series for the *St. Louis Post Dispatch* entitled "Through Russia With Guitar." Later, as the representative of the Kennedy Administration's Food For Peace program, he played and sang in barrio and countryside throughout Latin America; NBC's David Brinkley's *Journal of Christmas*—1963, depicted his inauguration of a school lunch program in Peru. He has performed on the Tonight Shows of Great Britain (Cliff Michelmore) and the United States (Johnny Carson), and has been recorded for the Voice of America and as commentator on the recent PBS series on the U.S. Civil War, which his Wadsworth and Symington ancestors fought on opposite sides.

Currently a partner in the Washington, DC law firm of O'Connor & Hannan, he continues to observe, smile, write, and sing—fulfilling the claim that:

> *"It is hard to find anyone in this testy town who doesn't like Jim Symington, and no one who doesn't appreciate his minstrelsy."*

Mary McGrory, Syndicated Columnist,
*Washington Post*

**Seconds, anyone?**

Paolo's Restaurant in Georgetown.
Washington, DC, July 1998.

# Photographs

Page

Outnumbered but still smiling—President George Bush, Senator
John Warner (R-VA), Congressman Robert Michel (R-IL),
and the author (D-MO). Alfalfa Club Dinner, Washington,
DC; January 25, 1992 . . . . . . . . . . . . . . . . . . . . . . . . . . . . . . . . . . . .Cover

Here's the scoop!—Howard Johnson's, during U.S. Senate
campaign. St. Louis, Missouri, July 1976 . . . . . . . . . . . . . . . . . . . . . . . vi

Art Buchwald, dean of Washington's humorists, as auctioneer
for a public television fundraiser calling for bids on an evening
of folksongs with the author. Washington, DC, 1970 . . . . . . . . . . . . . . 15

Strumming for father, Stuart Symington's Senate race.
Tarkio, Missouri, 1952 . . . . . . . . . . . . . . . . . . . . . . . . . . . . . . . . . . . . . 26

Oratory — Author's declaration of candidacy for Congress.
Chase-Park Plaza Hotel, St. Louis, Missouri; April 1, 1968 . . . . . . . . . . 28

Opening of first Congressional campaign headquarters. Clayton,
Missouri; May 19, 1968. Left to right: Author with wife, Sylvia;
mother, Mrs. Stuart Symington; and campaign manager,
Morton Bearman . . . Sylvia at the headquarters . . . . . . . . . . . . . . . . . 29

The author, his wife, and volunteer workers with the campaign
bus in first Congressional race. Clayton, Missouri, 1968 . . . . . . . . . . . . 30

Father and son on *Meet The Press*. NBC Studio, Washington, DC;
June 20, 1971. Left to right: John W. Finney, *New York Times*;
Carl Leubsdorf, Associated Press; Marquis Childs, *St. Louis
Post Dispatch*; Paul Duke, NBC News; and Lawrence Spivak
(Producer) . . . . . . . . . . . . . . . . . . . . . . . . . . . . . . . . . . . . . . . . . . . . . . 42

With Sylvia. St. Louis, Missouri, 1970 . . . . . . . . . . . . . . . . . . . . . . . . . . 52

Honeymoon. Miami, Florida, January 1953 . . . . . . . . . . . . . . . . . . . . . . 56

The author's arrival on Capitol Hill. Washington, DC,
January 1969 . . . . . . . . . . . . . . . . . . . . . . . . . . . . . . . . . . . . . . . . . . . . . 88

The author, House Science and Astronautics Subcommittee
Chairman, with Senator John McClellan of Arkansas and
astronauts of the *Apollo 11* moon landing (July 20, 1969):
Mike Collins (pilot) and Buzz Aldrin and Neil Armstrong
(moonwalkers). Washington, DC, 1969 . . . . . . . . . . . . . . . . . . . . . . . . 93

Yale Men in Congress. Speaker's Dining Room, U.S. House of
  Representatives, The Capitol; Washington, DC, 1970.  Left to
  Right: Rep. Thomas "Lud" Ashley (D-OH); Sen. J. Glenn Beall,
  Jr. (R-MD); Rep. Guy Vander Jagt (R-MI); Rep. George Bush
  (R-TX); Rep. Allard Lowenstein (D-NY); Kingman Brewster,
  President of Yale; Rep. William S. Moorhead (D-PA); Rep.
  Jonathan B. Bingham (D-NY); Rep. James W. Symington
  (D-MO); and Sen. William Proxmire (D-WI) ..................... 96

Among those who did make it to the "heartland" was Israeli
  Ambassador, later Prime Minister, Yitzak Rabin. In this
  photo he is greeted at Lambert Field by the author —
  then congressman. St. Louis, Missouri, 1972 ..................... 120

White House ceremony marking the first anniversary of the
  Alliance For Progress. Washington, DC; March 13, 1962 ............. 127

Lunch *al fresco* with Canadian counterpart, Chief of Protocol
  Henry Davis, during President Johnson's meeting with
  Canadian Prime Minister Lester Pearson. Campobello
  Island, New Brunswick, Canada, 1966 ......................... 129

Folksongs for Muscovites. Moscow, July 1958 ..................... 136

Tennis fundraiser to provide court time and lessons for the underprivileged
  at the Washington International Hotel. Washington, DC, June 1971. Left
  to right: General William Westmoreland, Cong. Robert McClory (R-IL),
  Senator Jacob Javits (R-NY), Senator Claiborne Pell (D-RI), and
  the author (D-MO) .......................................... 140

The Wall — Congressional visit to the Berlin Wall. Berlin,
  Germany, February 1970 ..................................... 144

Private First Class, U.S.M.C. Camp Lejeune, North Carolina, 1945 ..... 152

Author with grandmother, Alice Hay Wadsworth, on
  Christmas furlough. Washington, DC, December 1945 ............. 152

Author's grandfather, James W. Wadsworth, Jr. Member of
  the U.S. Senate (Republican) 1915-27, and the House of
  Representatives (R-NY), 1933-51 .............................. 154

John Hay, Private Secretary to President Abraham Lincoln,
  1861-65; later, Secretary of State under Presidents McKinley
  and Theodore Roosevelt ..................................... 188

Brigadier General James S. Wadsworth, United States Army.
  Killed at the Battle of the Wilderness, Spotsylvania, Virginia, 1864 . . . 188

Captain W. Stuart Symington of Baltimore, Maryland.
  Aide-de-Camp to General George Pickett, Confederate
  States of America, 1863 . . . . . . . . . . . . . . . . . . . . . . . . . . . . . . . . . . 188

Author and "Noble Regent" (the cow) with Food For Peace
  staples: milk, corn, and wheat. Beltsville, Maryland,
  Agricultural Station, 1961 . . . . . . . . . . . . . . . . . . . . . . . . . . . . . . . . 190

Deputy Director, Food For Peace, singing with Peruvian
  families at a school-lunch opening. Lima, Peru, 1961 . . . . . . . . . . . . . . 191

Father and son on a stroll. Washington, DC, 1985 . . . . . . . . . . . . . . . . . . 198

At home in Washington, DC, 1985 . . . . . . . . . . . . . . . . . . . . . . . . . . . . . 199

Mother, Eve Symington. New York City, 1938, and St. Louis, 1942 . . . . . 203

Family outing in second-hand pedicab purchased in Kuala
  Lumpur, Malaysia, 1967. Author, his wife Sylvia, Julie,
  Jeremy, and Brandy (retriever) . . . . . . . . . . . . . . . . . . . . . . . . . . . . . . 204

Music and words — Sylvia and Jim. New York City, 1953 . . . . . . . . . . . . 208

Arthur ("Punch") Sulzberger, front row left, and author, front
  row right, equally amused by Captain George Plimpton's
  deadpan expression. Undefeated "Giants" of St. Bernard's
  School, New York City, 1936 . . . . . . . . . . . . . . . . . . . . . . . . . . . . . . . 221

Juggling for girls softball team, the "Symington Patriots,"
  in the Kirkwood Bicentennial Parade. St. Louis County,
  Missouri; May 29, 1976 . . . . . . . . . . . . . . . . . . . . . . . . . . . . . . . . . . . 222

With Julie and Jeremy at home. Washington, DC, 1962 . . . . . . . . . . . . . . 227

Escorting young guest at a benefit performance for the United
  Planning Organization (UPO). Washington, DC, 1962 . . . . . . . . . . . . . 228

1960 Democratic Presidential contenders rally around Harry
  S Truman. Washington, DC, spring 1960. Left to right: Gov.
  Robert Meyner (NJ), Sen Hubert Humphrey (MN), Gov. Leroy
  Collins (FL), Gov. G. Mennen "Soapy" Williams (MI), Sen. Stuart
  Symington (MO), Sen. John Kennedy (MA), Gov. Edmund
  "Pat" Brown (CA). Missing — Sen. Lyndon Johnson (TX) . . . . . . . . . . 239

Men and machines, sharing a laugh. Overland, Missouri, July 1968 . . . . 250

With "the Master," Senator Hubert H. Humphrey, endorsing author's
Senate candidacy. St. Louis, Missouri; July 23, 1976 . . . . . . . . . . . . . . 254

With Jacqueline Kennedy Onassis at Averell Harriman's
Testimonial Dinner. Washington, DC; May 15, 1974 . . . . . . . . . . . . . . 259

Serenading President and Mrs. Johnson at the LBJ Ranch on
the Pedernales (near Austin, Texas). An evening for Israeli
Prime Minister and Mrs. Levi Eshkol, December 1967 . . . . . . . . . . . . 266

Performing "On The Road With LBJ" aboard *Air Force One,*
somewhere over Alaska, October 1966. Left to right behind
the President: Liz Carpenter (Presidential Aide), John Roche
(Foreign Policy Consultant), Bess Abell (White House Social
Secretary), the author (Chief of Protocol), and Connie Gerard
(Secretary to the President) . . . . . . . . . . . . . . . . . . . . . . . . . . . . . . . . . . . 271

President and Mrs. Johnson's arrival at a Royal Airport
reception (with Marvin Watson, White House Chief of
Staff, and the author). October 1966 . . . . . . . . . . . . . . . . . . . . . . . . . . . . 275

The author with President Johnson on the Truman balcony.
The White House, January 13, 1967 . . . . . . . . . . . . . . . . . . . . . . . . . . . . 279

Receiving line at the White House wedding reception for Charles
and Lynda Robb. Washington, DC; December 9, 1967 . . . . . . . . . . . . . 281

Sylvia Symington's dinner partner speaks. Washington, DC, 1970 . . . . . 285

*Washington Post* Book-and-Author Luncheon — Bill Moyers,
Katherine Graham, and the author. Washington, DC, 1970 . . . . . . . . . 295

Seconds, anyone? — Paolo's Restaurant in Georgetown.
Washington, DC, July 1998 . . . . . . . . . . . . . . . . . . . . . . . . . . . . . . . . . . . 313

# Index

1996 Presidential election, 19
1992 Presidential election, 303
1960 Presidential primaries, 253
1912 Democratic convention, 196
*1776*, 85, 87, 291


ABM (anti-ballistic missile), 86,
    87*n*
Abel, Elie, 276, 276*n*
Abell, Bess, 269, 271
Abu Simbel, 106
Acheson, David, 196, 197*n*
Achilles, 215
Adams, Henry, 187
Adams, John, 85
Adams, John, (Counsel, U.S.
    Army), 241, 241*n*
Adams, Robert, 8
Adams, Sherman, 241, 241*n*
Aegean Sea, 60
Air and Space Museum, 11
Air Force, U.S., 196, 211, 297*n*
*Air Force One*, 269-270, 270*n*, 271,
    274, 277
Alaska, 32, 247, 270-271, 277
Alceste, (Molière's *Misanthrope*),
    xvii
Aldrin, Buzz, 93
Alexander, Shana, 276, 276*n*
Alexis, Grand Duke of Russia,
    133-134
Alliance for Progress, the, 125-
    127
Alps, the, 59
America, xv, 41, 60, 70, 79, 85, 99,
    102, 106, 119, 122, 125, 133,
    143, 156, 172*n*, 181, 188-189,
    211, 217, 243, 247, 273*n*, 274,
    289, 292, 311-312

American Film Institute (AFI),
    293, 294*n*
American Revolution, vii
American-Russian Cultural
    Cooperation Foundation, 133
Anderson, Clinton, 31, 211
Angelo, Bonnie, 277, 277*n*
Annapolis, U.S. Naval Academy
    at, 50
*Apollo 11*, 93
Appomattox, 79, 182
Arcturus, 185
Argentina, 247
Arizona, 302*n*
Arkansas, 93, 111
Armstrong, Neil, 92-93
Armstrong, William, 74, 74*n*
Armstrong-Jones, Antony, 1st
    Earl of Snowdon, 121
Army-McCarthy hearings, 240,
    241*n*, 244, 255
Army-Navy game, 235
Army, U.S., 12*n*, 134*n*, 150, 153,
    175, 177, 181, 186, 188, 210,
    240, 241*n*, 244
Arnold, Fortas & Porter, 257
Arthur (King), 40
Ashley, Thomas "Lud," 96
Asia, 197, 276
Associated Press, the, 35, 35*n*, 42
Aswan Dam, Egypt, 106
Athens, Greece, 66-67
Atlantic Ocean, 217
Atlantis, 225
Austin, Texas, 266 270
Austria, 215-216
Autry, Gene, 212


Baghdad, Iraq, 202
Bailey, Chuck, 276, 276*n*

Baldridge, Malcolm, 13
Baldridge, Mrs. Malcolm ("Midge"), 13
Ball, George W., 7n
Baltimore, Maryland, vii, 13, 106, 107n, 182, 188, 196-197
Baltimore Inner Harbor, 106, 107n
*Baltimore Sun*, 35, 35n, 39
Barristers' Ball, 76n, 244
Barry, Marion, 293
Bartlett, Charles, 7, 7n
Beach Boys, the, 103
Beale, Sir Howard, 210
Beall, J. Glenn, Jr., 96
Bearman, Morton, 29
Beethoven, Ludwig van, 207
Beggs, Jeanne F., 293
Belleview Valley, Missouri, 111-112
*Bells, The* (Poe), 192n
Beltsville, Maryland, 190
Berlin, Germany, 144
Berlin Wall, the, 144
Berliner, Deborah E., xv
Berliner, Diane T., xv
Berne, Switzerland, 59
Bethany Beach, Delaware, 260
Bill of Rights, U.S., 80
Bingham, Jonathan B., 96
Blackhawk Indians, 182
Boca Grande, Florida, 291
Bolsheviks, 122
Borman, Frank, 92
Boston, Massachusetts, 134
Boswell, James, 185
Boxer rebellion, Chinese, 182
Boyden, Frank, 173
Brewster, Kingman, 96
Brinkley, David, 311
British Broadcasting Corp. (BBC), 311
Broadway, 85
Bronxville, New York, 50

Brown, Edmund "Pat," 239
Brown University, 181, 183
Brownell, Herbert, 241, 241n
Buchwald, Art, 15
Buffalo Bill (see Cody)
Buford, Anthony, 111
Buford Mountain, Missouri, 111-112
Bundy, William, 272, 273n
Burke, Edmund, 98
Burkley, George, Dr., 270, 270n, 272, 273n
Burns, Ken, 187n
Bush, George H. W., 21, 96, 292, 296-297, 300-302, 302n
Butler, John Marshall, 243, 243n
Butz, Earl, 68, 70n
Bynkershoek, Cornelius van, 246, 264n

Caesar, Julius, 280
Caledonia, 111
California, 248n
Camp Lejeune, North Carolina, 58, 152
Campobello Island, New Brunswick, 129
Canada, 113, 129
Cape Cod, Massachusetts, 32
Capitol Hill, 86, 88, 96, 261
Caplin, Mortimer, 71
Cardozo, (Washington, D.C.), 1
Carmichael, Dr. Leonard, 211
Carpenter, Liz, 266, 269, 271
Carson, Johnny, 312
Carter, Carlyn, 293
Case, Francis, 255n
Casey, William, 296, 297n
Catholic University, 210
Caudle, T. Lamar, 238, 238n
CBS, 36
Central Intelligence Agency, U.S., 297n

Central Park, (New York City), 102, 170
Chase Manhattan Bank, 131
Chicago, Illinois, 4
*Chicago Daily News*, 276n
*Chicago Tribune*, 241n, 243n
Chicago, University of, 149
Childs, Marquis, 42, 276, 276n
China, 151
Christmas, 105, 119, 152, 240, 243, 283, 299, 311
Civil War, the, 134n, 181, 187n, 312
Clark, Deena, 209
Clark, Mark, 236, 238n
Clayton, Missouri, 29-30
Clifford, Clark M., 196, 197n, 241, 241n, 270
Clinton, Bill, 303-304
Club Med, 194n
Coast Guard, U.S., 102
Cobbs, Armstrong, Teasdale & Roos, 74n
Cobbs, Thomas, 74, 74n
Cody, William F., ("Buffalo Bill"), 134, 134n
Cohan, George M., 139
Cohn, Roy, 242, 242n, 244
Coke, Sir Edward, 68, 70n
Collins, Leroy, 239
Collins, Michael, 93
Columbia, Missouri, 70
Columbia University, School of Law, 72, 76-77, 244, 311
Commerce Committee, House of Representatives, U.S., 36
Commerce Department, U.S., 13
communism, 143, 236
Confederacy, Army of the, 182
Confederate Constitution, 78-80
Confederate States of America, 79, 188
Congress, U.S., vii, 23, 27-28, 36-37, 79-80, 83, 85-87, 89-90, 92,

96-97, 119, 155, 172, 172n, 210, 245, 249, 265, 283-284, 291, 297, 305, 311
*Congressional Record*, 37, 94
*Constellation*, U.S.S., 106, 107n
Constitution, U.S., 36, 78, 97, 289
*Constitution*, U.S.S., 107n
Continental Congress, vii, 27n, 85-86
Cook, Val, 294
Cooper, Peggy, 293
Corcoran Gallery of Art, 293, 294n
Costa Rica, 211
Costello, Frank, 237, 238n
*Courrier Diplomatique*, 292
Crockett, William, 269
Cuba, 183, 262
Custer, George Armstrong, 134, 134n
Czar Alexander II, 133

Daedalus, 10
Dallas, Texas, 263
Daniel, Margaret Truman, 122
Dapron, Eugene, 74
Davis, Henry, 129
D.C. Arts Commission, 293, 294n
de Tocqueville, Alexis, 292
Dean, John W., III, 197, 287-288
Declaration of Independence, vii, 85, 87
Deerfield Academy, 142, 172-173
*Deerfield Journal*, 173
Defense Department, U.S., 36
Delaware, 187, 260
*Democracy In America*, (de Tocqueville), 292
Democratic National Committee, 284
Democratic National Convention, 31, 38
Democrats, 181

Demosthenes, 87
"Desert Storm," 298
Diaz, Ordaz (President of
  Mexico), 265
Dickinson, John, of Pennsylvania,
  85
DiMaggio, Joe, 176
Dionysus, 61
Dirksen, Everett, 85, 91, 91n
Disneyland, California, 119
Doerr, John, 174
Dole, Elizabeth H., 292
Dole, Robert J., 304, 304n
Dostoyevski, Feodor, 134, 134n
Douglas-Kerr debates, 86
Douglas, Paul, 91
Duke, Paul, 42
Dulles, John Foster, 252, 252n

East Room, the White House, 184
Einstein, Albert, 68, 70n
Eisenhower, Dwight D., 197, 235,
  241n, 245, 251-252
Elba Island, 267
Elliot, Richard, 175
Emerson, Ralph Waldo, 196
Enders, Gaetana, 292
England, 121, 141, 311
Eshkol, Levi, 266
Euphrates River, 298
Euripides, 61
Europe, 50, 60, 79, 150, 182
Executive Mansion, the, 184

Faisal, King of Saudi Arabia, 265
Falstaff, (Henry the Fourth), 185
Farragut, David G., 4
Farragut Square, (Washington,
  D.C.), 3-4
Faulkner, Ken, 174
Faulkner, Lieut., U.S. National
  Guard, 174

Federal Bureau of Investigation
  (FBI), 241n
Federal City Club, 7, 7n
Finney, John W., 42
First Amendment, the, 20, 36-37,
  39, 65
Fisher, Eddie, 76n
Five Forks, Virginia, 181
Florida, 38, 56, 193, 291
Food For Peace program, 189-
  191, 311
Ford, Gerald R., 70n, 197
Ford's Theatre, (Washington,
  D.C.), 185, 294n
Fort Myers, Virginia, 280
Fort Wadsworth, Staten Island,
  181
Founding Fathers, 80, 85, 87, 101
France, 11, 102, 289
Frankel, Max, 276, 276n
Franklin, Benjamin, 85-87
Fujimori, Alberto, 130
Fuller, Thomas, 68, 70n

Galápagos Islands, 8
Galileo, 161, 161n
Gallipoli, Turkey, 8
Gardner, John, 265
Garfield, James A., 187, 263
General Services Administration
  (GSA), 90
Genesee Valley, New York, 104
Geneseo, New York, 104, 150, 181
Georgetown, (Washington, D.C.),
  256, 313
Gerard, Connie, 271
Germany, 70n, 79, 144, 182
Gertken, John, 89
Gettysburg Address, the, 182
Gettysburg, Battle of, vii, 181-182,
  186, 196
Gettysburg, Pennsylvania, 252
Gibbon, Edward, 225, 225n

Gilbert & Sullivan, 170, 253
Ginsberg, Ina, 293, 294*n*
Goebel, Julius, 76
Government, U.S., vii, 20, 36-37,
  39, 69, 89, 97, 107*n*, 174, 197,
  245, 265, 311
Graham, Katherine, 293, 295
Grant, Ulysses S., 133, 134*n*,
  181-182
Great Britain, 11, 187, 311-312
Greece, 172*n*, 265
Greenfield, Meg, 290
Grotius, Hugo, 246, 246*n*
Groton School, 131
Guadalcanal Island, 155
Gulf of Mexico, 290
*Gungha Din*, (Kipling), 287
Guthrie, Woodie, 7

Hadrian, 194*n*
Hall, Leonard, 111
Halley, Rudolph, 237, 238*n*
Hamilton, George, 280, 280*n*
*Hamlet*, (Shakespeare), 68, 186
Hanoi, North Vietnam, 139, 283
Harriman, Mrs. J. Borden, 211
Harriman, Pamela, 123-124
Harriman, W. Averell, 7*n*, 122-
  124, 257, 259
Harrower, Tina, 294
Hartke, Rev. Gilbert, 210
Harvard University, 131, 149
Hassan, King of Morocco, 172*n*,
  265
Hay Adams Hotel (Washington,
  D.C.), 263
Hay, John, of Illinois, vii, 181-188,
  263, 311
Hay, Milton, 183-85
Head Start program, 85
Hearst, William Randolph, 243,
  243*n*
Heckler, Margaret, 293, 294*n*

Heidelberg University, 79
Henley, William Ernest, 128*n*
Henry, John, 161
Henry VIII, King of England, 70*n*
*Henry the Fourth*, (Shakespeare),
  185
*Henry the Sixth*, (Shakespeare),
  68, 185
Hensel, H. Struve, 241, 241*n*
Herald Square, (New York City),
  121, 165
Hercules, 196
Herodotus, 262
Hewitt, Frankie, 293
*Hiawatha*, (Shakespeare), 31
Hightower, John, 35, 35*n*
Hills, Carla, 293
Hirshhorn Museum, 10
Hiss, Alger, 236, 238*n*, 241, 241*n*
Hitler, Adolf, 141
Ho Chi Minh, 139, 139*n*
Ho Chi Minh Trail, 139
Holbrook, Hal, 177
Holiday, Wilhelmina ("Billie"),
  293, 294*n*
Hollings, Ernest E. "Fritz," 196,
  197*n*
Holloway, James L., III, 107*n*
Holmes, Oliver Wendell, Jr., 97,
  107*n*, 134, 134*n*
Hood, Thomas, 186
Hoover, J. Edgar, 241, 241*n*
Hope, Arkansas, 303, 307
House of Representatives, U.S.,
  27*n*, 31, 78-80, 94, 96,
  153-154, 185
Howe, Julia Ward, 294, 294*n*
Hullverson, James, 73, 73*n*
Hume, David, 236, 238*n*
Humphrey, Hubert H., 27, 27*n*,
  31, 239, 253-254, 258
Hungate, William, 300*n*
Hussein, Saddam, 296, 298-300

Hussein ibn Talal, King of
  Jordan, 296

IBM, 192
Iceland, 211
Illinois, 91, 181, 183, 311
India, 9, 211
Indiana, 184
Internal Revenue Service, 20, 71,
  94, 238n
*Invictus*, (Henley), 128n
Iran, 261, 296
Iraq, 296, 299
Iron County, Missouri, 111
Isham, Sheila, 293
Israel, 211
Istanbul, Turkey, 4
Italy, 210

Japan, 236
Japan, Embassy of, 130
Javits, Jacob, 140
Jefferson, Thomas, vii, 85, 87
Jenner, William E., 243, 243n
Joelson, Charles, 95
Johannsen, Ingomar, 217-218
Johnson Administration, the, 119
Johnson, Lady Bird, 266, 273-275
Johnson, Luci, 267
Johnson, Lyndon B., 31, 129,
  172n, 197, 239, 255, 265-267,
  269-270, 270n, 271, 275-276,
  279
Johnson-Robb, Lynda Bird, 122,
  280-281
Johnson, Samuel,Dr., 68, 70n
Johnston, Ed, 74
Joliet, Louis, 113
Jordan, Kingdom of, 296
Judiciary Committee, House of
  Representatives, U.S., 97
July 4th, 85

Justice Department, U.S., vii,
  175, 177

K Street, (Washington, D.C.), 3
Kansas, 60, 294n
Kansas City, Missouri, 116, 235
Kansas-Nebraska Act, 78
Kant, Immanuel, 246, 246n
Kasparov, Gary, 161
Kassebaum, Nancy, 293
Katzenbach, Lydia, 121
Katzenbach, Nicholas, 121, 174,
  265
Keating, Kenneth, 210-211
Kefauver, Estes, 211, 237, 238n
Kelley, P.X., 102
Kenilworth Hotel, 193-194
Kennebunkport, Maine, 297
Kennedy Administration, the, 7,
  189, 262, 267, 311
Kennedy, John F., 31-32, 40,
  92, 197, 239, 253, 255-258,
  260, 263
Kennedy Onassis, Jacqueline,
  122, 257, 259
Kennedy, Robert F., 174, 210, 311
Kernan, Michael, 172
Kerr, Robert, 91, 91n
Key Biscayne, Florida, 286
Khomeini, Ayatollah Ruhollah,
  296
Kiel Auditorium, St. Louis, 251
Kiev, Ukraine, 133, 311
Kilpatrick, James J., 276, 276n
Kipling, Rudyard, 131n, 287
Kissinger, Henry, 7n, 283-284
Knowland, William, 243, 243n
Koch, Edward, 102
Kraft, Polly, 293
Kramer, Harry, 74
Krock, Arthur, 40, 40n
Kruschev, Nikita, 260
Kuala Lumpur, Malaysia, 204

Kuwait, 296, 298

Lafayette Square, (Washington, D.C.), 263
LaGuardia Airport, (New York City), 166
Lambert Field, St. Louis, 97, 120
Lamkin, Henry, 74
Lanahan, Mrs. Samuel J. "Scottie," 210
Latin, 170, 178
Latin America, 125, 311
Lawrence, William H., 31, 243, 243*n*
Lebed, General Alexander, 133
Lee, Robert E., 182
Legend Singers, of St. Louis, 119*n*
Lehman, John F., 103
Lemos, Gloria, 293
Leningrad, Soviet Union, 133, 311
Leubsdorf, Carl, 42
Liberia, 211
Library of Congress, U.S., 79, 210
*Life Magazine*, 85, 87, 276*n*, 277*n*
Lima, Peru, 130, 191
Lincoln, Abraham, vii, 37, 181 188, 263, 311
Lincoln, Mary, 183
Lincoln, Robert, 186
Lion's Club, 174
Lippmann, Walter, 7*n*
Lisagore, Peter, 276, 276*n*
Literary Enterprises International, iv
Little Rock, Arkansas, 306
Livingston, Jane, 293, 294*n*
Locke, John, 68, 70*n*
Lodge, Henry Cabot, 241, 241*n*
London, England, 135, 166, 229, 282, 311
Long Island, New York, 278
Longfellow, Henry Wadsworth, 197, 197*n*

Longworth, Alice Roosevelt, 7*n*, 122
Lord Byron, George Gordon, 195, 195*n*
Los Angeles, California, 31
Lowenstein, Allard, 96
Lucerne, Switzerland, 59
Lustron Corporation, 242, 242*n*

MacArthur, Douglas, 236
MacGregor, Clark, 94
McCarthy, Joseph, 197, 197*n*, 237, 240, 241*n*, 242, 242*n*, 244, 251, 255
McClellan, George B., 181
McClellan, John, 93
McClory, Robert, 140
McCormack, Robert R., 243, 243*n*
McCullough, David, 187*n*
McFarlane, Robert C. "Bud," 296, 297*n*
McGovern, George, 189, 255, 255*n*
McGrory, Mary, 312
McHugh, Godfrey T., 211
McKinley, William, vii, 187, 189, 263, 311
McNamara, Robert S., 273, 273*n*
McPherson, Harry, 272, 273*n*
*Macbeth*, (Shakespeare), 186
Madison Square Garden (New York City), 217
Madrid, Spain, 187
Major League, the, 95*n*
Manatos, Michael, 211
Manila, the Philippines, 269
Mansfield, Anne, 211
Mardi Gras, 134
Marine Band, the, 265
Marine Corps, U.S., 58, 150-153, 155-156, 280
Marine Corps Hymn, 280
Marines, the, 103, 151, 236

Marquette, Jacques, 113
Marquis of Queensberry, 244
Maryland, 181-182, 188-190
Massachusetts, 31, 142
Maul, Bill, 72
Mayo, William J., Dr., 161, 161*n*
Medal of Freedom, U.S., 11
Mediterranean Sea, 60
*Meet The Press*, 42
Melbourne, Australia, 166
Memorial Day, 102
Meredith, James, 174, 262
Mesopotamia, Iraq, 298
Metternich (see von Metternich)
Mexico, 184, 265
Meyner, Robert, 239
Miami, Florida, 38, 56, 193
Miami Beach, Florida, 193, 226
Michelmore, Cliff, 312
Middle East, the, 131, 296
Military Affairs Committee,
     Senate, U.S., 150
Milwaukee, Wisconsin, 280
*Minneapolis Star and Tribune*, 276*n*
*Misanthrope, The* (Molière), xvii
Mississippi, 177
Mississippi River, 113, 115, 181
Mississippi, University of, at
     Oxford, 174, 262
Missouri, vi, vii, 26, 28-32, 51-52,
     65, 67, 70, 90, 98, 108-109,
     111-112, 112*n*, 113, 116, 120,
     175-176, 197, 222, 250-251,
     254, 300*n*, 311
Missouri, University of, School
     of Law, 68
Mizell, Wilmer "Vinegar Bend,"
     95, 95*n*
Molière, Jean Baptiste, xvii
Montgomery, Alabama, 78
Moorhead, William S., 96
More, Sir Thomas, 68, 70, 70*n*
Morocco, 172*n*, 265

Moscow, Soviet Union, 109, 133,
     136, 311
Moss, Annie Lee, 197, 197*n*
Moyers, Bill, 270, 276, 278, 295
Mundt, Carl E., 243, 243*n*, 255
Murphy, George, 172
Muskie, Edmund, 27, 27*n*
Mussorgsky, Modest Petrovich,
     134, 134*n*

National Aquarium, 13
National Association of Retired
     Federal Employees, 80
National Museum of Women
     in the Arts, 294*n*
National Portrait Gallery, 11
National Press Club, 172
National Security Council, U.S.,
     297*n*
National Security Resources
     Board, U.S., 32
National Soccer Coaches
     Association, 219-220
National Society of Arts and
     Letters, 209-210
*Naval History*, 107*n*
Navy, U.S., 103, 153
NBC, 42, 209-210, 276*n*, 311
Nebraska, 134
Nebuchadnezzar, 298
Nef, John, 149
Nef, Louisa, 149
Neptune, 13
Nero, 175
Netherlands, the, 211
New Jersey, 95
New Mexico, 31-32
New Mexico Democratic
     Convention, 31
New Orleans, Louisiana, 114, 134
New York, vii, 48, 57, 103-104,
     119, 122, 150, 171, 172*n*, 181-
     182, 210, 218, 244, 311

New York City, 8, 170, 181, 203, 208, 221
*New York Herald Tribune*, 40
*New York Times*, 31, 40, 40*n*, 41-42, 121, 243*n*, 276*n*
*New York Tribune*, 183, 187
Newport News, Virginia, 165
Newton, Sir Isaac, 161, 161*n*
Nicolay, John, 183
*Nieu Osterreich Zeitung*, 216
Nile River, 106
Nixon, Richard M., 85, 122, 243, 243*n*, 252, 252*n*, 256, 282-283
Noah, 161
Norfolk, Virginia, 151
North, Oliver, 297, 297*n*
North Carolina, 58, 152
North Korea, 236
Northern Lights, the, 218
Northern Virginia, Army of, 79, 181, 196
Norway, 211

*Observer*, 282
Ochs, Adolph Simon, 40, 40*n*
O'Connor, Sandra Day, 292
Office of Management and Budget, 304*n*
Ohio, 241*n*
Okamoto, Yoshi, 272, 273*n*
Okinawa, Japan, 155
Oxford, Mississippi, 174, 176-177
Oxford, University of, 71

Pacific Ocean, 150, 263, 274
Pakistan, 211
Pandora, 237
Panetta, Leon, 304, 304*n*
Paris, France, 187
Parnassus, 11
Parris Island, South Carolina, 150-151, 155-156
Parthenon, 65

*Patience*, (Gilbert & Sullivan), 170
Patterson, Floyd, 217-218
Patton, George S., 131
Payson, Daniel, 150
Peace Corps, U.S., 270*n*, 276, 278
Pearl Harbor, Hawaii, 141
Pearson, Lester, 129
Pedernales, the, 266, 269
Peking, China, 182
Pell, Claiborne, 140
Pennsylvania, 85, 87
Pentagon, *see* Defense Department, U.S.
Perrone-Capano, Kinga, 210
Peru, 130, 191, 312
Petrarch, 195, 195*n*
Philadelphia, Pennsylvania, vii
Pickett, George E., 176, 181, 188
*Pinafore*, (Gilbert & Sullivan), 253
Plato, 61
Plaza Hotel, (New York City), 8, 28
Plimpton, George, 170, 221
Poe, Edgar Allan, 192*n*
Poindexter, John, 297, 297*n*
"Pony Express Band," 235
Pope, Alexander, 292, 294*n*
Pope, John, 181
Porter, Cole, 130*n*
Porter, Paul, 265
Poseidon, 13
Potomac River, 7, 240
Poussaint, Renee, 294, 294*n*
Presidential Prayer Breakfast, 119*n*
President's Committee on Juvenile Delinquency, 265, 311
Press, the, 33, 35-36, 39, 65-66, 107*n*, 216-217, 276, 282-283, 288, 301
Princess Margaret, The (Countess of Snowdon), 121
Proxmire, William, 96

Public Broadcasting Service
(PBS), 312
Puerto Rico, 153
Pulitzer prize, 35
Punta del Este, Uruguay, 126
Pyongyang, North Korea, 236

Qaddafi, Muammar al-, 298

Rabin, Yitzak, 120
Rayburn, Sam, 31
Reagan, Nancy, 293, 294*n*
Reagan, Ronald W., 11, 292, 296-
297
Reid, Whitelaw, 183
Republicans, 95, 164, 181, 251,
303
Reston, James B. "Scotty," 40
Reynolds, Nancy, 293, 294*n*
Ribbon Creek incident, 155
Ribicoff, Jane, 210
Ribicoff, Mrs. Abraham, 211
*Richard the Third*, (Shakespeare),
185
Richardson, Elliot, 7*n*
Richardson, Orville, 73, 73*n*
*Richmond Times Dispatch*, 276*n*
Ripley, Mary, 11
Ripley, S. Dillon, 8-12
Riyadh, Saudi Arabia, 300
*Road to Mandalay*, (Kipling), 131,
131*n*, 269
Robb, Charles, 280-281
Robb, Lynda (see Johnson-Robb)
Roberts, Chalmers, 35, 35*n*
Roche, John, 271
Rock Creek Park, (Washington,
D.C.), 7
Rockefeller, Nelson, 7*n*
Rogers, Will, 85
Rogers, William, 241, 241*n*, 283
Roman Circus, the, 219
Romans, the, 61

Roos, Walter, 74, 74*n*
Roosevelt, Archibald Bullock,
131-132
Roosevelt, Eleanor, 251
Roosevelt, Franklin D., Jr., 122
Roosevelt, Selwa "Lucky,"
131-132, 293, 294*n*
Roosevelt, Theodore, vii, 132,
187-188, 311
Ross, Betsy, vii
Rostow, Walt, 272, 273*n*
Ruckelshaus, William D., 7*n*
Rucker, Evelyn Symington, v
Rucker, Hayley Rose, v
Rusk, Dean, 265, 269, 272, 273*n*
Russia, 78, 133-135, 298, 311
Russia, Embassy of, 133

Saigon, South Vietnam, 139
Saks Jandel, 294
Salonika, Greece, 60
Salvation Army, 4
Samarkand, Soviet Union, 131-
132
San Clemente, California, 286
*San Francisco Examiner*, 243*n*
San Juan, Puerto Rico, 131
Sandanistas, the, 296
Santa Claus, 240-242
Sante Fe, New Mexico, 31-32, 116
Sarah Lawrence College, 50, 311
Saudi Arabia, 132, 265, 300
Schine, David, 242, 242*n*, 244
Schlesinger, Arthur, 262, 267
Schmeling, Max, 217
Science and Astronautics
Subcommittee, House of
Representatives, U.S., 93
Secord, Richard, 297, 297*n*
Securities and Exchange
Commission, 292, 294*n*

Senate, U.S., vi, 23, 26, 31-32, 50, 91, 111, 150, 154-155, 185, 196, 254, 255*n*, 304*n*
Seoul, Korea, 265
Seymour, Horatio, 181
Shah of Iran, 261
Shakespeare, William, 31, 68, 185, 209
Shankar, Ravi, 122
Shaw, Charlie, 75
Shaw, Lucinda, xv
Shenker, Morris, 75
Sheraton Park Hotel, (Washington, D.C.), 124
Sherer, Ray, 276, 276*n*
Sheridan, Philip H., 134, 134*n*
Sholokhov, M.A., 278*n*
Shultz, George P., 296, 297*n*
Sidey, Hugh S., iii, vii, 277, 277*n*
Sidney, Sir Phillip, 210
Smith, Merriman, 277, 277*n*
Smithsonian Institution, 8, 10, 211
Snowdon, Lord (see Armstrong-Jones)
Socrates, 65-67
Sokolsky, George E., 241, 241*n*, 243, 243*n*
Sollazio, Louis, 238, 238*n*
South Dakota, 255
Soviet Union, 108*n*, 122, 135, 147
Space Committee, House of Representatives, U.S., 92, 210
Spain, 183
Spalding, Charles, 258
Spaniards, the, 153
Spartans, the, 197
Spivak, Lawrence, 42
Spotsylvania, Virginia, 188
Spring Valley, (Washington, D.C.), 1
Springfield, Illinois, 183
Squirrel Hill, Pennsylvania, 35
St. Bernard's School, 170-171, 221

St. Louis, Missouri, vi, 27-28, 51-53, 55, 59, 65, 67, 72*n*, 73, 73*n*, 74, 74*n*, 75, 89, 105, 108, 110, 113-115, 119*n*, 120, 169, 203, 212, 222, 238, 243, 249, 251, 254, 311
St. Louis Bar Association, 72*n*
*St. Louis Post Dispatch*, 42, 133, 135, 276*n*, 311
St. Louis Zoo, 210
St. Paul's Cathedral, 196
St. Petersburg, Russia, 133, 311
St. Regis Hotel, (New York City), 8
Stahr, Elvis J., Jr., 210
Stalin, Joseph, 143, 236, 240
Stanley, Timothy Wadsworth, 230*n*
Stanton, Edwin M., 186
State Department, U.S., vii, 107*n*, 270*n*
Statue of Liberty, 102-103
Stennis, John, 177
Stevens, Robert, 244
Stevenson, Adlai, 241, 241*n*, 251
Stewart, Potter, 210
Stuart, James Ewell Brown (J.E.B.), 79, 182
Sulzberger, Arthur Ochs, 40, 40*n*, 221
Sununu, John, 21
Supreme Court, U.S., 248*n*, 294*n*
Symington, Anne, xv
Symington, Dylan Stuart, v
Symington, Evelyn W., 29, 151, 182, 197*n*, 200, 202-203
Symington, Harriet Hay, v
Symington, Jeremy Wadsworth, 204, 227
"Symington Patriots," the, 222
Symington-Rucker, Julia Hay, 178, 204, 227
Symington, Sawyer Wadsworth, v

Symington, Stuart, vii, 26, 31-32,
32*n*, 42, 50, 155, 196-198, 210,
239, 241, 241*n*, 242, 242*n*, 244,
258, 311
Symington, Stuart, Jr., 104, 150,
197
Symington, Sylvia, v, vii, xv, 2,
11, 14, 25, 29, 41, 46, 51-53,
59, 61, 98, 101, 110, 112, 116,
119, 134, 146, 162, 193, 195,
204, 208, 235, 258, 285, 311
Symington, Thomas, 79, 182
Symington, W. Stuart, 79, 181-
182, 188,
Syria, 298

Taft, Robert, 241, 241*n*
Tarkio, Missouri, 26
Taylor, Maxwell D., 211
Teasdale, Ken, 74, 74*n*
Tennessee, 6
Texas, 31-32, 133, 266, 270
Thanksgiving, 97
Thayer, William Roscoe, 183
Thermopylae, Greece, 197
Thieu, Nguyen Van, 283, 283*n*
Tho, Le Duc, 283, 283*n*
Thomas, Barbara, 292
Thor, 211, 217-218
Thyrssis, 209
Tigris River, 298
*Time Magazine*, 277*n*
Tin-Pan-Alley, (New York City),
1, 298
Tobey, Charles W., 237, 238*n*
Tokyo, Japan, 4
Tolstoy, Count Leo, 134, 134*n*
Topeka, Kansas, 60
Toynbee, Arnold J., 225, 225*n*
Treasury Department, U.S., 94
Truman Balcony, the, 307, 307*n*

Truman, Harry, 32, 197, 235-236,
238-239, 241, 241*n*, 279, 307,
307*n*
Truman, Margaret, 122, 235
Tunisia, 211
Tupac Amaru, the, 130
Turgenev, Ivan Sergeevich, 134,
134*n*
TWA, 166
Twain, Mark, 134, 134*n*, 177, 187

Ukraine, Soviet Union, 133
Ulysses, 60
Uncle Sam, 19, 139
United Planning Organization
(UPO), 228
United Press International, 277*n*
United States, the, vi, 20, 70*n*, 89,
92, 97-98, 102, 106, 108*n*, 109,
111, 116, 131, 133, 134*n*, 139*n*,
154-156, 172*n*, 188, 197*n*, 211,
238*n*, 240, 248*n*, 270, 282,
294*n*, 297*n*, 302*n*, 311-312
Untermeyer, Louis, 210
Uruguay, 126
U.S. Naval Institute, 107*n*
U.S.S. *Constellation*, 106, 107*n*
U.S.S. *Constitution*, 107*n*
U.S.S. *Iowa*, 102
U.S.S. *John F. Kennedy*, 102
Utah, 240

Valenti, Jack, 272, 273*n*
van Wijnen, D.J., 211
Vander Jagt, Guy, 96
Vatican, the, 236, 238*n*
Vienna, Austria, 187, 215, 260
Vietnam, North, 139*n*, 283*n*
Vietnam, South, 119, 139, 280,
283*n*
Virginia, 79, 181, 188, 196, 231,
280
Voice of America, 125, 189, 312

von Borcke, Heros, 79, 182
von Metternich, Clemens W.N.L., 283, 283n
Vorontsov, Yuli, 133

Wachtmeister, Count (Willem), 293, 294n
Wachtmeister, Countess (Ulla), 293, 294n
Wadsworth, Alice Hay, 152, 182
Wadsworth, James S., 181-182, 188
Wadsworth, James W., Jr., vii, 104, 150, 154, 311
Wadsworth, Jim, 182
Walker, John, 196, 197n
Ward, Julia (see Howe)
Ward, Paul, 35, 35n
Washington, D.C., v, xix, 1-4, 6-7, 11-15, 19, 22, 24-25, 35, 41-42, 45-46, 49, 61, 68, 80-81, 88, 92-93, 96, 98, 101, 107, 110, 119, 121, 124, 127-128, 130, 132, 134, 139-140, 146, 148-149, 152, 159-160, 162, 165, 181, 183, 187, 192, 195, 197, 197n, 198-199, 207, 209, 211, 219, 227-228, 230, 230n, 239, 253, 256-257, 259, 261-262, 264, 268, 270n, 278, 281, 285-288, 293-295, 297-307, 311-313
Washington, George, 87
Washington International Hotel, 140
Washington Monument, vii, 196
Washington National Cathedral, 197, 197n
Washington Post, 4, 20, 35n, 106, 172, 211, 238n, 294n, 295, 312
Washington Redskins, the, 219
Washington Star, 276n
Watergate affair, 284, 286, 288, 289n, 291

Watergate Hotel, 284
Watkins, Arthur V., 240, 240n
Watson, Marvin, 172n, 272, 273n, 275
Ways and Means Committee, House of Representatives, U.S., 94
Webster, William, 74
Weed, Thurlow, 37
Welker, Herman, 243, 243n
West Point, U.S. Military Academy at, 182
Westmoreland, William C., 140
WETA, 207n
White House, the, iv, vii, 20, 125, 127, 172n, 181-183, 186-187, 209, 211, 262, 265, 267-269, 270n, 271, 275, 278-281, 284, 287, 289, 303, 304n, 307, 307n, 311
White House Press Corps, 276
White House Rose Garden, 280
Whitewater affair, 306
Whitman, Walt, 134, 134n
Wilderness, Battle of the, 176, 181, 186, 188
Williams, G. Mennen "Soapy," 239
Wilmington, Delaware, 187
Wilson, Charles, 252, 252n
Wilson, James, of Pennsylvania, 87
Wilson, William, 211
Wilson, Woodrow, 10, 196
Winnie the Pooh, 87
Wirtz, Willard, 265
Wisconsin, 240
Wordsworth, William, 197, 197n
World War I, 150, 170
World War II, 141, 150, 311
WRC-NBC, 210
Wren, Sir Christopher, 196

*Yale Literary Magazine*, 147
Yale University, 96, 143, 147, 181-
    182, 219, 311
Yuma, Arizona, 302*n*